PAYBACK

A Dan Ballantine Novel

Mark Travis

Books by Mark Travis:

Dan Ballantine series:
EXPRESS MALICE*
INTENT TO DEFRAUD
CRASH AND BURN*
PAYBACK*
COLD LEG*

Michael Hunt series:
DRAFTEES, US ARMY, 2 EACH*
The BAD BOY MURDERS*
REBELLION*

Ethan Cooper series:
MURDER FOR A BUCK*
DESTROY PHOENIX*

Others:
STUMPED
DEAD DRUNK*
COMMITMENTS*
RAID ACROSS THE RIO BRAVO*

*Published by Virtualbookworm.com

"PAYBACK," by Mark Travis. ISBN 978-1-60264-349-9.

Published 2009 by Virtualbookworm.com Publishing Inc., P.O. Box 9949, College Station, TX 77842, US. ©2009, Mark Travis. All rights reserved. No part of this publication may be reproduced, stored in a retrieval system, or transmitted in any form or by any means, electronic, mechanical, recording or otherwise, without the prior written permission of Mark Travis.

Manufactured in the United States of America.

ONE

The battery-powered hallway light aimed Linda Coleman's fuzzy shadow into the mountain cabin's bedroom. The rough dark roundness of her head stretched across the naked legs of Steven David Reynolds, M.D., whose drugged sleep resulted from the chemical she had added into his Irish Whiskey an hour earlier.

Linda held in her right hand a hypodermic syringe containing a sufficient amount of morphine to kill Reynolds, but she hesitated to murder the man she had until recently loved.

Since Linda had known Steven, they had engaged in many serious conversations. She could imagine the one they might have if he woke and found her ready to push a needle into his thigh.

"What are you doing, Linda, dear?"

"I am injecting you with a fatal dose of morphine with hopes the police will believe you committed suicide."

"What makes you think people will believe I committed suicide?"

"The facts, Steven. You found and converted your son's stock certificates into one point six million dollars in cash which you did not report to your wife or the I R S. Then you stole a corpse, cut off its head, placed the body in the pilot's seat of your plane, crashed the plane in the desert, then burned the body to a crisp. Finally, the woman you love stole the money and left you."

"You helped me with all that except the last part, Linda, dear. Are you stealing my money and leaving me?"

"Yes, Steven, I am."

"The police will look for you, you know? When they find my body, they will know I was not in my plane. It won't take too much digging to discover the stock business and your brother's name on this cabin. They may not care about the missing money, but they will want to talk to you about my death."

Linda thought about that a moment.

"And when they talk to Marva about the missing money, she may pay a private investigator to find you. She will believe, rightfully so, the money is hers."

"Well, Steven, darling," said Linda, "my first thought is that I didn't want you looking for me."

"I wouldn't do that, darling," said Steven. "First, I'm supposed to be dead, remember? I can't go to the police and report you've stolen one point six million dollars from me.

"Second, and more important, I love you."

"Well, Steven, I've got a feeling the authorities will soon find us and arrest us for that fraud. I don't want to go to jail."

"You shouldn't murder me, Linda. If you leave me alive, I will be the criminal they prosecute. They might not even look for you. They won't care about you or the money. All they want is the unpaid taxes which I can pay back when I get out of jail."

Linda ended the imaginary conversation with the conclusion Steven was correct. The police might even think he hid her and the money in some place safe because he feared imminent arrest.

Linda looked down at the syringe in her hand then back at her target. "Good-bye, Steven," she said softly. "It was fun for a while, dear, but it would not have lasted. You became a bore when you no longer had patients to treat. And I really did not want to get pregnant."

Linda stepped into the bathroom, turned on another battery-powered light, squirted the fatal liquid back into the bottles, put the plastic cap over the needle, and dropped the tools into her purse. As she left the small, white pine-paneled room, she intentionally left the light on then closed the door behind her. She thought Steven might awaken, notice her absence from the bed, look for her, see the light at the bottom edge of the door, and return to sleep. She turned off the hall light and stepped through a door into the single-car garage attached to the cabin.

After switching on a third dim light, Linda squeezed beside her Jeep to the garage door and raised it. Back at her driver's door, she peeked behind the seat and smiled at the sight of the fat, dark blue suitcase containing a lifetime's supply of cash.

Linda backed her Jeep from the garage and left the vehicle with the engine running and the parking lights showing her way. She stepped back into the garage and switched off the inside light. From the outside she lowered the main door.

Linda reversed the Jeep's direction in the circular drive at the front of the cabin. She accelerated slowly on the hard-packed dirt swath through the trees then used her emergency brake to slow before she reached the graveled public road. Flashing brake lights would reveal her position in the dark forest.

A hundred feet from the junction, Linda turned off her parking lights, cut left into the forest, and eased the white vehicle through the trees. She wanted to avoid breaking the infrared beam Reynolds had rigged across the drive between a pair of larger trees. She doubted the alarm would immediately awaken him, but the longer he slept the better.

When Linda approached the road, she again used the emergency brake to slow the Jeep. She let momentum carry it across the loose berm and onto the width of gravel-packed dirt which serviced the several widely separated cabins.

Linda believed the watchers in the US Forest Service truck she had seen twice the day before would park farther west because maps of the area showed the gravel road ended at the Arrowrock Reservoir several miles east of the cabin. When her reclusive brother, Peter Hodges, still lived, he had often taken Linda to fish the lake on unmarked roads around it.

Linda drove her Jeep slowly along the white band through the dark forest and soon reached the reservoir. There she engaged four-wheel-drive, turned north, and chanced her parking lights again as she made her way along the perimeter of the lake. When Linda came to another faint road heading away from the lake, she turned onto it and, forty minutes later, reached State Route 21 a few miles south of Idaho City.

Her goal was to put many miles between her Jeep and the cabin as quickly as possible. She would have preferred to turn south and drive twenty-five miles to Boise. The interstate highway would carry her from the area faster, but she feared the people watching the road to the cabin might have a man parked on the state highway, too. She could not risk being stopped and questioned, so she turned north and spent three dark hours on the winding, twisting mountain route.

The rising sun shined on Linda's Jeep stopping at the junction of Idaho State Route 75 with US Highway 93 two miles below Challis. She drove to the mountain town sitting below the western edge of the Lost River Range and found a gasoline station/convenience store business. In addition to paying cash to top her fuel tank, Linda visited the restroom then bought a large coffee, a package of English muffins, and a small jar of creamy peanut butter.

While driving southeasterly on US 93, Linda ate two muffins and several fingers of peanut butter while the coffee cooled.

Behind her, as the first light of morning struck the cabin, FBI agents awakened and arrested Steven Reynolds for income tax evasion and commenced a search of the cabin for his cash.

Two and a half hours Challis, at Arco, Linda left US 93 for US 26 and continued southeasterly until she reached Interstate 15. She turned toward Salt Lake City and reached the outskirts in three uneasy hours. Though she held her pace to five miles an hour above the speed limit, she feared every policeman in several states searched for her.

Linda visited another fuel station and store. After using the toilet, she bought a sandwich, warmed it in a microwave oven, and added a bottle of cold tea. She also purchased two newspapers and a city map.

While eating her sandwich in the parking lot, Linda found an advertisement for a new apartment complex and memorized the address. In the private vehicle section of the classified advertisements, Linda circled several vehicles which would carry her to Mexico without attracting attention. Her third telephone call from a public phone got her an address that fit her criteria.

Linda removed eight thousand dollars from the money suitcase and parked her Jeep in a shopping center parking lot. Then she called a taxi from another public phone and tried to calm herself while she waited for it. When it arrived she gave the driver an address less than three miles away. She apologized for the short trip with the explanation a friend she shopped with had to leave in a hurry and stranded her.

The middle-aged man selling the five-year-old Toyota Corolla explained he had bought it two years earlier for his daughter's sixteenth birthday. The high school graduate had left for college and lived in the dorm where freshman were discouraged from having a car. Rather than let it sit, he decided to sell it.

The seller lifted the hood, started the engine, turned on the air conditioner, and presented receipts for the new tires and the brake job he had done on the car shortly after he bought it. He assured Linda the car had given his daughter no trouble.

The seller rode with her while she tested the car. He directed her to the interstate so she could see how the Toyota performed.

When they closed the deal, Linda paid in cash and gave the seller a false name and the memorized apartment address. She drove back to the Jeep and transferred her three suitcases to the trunk of the Toyota. She left the Jeep's driver's door window down and a key in the ignition. She considered removing the license plates, but she could not think what she might tell a curious police officer in the event she got caught doing so.

Linda returned to the southbound interstate in the Toyota, got off twenty minutes later at Riverton, found an older motel, paid cash for a room, showered, and tucked herself between cool, clean sheets.

TWO

"There was a phone message from Doctor Steven Reynolds on my machine. He wants you to call him. Here's the number."

Lansing Ballantine, my University of California at Davis professor father, recited the number, and I wrote it while sitting at the table inside my fifth-wheel travel trailer. Outside a hard August rain pounded my roof and the roofs of all the other recreational vehicles sitting in the RV park behind the Boomtown casino just inside the Nevada border a few miles west of downtown Reno.

Unlike most other citizens under forty, I do not like cell phones. I don't like land line phones, either, but in my business I am occasionally required to talk with people. I have advised the few folks who have my number I will activate my phone at eight o'clock every Saturday morning I am within range of a cell tower.

By reading part of the thick instruction book, I taught myself how to answer the phone, make calls, and retrieve voice mail messages. My phone has the electronic ability to speed dial, text message, and provide me with alarm clock service, but I don't use those features.

No, I am not retarded. I have a law degree from UCLA, and I was a patrol cop for the LAPD until I took a bullet in the hip and a medical retirement. I simply do not like my life interrupted by people who believe they must talk with me. I don't like traffic, either. Or smog, or fast food except Original Tommy's chili burgers, or wives, or cats.

The latter two reciprocate my feelings.

Actually, I like cats. I just can't eat a whole one by myself.

That Saturday found me and my mixed-breed mutt, Penny, in Boomtown because I periodically visit my severely autistic son, Danny, Junior, and my part-time girlfriend with benefits, Kyra Simmons, both of whom reside in Reno.

I finished my chat with my father, closed my phone, and thought about Steven Reynolds.

About two years ago FAA investigators believed they extracted Doctor Steven David Reynolds' burnt and headless corpse from his fire-blackened and partially melted single-engine Piper which had crashed into a dry lake in the desert near the Oregon-Nevada border. Ed Logan, CEO of a private insurance adjusting firm he owns in Los Angeles, had called me. He told me his gut started rumbling when Marva Reynolds, the physician's widow, called her local agent and asked how to file a claim for her million dollars in life insurance benefits.

I met Logan during the short time I actually did law, but I found the investigative work he offered, and continued to provide, much more interesting than handling cops' divorces. This work also took me out of Los Angeles which was a larger perk than I realized at the time.

Logan reported that Reynolds, a dozen weeks before his plane crash, had changed his life insurance policy in a highly unusual way. The physician reduced his coverage from a million dollars to one hundred thousand and made his student loan bank, to which he owed nearly ninety thousand dollars, his primary beneficiary. That meant Marva would receive about ten grand on her husband's death.

After talking with Marva, the Sacramento agent told Logan he felt the doctor had not mentioned the changes to his wife.

Logan had asked me to look into the case with the advisement he could not pay Marva's claim until a laboratory confirmed the crispy corpse was her husband's. I visited four hundred pound Marva who mentioned her husband's affair with an ER nurse. When I tried to talk with Linda Coleman, her landlady told me Linda's mother in Idaho had a health emergency. The nurse broke her lease and left town.

On the way from Sacramento to the phony Twin Falls address Linda gave her landlady, I visited my pal, Brad Gunn, and his family. Brad is the agent in charge of the FBI's Reno office. I mentioned the case.

Brad did some computer searching and found that Steven Reynolds, Junior, had, during 1988 and 1989, purchased what brokers call "penny stocks," that is, those which cost less than five dollars per share. He had the wisdom or good fortune to buy Microsoft at less than two dollars per share, Cisco Systems for thirteen cents per share, Linear Technology Corporation shares for ninety-eight cents, and so on. He bought a few losers, but the total appreciated value, at the time he sold them, exceeded a million six hundred thousand dollars.

But Brad discovered the Steven Reynolds, Junior, a US Army tank commander, got killed in Operation Desert Storm.

The FBI concluded Doctor Reynolds, Senior, found the old stock certificates, sold them in his son's name and social security number, converted the money to cash, and declined to pay taxes on the profits.

I found Reynolds and Coleman in a mountain cabin, told Brad, and the FBI let me watch them arrest him. I could see their unhappiness when they discovered the nurse and the cash were not present.

So the doctor remained with the living, Ed Logan deposited ten percent of what I saved him into my bank, and I went fishing which is what I do when the season is open.

I tapped the numbers my father had given me. After identifying myself to a phone answerer, I got put on hold and forced to listen to classical music for two minutes.

"Doctor Steven Reynolds."

"Dan Ballantine calling."

"Thank you for calling me, Mister Ballantine," said Reynolds. "I came into the clinic this morning because your father said you would not receive my message until now."

"What do you want to talk about, Doctor Reynolds?"

"I want to hire you."

"To do what?"

"To help me find Linda Coleman. I have reason to believe she still has most of the money she stole from me."

"Do you have any idea where she might be?"

"I think so."

"What do you have?"

"I would rather not discuss it over the telephone, Mister Ballantine. I would like to meet with you in person, and I am willing to pay you to come to Boise, Idaho."

One benefit of my life style is that I am free to move about the country with my dog to do my work and search for new fishing holes. I knew from my previous search for Reynolds and Coleman I would have to drive a full day to reach Boise from Boomtown. I also remembered I enjoyed a week of good fishing in the lakes north of that city after Reynolds' arrest.

"How much are you willing to pay for what will probably consume a week of my time?" I asked.

"I don't know where you are, Mister Ballantine, but if you're in the United States I am willing to reimburse you for a round trip commercial plane ticket to Boise. I will also reimburse you for a night in Boise, your meals, and I will pay you a hundred dollars an hour while we talk.

"I don't see how you could lose more than two days."

"I don't fly," I said. "My work requires that I move around, so I live and work from a travel trailer. Considering the price of gasoline and the travel time required to reach Boise, I will need two thousand dollars, in advance, and I won't arrive until next Tuesday at the earliest."

"Well," said Reynolds hesitantly, "okay. I guess I can afford that, but I don't have it all today. May I send a thousand now and pay you the second thousand when you get here?"

"Does Boise have a branch of the Bank of the West?"

"I don't know. Let me check my phone book. I need to put the receiver down for a moment."

"I'll wait."

I heard a clunk, a drawer rolling, a soft thud, then flimsy pages turning.

"Yes," said Reynolds after lifting the phone. "Two."

"If I give you my account number, could you deposit the first thousand today? I believe some branches are open until noon on Saturdays."

"It's a few minutes before ten here. Yes, I can do that."

"I will check my account on line a few minutes after noon," I said. "If I see you have made the deposit, I'll start for Boise as soon as I finish some local business.

"If you don't make the deposit today, I'll check my account Monday about noon."

"I'll make it today," said Reynolds. "I'm still living in that cabin where the F B I arrested me. I don't have phone service there, and I use a generator for power. You are welcome to park your travel trailer there while we talk."

"Will you be near this telephone number on Tuesday?"

"Yes. This is the clinic where I work. I probably won't answer myself because I see patients on week days, but somebody will answer and will know where I am."

"I will call this number next Tuesday."

"Thank you, Mister Ballantine. I look forward to talking with you Tuesday evening."

"Good-bye," I said.

My "local business" was a date with Kyra Simmons which, at the moment, meant more to me than Steven Reynolds or Linda Coleman.

I punched the buttons for Brad Gunn's home phone.

"Gunn residence," said Brad's wife.

"It's Dan Ballantine, Melanie. How are you?"

"Hey, Dan! Long time no see. I'm fine. How are you?"

"I'm well. Say, do you remember me telling you and Brad about Doctor Steven Reynolds about two years ago?"

"I do, Dan. Whatever happened to the doctor?"

"I just talked with him," I said. "He's still in Boise and says he works in a clinic. He said he wants me to help him recover the money that disappeared with Linda Coleman. I thought I'd ask Brad for a follow-up on Reynolds' tax evasion case. Is he there?"

"No, Dan. He went into the office this morning. I do expect him home for lunch soon."

"I'm camping at the R V park next to the Boomtown casino. Would you ask Brad to give me a call?"

"Sure, Dan."

THREE

Linda Coleman planned to hide in San Felipe, Mexico. She had once read a travel magazine article describing the resort town on the west side of the Gulf of California. With a large population of semi-permanent Norte Americano residents, she assumed she could blend in and enjoy a vacation which could last as long as she wished.

She had left untouched the five hundred thousand dollars

she "earned" for murdering her first husband. Linda had always considered that money her retirement fund with the understanding she could retire whenever she desired. Her employment position as a supervising emergency room nurse had helped fill her time, and, when Doctor Steven Reynolds joined the day shift, she began to enjoy her work.

That the physician fell in love with her complicated matters as his fat wife refused to give him a divorce. Though Linda often told Steven she dreamed of married life and making babies with him, part of her enthusiasm came from the hard fact she knew neither of those events would ever occur.

Reynolds discovery of his son's stock certificates initially threatened Linda. Though he stated a desire to avoid sharing the proceeds from the liquidation with Marva, Linda feared he would declare his find and pay whatever it cost to divorce his ugly wife. Linda predicted their relationship would end when she confessed to Steven she would neither marry him nor bear his child.

As she watched Steven turn stocks into cash, greed led her to suggest Steven fake his death so they could live together in her brother's Idaho cabin.

After dark the day she purchased the Toyota, Linda awakened from her sleep ready to travel. She drove the small car south on Interstate 15 to Nephi where she stopped for a café dinner. She topped her fuel tank in St. George, drove through the dark desert, and reached Las Vegas as the sun lightened the eastern sky and early commuters entered the freeway system.

At the first motel Linda visited, the morning clerk wanted to copy her credit card. When Linda said she had been a victim of identity theft and had not yet cleared her credit problems or obtained a new credit card, the clerk apologized and declared she could not register Linda as a guest without a card.

Linda found a clean, modern non-franchise motel where the clerk accepted her false name, phony Salt Lake City address, Toyota license plate number, and cash in advance for three days. After she placed two of her suitcases in the room, the money case remained in the Corolla's trunk. Linda had decided the odds she might be robbed in her room were higher than having her compact economy car stolen.

While driving across the desert, Linda decided she needed different identity documents as soon as possible. Because she had no need to apply for credit or social security benefits, she concluded a driver's license and a passport would be sufficient.

After a shower, a nap, and lunch, Linda found a computer store, paid cash for an expensive laptop and took it to an internet café. She entered "new identity" in a search engine and felt amazement when eighteen million English language pages appeared. She modified her search to "get new identity," and the engine rewarded her with over thirty-four million pages.

Though Linda expected such businesses to be outside the country, she found a Las Vegas store and printed a map.

Before she closed her laptop, Linda searched for a Boise, Idaho, newspaper, and read an article describing the booking into the county jail of a Doctor Steven David Reynolds for federal income tax evasion. When the reporter sought to question the local FBI liaison officer, she received the 'there is an ongoing investigation and no facts can be released' response. The reporter visited the prisoner who declined to discuss his pending case.

I knew it! thought Linda. *A man in that Forest Service truck watched for us to leave the cabin. I got out just in time.*

It did not surprise her that she felt no twinge of conscience for Steven Reynolds.

Linda logged off, closed her laptop, drove twenty minutes, and found a less than pristine strip mall containing a small store bearing the sign A NEW YOU on the glass door.

Linda parked where a person inside the store looking outward could not see her car, walked to the door, and pushed it open. A ruddy, chunky man with a terrible comb-over sat at a well-used wooden desk on the opposite side of a store-wide counter. She watched him get to his feet and step to his side.

"Good afternoon. I am Joseph Smith," said the man. "How may I help you?"

Joseph Smith? thought Linda. Come on. Don't you have more imagination than that?

"I need a new driver's license and passport in a name different from my own," said Linda.

Smith smiled and said, "I think, perhaps, you misunderstand the services we offer, Ma'am." He reached under the counter, retrieved a colorful brochure, and placed it on the surface so Linda could read it.

"As you can see," said Smith, "we primarily offer seminars." He put his finger on the brochure and added, "This coming weekend we have a lecture entitled 'Why Credit Bureaus No Longer Serve Any Functional Purpose' at the Mandalay Bay Hotel and Resort.

"And the following weekend we offer our popular 'How to Identify and Acquire New Identities' seminar. Perhaps I could enroll you in that. Many of our clients have found it helpful.

"We also have online seminars through the University of Nigeria which you can pay for here or use your credit card on your computer."

Linda frowned. "I guess I did misunderstand your business, Mister Smith. I've recently left my lying, cheating husband, and I managed to get away with a good deal of his cash. He is very angry, and I know he will pay people to search for me. I need a passport to enter Mexico and a driver's license which would pass a routine examination by a police officer should I be stopped for some infraction.

"Could you refer me to someone who might provide me with those documents?"

"Do you realize what you are asking for is illegal?"

"Of course. I expect they will be rather expensive, too."

"Are you employed by any law enforcement agency?"

"No."

"Of course you aren't," said Smith, "and I believe you."

"From the tone of your voice I can tell that you do not."

"Can you return after dark?"

"I suppose," said Linda. "If it's really necessary."

"My back door is marked one fourteen. Remove all metal from your person and your purse, return at eight o'clock, and knock on the door eight times. Be prepared for me to pass a metal detector over you. Bring two thousand dollars in cash."

Linda met his eyes. "You won't mind if my sister waits in her car outside your door with her cell handy, will you?"

"No. Tell her you will be inside about ten minutes."

"Thank you, Mister Smith. See you at eight."

In the back office of A NEW YOU at eight o'clock, Smith asked Linda to hold her car key in her outstretched hand then he passed a sensitive metal detector up, down, and around her body. "You understand I must assure myself you are not wearing a transmitting or recording device, right?"

"I do," she said.

When Smith finished his test, he turned, leaned against the counter, pointed to a four foot high stool placed near the back door, and said, "Please have a seat."

Linda climbed onto the stool.

"I can offer you several different types of new identities," said Smith. "I have available actual documents which were stolen by purse snatchers or burglars. We must assume they have been reported stolen and, accordingly, have limited use.

"I have similar documents acquired from deceased persons. By 'acquired,' I do not mean I have the deceased person's personal documents but duplicates which have been obtained from the issuing agencies. For example, Mrs. Jones dies in Las Vegas. Before her death certificate gets into the state's computer system, a person who looks like Mrs. Jones appears at various agencies, claims she has lost her purse, and obtains a new driver's license, birth certificate, and so on.

"These documents are real, but they, too, have obvious limitations.

"The best documents have been created from a person long deceased and are absolutely clean. They are quite expensive, but you actually become a new person and can use these documents as if you had obtained them legitimately.

"Though I would try to match your height and weight to these documents, their use would probably require you to change your hair style and possibly your make up.

"Finally, I could take your picture and have the documents you need prepared with whatever name you choose, but common sense should tell you that such forgeries are the easiest to break by authorities."

Smith stopped talking and looked at Linda.

"I only need to get into Mexico where I can blend in with

tourists for a few months until my husband quits looking for me. Though he has a fortune, he's a cheapskate. I doubt he is willing to pay searchers for more than six months."

"Where do you plan to enter Mexico?" asked Smith.

"At Calexico."

"If you have a car, I've been told the Mexicans at San Luis, below Yuma, are more relaxed, and, if questions arise, are more susceptible to la mordita, the little death."

"The little death?" asked Linda.

"A bribe," said Smith. "For example, under certain circumstances one might say to a Mexican border guard, 'I am certain my papers are in order, sir. May I give you one hundred dollars to verify that they are?'"

"I see. What if I did not plan to drive into Mexico?"

"Then, unless you have someone with a car waiting on the Mexico side of the border, San Luis is not a good choice. Walking across from Calexico into Mexicali for a day of shopping should present no problems except you can't take much with you. For a relatively small fee I could have trunks and suitcases transported across the border for you within a day or two of your crossing."

The San Felipe article Linda read suggested vacationers might not want to take their personal vehicles into Mexico. In Mexicali one could find safe and reliable bus transportation for the one hundred mile trip to San Felipe. Linda had planned to deposit her money in an El Centro bank and make that bus trip every few months as needed for living expenses.

"I'm traveling light and will buy clothes in Mexico," said Linda. "How much would you charge for a driver's license and passport which would pass scrutiny at Calexico?"

"Any particular state?"

"California, I think, would be best, but Nevada is okay."

"Three thousand for California. Twenty-five hundred for Nevada. And I'll need three days."

"California it is. May I have a Palm Springs address?"

Smith nodded and studied Linda's face a moment. "I'm happy to do that for you, but I was just thinking you look very much like a package we have in inventory."

"What does that mean?"

"About six months ago a Long Beach, California, woman named Lorraine Portman went sailing with friends to Catalina. She was about your age and looked a lot like you. They ran into unexpected bad weather, and their small boat capsized. Everybody wore life vests, and all were rescued except Lorraine. Her life jacket washed up on shore two days later, but her body was never found.

"The search made the news and, before Lorraine's husband returned home, an enterprising burglar broke into their house. He found one of those small, cheap, hopefully fire proof safes people buy, and he stole it. After he forced it open, he sold us her birth certificate, social security card, and passport.

"We could make a duplicate of her California driver's license and let you have the whole package for ten thousand dollars. Since Lorraine's body was never found, she has not officially been declared dead. In fact, I suppose it's possible she got picked up by a Good Samaritan and used the episode as an opportunity to get away from an abusive husband."

"She probably slipped her life jacket and drowned."

Smith nodded. "Probably, but California computers won't show her dead until her husband waits the statutory amount of time and secures a court declaration."

"You say I look like her?" asked Linda.

"Your facial structures are similar," said Smith. "She had short blond hair and a tan which you could duplicate quite easily. You may be an inch or two taller and a few pounds lighter than she was, but that does not show in a head shot."

Linda wondered if Smith flattered her as part of his sales pitch. She lied, "I must make my cash last a long time, and I didn't plan to spend so much for identification."

Smith frowned. "That's unfortunate. Our prices are nonnegotiable. I'm sure you can understand why such a package would command a premium."

Linda nodded.

"If you still want a California license and passport, I'll take your picture and two thousand dollars down and have them for you Monday. You bring in the balance when you pick them up. Cash, of course."

"Could I examine the Portman passport?"

"You may," said Smith, "but it is not in Las Vegas at the moment. I could have those documents here tomorrow evening for your review. If they are not to your liking, I will take your photo for the others. Okay?"

"That is acceptable," said Linda. She slid off the stool.

"I need a non-refundable five hundred dollars cash to have the Portman documents brought to Las Vegas," said Smith.

Linda opened her purse, removed five bills, and handed them to Smith.

Smith stepped to the door and opened it. "Come to this door tomorrow evening at eight. Again, no metal."

Linda nodded. "I'll be here."

Smith said, "Have a good evening."

"Thank you," said Linda.

FOUR

Brad Gunn called me an hour after I talked with Melanie.

"Dan! How are you?"

"I'm good, Brad. How are you?"

"We're all most excellent. Will you join us for lunch? Tim and Emily would like to see you and Penny."

"I would like that. What can I bring?"

"Just you and the mutt, Dan. Come as soon as you can. Melanie is assembling sandwiches as I speak."

"Did Melanie tell you why I called?"

"She did, and I will update you on Doctor Reynolds when you get here."

"Great. See you in about twenty minutes."

Penny sat still while Brad's elementary school age children petted and scratched her. Then the children washed their hands, and we all sat in a kitchen nook to a lunch of sandwiches, grilled cheese for Tim and Emily, and ham and cheese on a fresh, light rye for the adults. Melanie also had pickles, chips, milk, and soft drinks on the table. After we ate, she took the kids and Penny into the den to play a few minutes before the children napped. Brad and I moved to the living room.

"Marty Pemberton told me Doctor Reynolds found a rabbi in the Boise jail," said Brad after we dropped into arm chairs.

"I'd bet that doesn't happen often." I glanced out a window and noted the rain had stopped, and the sun again shined.

"Well, the rabbi was not among his fellow inmates.

"Reynolds declined to make any effort to raise bail and, after a couple of days of doing nothing in his cell, he volunteered to work in the medical facility. There he met Doctor Samuel Trenton who, in addition to running that facility for the county, operates a clinic in Boise."

"Wasn't Pemberton that officious agent in charge of the Boise office?" I asked.

"Right. He said Trenton got Reynolds a local lawyer who came up with an interesting argument regarding Reynolds' tax liability. He took the position the Reynolds, both Steven and Marva, should only be responsible for the increase in the value of their son's securities from the date they discovered them."

"That must have reduced the government's money claim," I said. "What did the federal judge think of the argument?"

"It did cut the Reynolds' liability, but I don't think a judge ever heard the argument. According to Pemberton, the government lawyers' first conclusion was to take the case to trial and see what a judge or jury might say. But a couple of factors weighed on them. One, they would be seen as putting the squeeze on the parents of a deceased Desert Storm war veteran who was killed in the line of duty. Lieutenant Steven Reynolds, Junior, was an only child who happened to get lucky with some penny stock buys. And, two, with the passage of time and Pemberton's failure to actually find Linda Coleman or the cash, the government's lawyers asked if Reynolds might be willing to plead guilty to income tax evasion and pay all taxes, penalties and interest without a fiscal battle over the amounts."

"I don't see how Linda Coleman's disappearance with the money was Pemberton's fault."

"It wasn't, but he was the man in charge," said Brad. "The fibbie rumor mill says he took the first cloud, however light, on his career pretty hard. Fortunately for the troops under him, he got off the dictatorship horse he'd been riding and became reasonable agent."

"Is that why you referred to him as 'Marty' instead of something more formal?"

Brad nodded. "He told me to call him 'Marty.'"

"Interesting," I said. "I remember him as having a pretty stiff rod stuck up where the sun does not shine."

Brad grinned. "He did, and he would like to be kept in the loop regarding any efforts to find Coleman or the cash."

"It's human nature to remember the failures."

"I certainly remember mine," said Brad. "Anyway, Reynolds' wife jumped into his tax evasion prosecution with a lawsuit against him for conversion of marital property. She also sought to divorce him. Through his attorney, Reynolds offered to plead to one felony count of income tax evasion for a total of one year custody time. He also offered to take full responsibility for all back taxes, penalties, and interest arising in the case from the date he found the securities."

"I'm surprised he was willing to let fat Marva off the hook," I said. "I remember thinking he must have seriously hated her to come up with the crash and burn plan and try to make it work."

"It probably would have worked except for Bulldog Ballantine," said Brad with a smile.

"I'll take that as a compliment, but didn't you give me the code name 'Traveling Dick' at some point in time?"

"I thought that was better than 'Tahoe Gumshoe.'"

"Right," I said. "That was much better, of course."

Brad grinned. "Anyway, the government wanted two years custody time but gave up the fight on the dollar figures. And, after one of the lawyers had a chat with Marva Reynolds in her attorney's office, they also decided to let the doctor take full responsibility for the money owed on the case."

"One look at Marva probably convinced the lawyer she has little income potential when compared to her doctor husband," I said. "When I interviewed her I estimated she weighed over four hundred pounds. Her body odor suggested she had not bathed recently, and I would have bet serious dollars she had not cleaned her home in several weeks."

"Sounds like she made an impression on you," said Brad

with a smile. "No pun intended."

"That she did, and, after seeing lovely Linda Coleman in the flesh near that cabin, I thought I understood part of Reynolds' motive for his fraud scheme."

"I hear you," said Brad. "To continue, Doctor Trenton, a well-respected Boise citizen and a popular man with law enforcement up there, wrote letters to the Attorney General and the F B I Director declaring Doctor Reynolds was basically an honest man and an excellent physician. He stated he was assisting Reynolds in securing an Idaho medical license because he had promised Reynolds employment in his clinic upon his release from custody."

"Just what you would expect from a good rabbi."

"The government prosecutor compromised at fifteen months custody time. After giving Reynolds credit for the time he spent in the Boise jail, he spent a little over a year in Lompoc. He's been back in Boise working for Trenton, keeping his nose clean, and suffering a fifty percent federal wage attachment for ten months now."

"And he wants me to go after Linda Coleman," I said.

"Did he say he had any reason to know where she is and whether she has the money?"

"He has something, but he wouldn't tell me what it is. He agreed to pay my expenses for a face-to-face meeting in Boise. When I told him I would need two thousand dollars for a week of my time, he hesitated then said he would deposit half that amount in the Boise branch of my bank today and pay the balance upon my arrival."

"If he's willing to pay two thousand dollars for some face time, he must have something he believes in."

"My main reason for charging an exorbitant fee was to gauge his level of involvement."

"Will you let me know what he's got?"

"I may have to do that off the record."

"Okay, but I'm surprised to hear you speak those words."

I thought a moment. "You're right, Brad. I consider you a friend, and I want to continue doing so.

"Do you recall our conversation about Reynolds' threatening to kill Jack Roeper's son if Jack continued to search for his deceased brother's body?"

"Yes. I particularly remember Melanie's concern."

"You recall I told you I believed Reynolds stole a corpse, probably Jack's brother, beheaded it, and put it in his plane before he crashed it?"

"Yes."

"What I didn't tell you then was that I visited Reynolds in his jail cell the day after his arrest."

Brad looked at me but said nothing.

"I felt a little guilty about withholding that information."

Brad maintained his poker face.

"I presented my attorney I D to the jail and told them Reynolds' wife had hired me to talk to him. That was a lie and probably unethical."

"You wanted a conference room without recording devices?"

"Right. I asked Reynolds to write a personal letter to Jack Roeper advising him the feds had caught up with him for tax evasion. I asked him to tell Jack he knew Jack had nothing to do with his capture, and he would never harm Jack's son as he had previously threatened.

"I use the word 'asked,' but I told Reynolds what I would do if he failed to write the letter. I threatened to advise the Ely authorities of Reynolds' assault with a deadly weapon on Jack, and, more important, I threatened to open a murder investigation in Sacramento against Reynolds and Coleman. I assured Reynolds a 'Murder One' arrest warrant would issue against Coleman, and I assured him she would be caught. I suggested she would point the murder finger at him rather than take the fall, and, as the physician in charge of the E R, the possibility of his conviction of at least second degree murder was very strong.

"At that point in time, and maybe still, Reynolds believed something had frightened Linda and caused her to go into hiding with the money. He expected her to communicate with him some way, and he definitely did not want anybody looking for her."

When I paused, Brad asked, "Did he write the letter?"

"He did. His guard let me give him paper, a pencil, and a

stamped, addressed envelope. I called Jack a week after I talked with Reynolds. He had received the letter which included an apology. Jack had also made arrangements to get the headless and burned corpse from the F A A and bury it in the family plot in Utah."

"Do you think I would have instigated those criminal investigations if you had asked me to?" asked Brad.

"Yes, Brad. You're a straight shooter. I put Melanie's concern for Jack Roeper's state of mind above our mutual desire to see justice completed in Reynolds' case."

Brad smiled. "You think I enjoy living with Melanie?"

"You repeatedly present evidence of such, and I wanted to avoid creating any conflict between you."

"I appreciate that, Dan, and you may be right. I may have passed a word to the Ely and Sacramento authorities. And, while there is no statute of limitations on the Sacramento murder, Reynolds' A D W on Roeper is too old to pursue.

"Most important," added Brad, "our friendship has to include the discretion to withhold some information. I did not need then nor do I want now a battle with Melanie over Roeper's son's jeopardy, real or perceived.

"And you can tell me what you deem appropriate about Steven Reynolds, Linda Coleman, and the missing cash."

"Thanks, Brad."

FIVE

Linda Coleman could have been looking at a tiny photo of a twin sister in the passport she held. She lifted her eyes and said, "This is a very good likeness of me, Mister Smith."

"I agree," said Smith. "If you look at the stamped pages, you'll see she only used the passport twice for brief trips into Mexico. The government had to add extra staff to meet the demand for passports when they changed the rules regarding travel to Mexico and Canada."

"That's when I got mine," said Linda.

"So," asked Smith, "do you want the Lorraine Portman

package for ten thousand dollars or shall I put together a California package?"

Linda looked around Smith's back office a moment then looked back at Lorraine Portman's passport photo. Smith had again wanded her with his hand-held metal detector which reminded her use of the new documents carried risk. How much risk she did not know, but she decided possessing documents for a real person who was probably dead carried less chance of apprehension than false documents for a fictitious person. And, when she put ten thousand dollars on the table against her freedom, the choice seemed much easier.

"I want the Portman documents," said Linda. "I'll need two days to retrieve the balance of the cost."

"That's fine except I need another non-refundable thousand before I can ask my people to start on a California driver's license for you."

"I brought that amount," said Linda. "Do you need to take my photograph?" She opened her purse and held a small stack of one hundred dollar bills toward Smith.

He took the cash. "No. We can use the passport photo."

"Could you make the hair a little longer on the driver's license?" asked Linda. "I'll visit a salon tomorrow and attempt to duplicate the color and style."

"How much longer?"

Linda glanced at the photo as she answered. "Lorraine had what I call a 'short bobber' hair style. It's easy to care for. She probably played tennis or swam a lot.

"Her hair just covered the tops of her ears," said Linda. "While I'm willing to trim mine much shorter than it is now, I'd rather my hair completely covered both ears and my neck down to a collar. The length of the bangs could be brought down to just above the eyes, too."

"I'll pass those requests," said Smith. "Can you return Monday afternoon at five o'clock? You may enter through the front door."

"A weekend in Vegas? However will I fill my time?"

Smith smiled. "Yeah. It's a one-horse town all right. They roll up the sidewalks at sundown."

The next morning, Saturday, Linda searched the yellow pages for upscale hair salons. She felt excitement about trimming her shoulder-length dirty blond hair shorter, lightening it, and becoming Lori Portman. She had already decided Lorraine sounded too old, and she believed the former Mrs. Portman used the nickname.

When Linda considered becoming Lori, she returned to the internet café and used her computer to search the archives of the Long Beach Press-Telegram and the Los Angeles Times for stories about the missing woman. She learned Portman, age thirty-three and married to private attorney Michael Portman, sold real estate for Red Carpet before she went on her ill-fated sailing excursion. There were no Portman children, but Michael, in a later personal interest article interview given to a local reporter in his small but richly furnished Belmont Shore home, said they had talked about starting a family.

Right, thought Linda as she read the final story. *So what was the real reason Lori was not rescued?*

In her mind Linda added these "facts" to the wonderful Portman marriage: Michael regularly got drunk and slapped Lori around to the point she planned to leave him. An excellent swimmer, Lori took advantage of the storm to swim to shore. The incoming tide helped her. While her husband, their friends, and the Coast Guard searched for her, she reached their home. She hurriedly packed a bag, retrieved her vital documents from the family safe, pulled the cash stash she had been building from its secret place, and caught a plane leaving Long Beach Airport to Las Vegas.

No, Linda interrupted her own thoughts. *Lori would have to identify herself to purchase a plane ticket. She took the train to Las Vegas.*

Wait? Why didn't Lori run home to her parents? Her sister? What would she do in Las Vegas?

After a few minutes Linda decided she, as Lori Portman, did not need a detailed back story. Experience had taught her that the less she said about herself the better off she remained.

Linda decided she liked the idea of being a Wealthy Woman of Mystery, a WWM, and four years younger, too.

She also decided a true WWM would appear better dressed

than she did. She put on her most expensive casual skirt, blouse, and sandals, dropped a small stack of one hundred dollar bills into her purse, called a taxi, and, when it arrived, told the driver, "The Bellagio, please."

At the Bellagio salon, Linda examined a brochure describing the many services available. She approached an attractive young female employee and said, "My husband gave me money and told me to have a good time while he golfs the day away with his buddies. He probably meant for me to gamble, but I've decided I'd rather spend it here."

The employee smiled. "We are happy to help you do that. Would you like to make an appointment for a spa package?"

"Well, I was hoping you would have time to help me right now," said Linda. "Do you take 'walk-ins'?"

"Yes. We do."

"May I select what I want a la carte instead of a package?"

"You may. What did you have in mind?"

"Well," said Linda as she looked at the brochure, "in no particular order I would like a hair cut with a lightening of the color to medium blond, a manicure with a full set of acrylic nails, and a pedicure. Also, before I start working on my tan, I'll need a bikini wax and brow shaping session. If we have time, I would like my teeth whitened."

The young woman lifted a form, checked several boxes, then looked at Linda and said, "You've requested about seven hundred dollars in services. I think we can complete them all this afternoon, but there may be a short wait now and then. We have complimentary drinks and snacks available, of course."

"Great. I promise to make an appointment next time."

"Will you be paying for these services with a credit card or do you want me to add them to your room charges?"

Linda opened her purse and counted out eight one hundred dollar bills. "My husband gave me cash. May I put this amount on account?"

"Certainly. May I have a name for our staff and our file?"

"Lori Portman," said Linda with a return smile.

While the Bellagio staff pampered Linda/Lori, she decided she could enjoy such treatment more often now that she was

Lori Portman, Wealthy Woman of Mystery. With her make over completed before five o'clock, she visited the Gucci store and spent nearly nine hundred dollars on a cotton poplin shirt dress, matching shoes, and a small clutch purse. She carried her old clothing from the store in a fancy Gucci bag.

Linda had snacked during the day and had promised the ladies in the salon she would watch at least one of the evening Fountains of Bellagio shows. As she left the salon, the Director had placed a small card in her hand and suggested she use it to secure a small table from which she could enjoy a complimentary drink and watch a Fountain show.

SIX

After the last morning Mass of summer, Hernando Perez waited to speak to his priest, Father Roberto Mayaguez. When it appeared to him the final churchgoer had exited the church, Hernando climbed the stairs and called, "Father Mayaguez. May I speak with you a moment?"

"Certainly Hernando. What may I do for you this fine morning?"

"My foolish seventeen-year-old daughter, Juanita, wants to go north."

"I am sorry to hear that, Hernando," said the priest. "Should I have a talk with her?"

"I'm afraid it would do no good, Father. My oldest son, Rubio, has written her many letters describing how grand life is in Stockton, California. He has been working building houses there. He sends some of his money to his mother and I even though we tell him we don't need it and urge him to return home before he gets caught by La Migra and sent to prison."

"Surely Juanita does not think she could work construction with Rubio," said Mayaguez.

"No, but Rubio writes there is plenty of work cleaning houses for rich Americans." Hernando chortled. "She does not keep her own room in our home clean nor does she help her mother much with the rest of the house, but she believes she can get rich cleaning American homes."

"Cannot she find work here in Hermosillo?"

"She could, Father," said Hernando. "They would hire her at the Ford plant where I work if she would only complete an application and give it to them. But, as I said, she is set on going to Stockton. Her mother and I have done everything we can think of to discourage her.

"I tell you this, Father, because I fear she will run away and try to make the crossing alone if her mother and I do not help her. Of course, we fear for her safety should she attempt that."

"It is she who should be afraid, Señor Perez," said the priest. "Very afraid. I have heard many stories of young women such as Juanita who have disappeared while making the difficult and dangerous trip to the United States."

"Unfortunately, Father, like many young people, Juanita does not believe bad things will happen to her. We have let her read Rubio's letter in which he tells of how he did not make it across the desert on his first try," said Hernando. "After several days he stumbled into Altar severely dehydrated and had torn his shirt to wrap around his feet because his sandals fell apart. The Red Cross and then the Church helped him recover."

"I did not know this," said Mayaguez. "And still you think Juanita would run away?"

"Sí, Father, because after he got healthy again, Rubio got a job in a restaurant where he heard stories which helped him prepare for a second attempt," said Hernando. "He saved his money and bought proper shoes, socks, a hat, and a backpack which he filled with cans of tuna, beans, water, and energy drinks. He also paid a coyote to guide him into Arizona through the Tohono O'odham Indian Reservation. He wrote that he had heard La Migra lets the Indian police patrol much of that section of the border."

"I am glad to hear Rubio made it and is prospering."

"Thank you, Father," said Hernando. "His mother and I are happy, too, except Rubio's letters tell of much money and good times he has, and Juanita insists she must join him there."

"I feel the Church has failed in its mission to guide our children," said the priest with a shaking of his graying head.

Hernando did not disagree. "One story Rubio heard while

in Altar told of a coyote, a gringo coyote, who guarantees a safe journey to Tucson with very little walking in the desert. No one who pays this gringo coyote has ever been caught by La Migra. He supposedly has a secret place to cross the border, but no one knows where it is except him.

"The problem is this gringo coyote charges five thousand American dollars which must be paid before he will take a person with him."

"That is a lot of money," said Mayaguez.

"It is," said Hernando. "Rubio wrote that it is more than twice what he paid his own coyote, but Juanita's mother and I would pay it if the guarantee were true. We have saved most of the money Rubio has sent us, but we are willing to use it to pay this gringo coyote to take Juanita to the United States. Since Rubio has convinced Juanita to go to Stockton, his mother and I think it fair he pay for part of her trip."

"I can see the logic in that," said the priest with a nod.

"Can you help me find out if this gringo coyote really exists, Father?" asked Hernando.

"Perhaps I can. The priest in Altar is a friend of mine. He should have completed his morning Masses by now. Let's go telephone him."

"Thank you, Father," said Hernando.

The following Wednesday morning Hernando and Juanita left Hermosillo before dawn in the family's Volkswagen Beetle. They took Highway 15, a toll road, north a hundred and seventy miles to the junction with Highway 2. They turned left, and, seventy-three miles later, they stopped in Altar for lunch at a café described by the local priest to his colleague in Hermosillo. With the help of a waitress they met the gringo coyote who introduced himself as El Hombre.

The coyote wore a United States Marine desert colored baseball-style hat, a military-style long-sleeve shirt which he had rolled above the elbows, faded blue jeans, and sturdy boots. His leather vest sagged on the left side because it held a nine millimeter semiautomatic pistol in an inside pocket. A three-day beard under sunglasses with half-egg-shaped lenses enhanced the semi-threatening look on his tight lips.

"I am sorry, Señor Perez," said El Hombre in flawless Spanish, "but I cannot help you today."

Hernando looked around the café, lowered his voice, and said, "But our priest, Father Mayaguez, said you would be making a crossing tonight. I am sorry I did not have time to make a payment to you to reserve a place for my daughter, but she is here now and I have the cash money you demand. I have already called her brother who lives in Stockton, California, and convinced him to drive to Tucson."

El Hombre verified no other person paid attention to them. "Most of my travelers arrange to make this trip many weeks in advance. I can only take so many, and this trip is full."

"When will you make another uh, trip?" asked Hernando.

"I do not speak of such things to strangers, Señor," said El Hombre. "People who travel with me make a down payment and provide a safe way for me to communicate with them. A way that cannot be monitored by the police."

Hernando looked at Juanita. "I am sorry, Juanita. I will give this man money, and he will tell us when you may travel with him at some future time."

Juanita's eyes began to tear. She looked at El Hombre and said, "Surely you have a small bit of room for a tiny little girl like me. I promised I would take almost no space and I would be so quiet you would not know I was even there."

El Hombre stared at the teenager.

"Please, Señor," said Juanita. "My brother will be waiting for me in Tucson. Perhaps I can take the place of another traveler who got sick."

"He can't know that will happen, Juanita," said the father.

"Then we must find another coyote, Papa," said the girl.

El Hombre feared for such a pretty little girl who might try to cross with another coyote. He had heard stories of girls and young women sold into slavery and transported abroad instead of led into the United States as promised. When he and his brothers decided to get into the coyote business, they agreed it was not merely for the money. They wanted to provide the highest quality and safest crossing possible with a guarantee the U S Border Patrol would make no arrests.

"Part of the journey is by bus," said El Hombre. "Are you

willing to sit on the floor?"

"Oh, yes, Señor," said Juanita eagerly. "I will sit on the floor in the back where you won't have to step around me."

El Hombre looked at Hernando. "Are you willing to give me information about you and your family here in Mexico?"

"I am, but why do you request such information?"

"Insurance. I do not know you, Señor Perez. You may be a police spy. If my business suffers police troubles because of you or Juanita, I want to know where I may find you so that I may discuss it with you."

I will take that as a threat, thought Hernando. "My wife and I live in Hermosillo," he said. "I work for Ford." He provided the information El Hombre requested and watched the coyote write it in a notebook.

"I do not let my travelers make cell phone calls," said El Hombre. "If you give me the number of her brother, he will be called about half an hour before we reach the location in Tucson where we will drop Juanita. We only drop a few people at each location, so he needs to be in Tucson waiting for our call by three o'clock tomorrow morning."

"He should be near there as we speak," said Hernando before he recited Rubio's cell phone number.

El Hombre wrote the number next to 'Rubio Perez' in his notebook. "I collect my travelers in an old school bus. I pick them up in small groups at prearranged places. You must drive up Road Sixty-four such that you reach Saric at exactly nine o'clock tonight. It is seventy-five miles, so allow yourself plenty of time. Park your car near the Santa Gertrudis del Saric Mission and wait in it with your lights off.

"If you are late for any reason, I will keep your payment and leave without Juanita."

"We will be there, Señor," said Hernando. "I promise."

"Juanita may bring one small suitcase, nothing more. We provide water and food during the journey which will be complete before dawn."

Hernando nodded and gave El Hombre twenty-five hundred United States dollars. "Muchas gracías, Señor."

Hernando and Juanita left the café and returned to their

Volkswagen. After a review of his map, Hernando decided he and Juanita had time to visit the church before they started on the drive. On their knees they prayed for Juanita's safe journey to Tucson and asked that her brother Julio find her and take her safely to Stockton.

Hernando parked his VW near the Saric mission before nine o'clock. A few minutes later an old school bus which had been painted light brown and had the words 'Jose's Desert Tours' lettered on each side stopped behind his car.

Hernando and Juanita left their VW. In the fading dusk both could see the bus contained at least thirty people of all ages and both sexes. Had Hernando looked under the vehicle he would have seen a reinforced frame, extra shock absorbers, and a drive train protected by sheets of quarter-inch thick diamond-plate aluminum.

El Hombre left the bus driver's seat, approached Hernando, and held out his hand for the balance of the payment. When he received it, he directed Juanita onto the bus.

"She will be fine," said El Hombre to the already worried father. "She can telephone you from Tucson mañana."

"Her mother and I will be waiting impatiently for that call," said Hernando

El Hombre nodded and said, "You need not worry, Señor Perez. I promise you I will deliver Juanita safely to her brother if he is waiting where we tell him."

"What about the fence the Americans are building? How do you get into the United States with that fence in place?"

El Hombre smiled. "I doubt that fence will ever be complete, Señor Perez. It costs more than forty dollars per foot to build, and many ranchers do not want it on their property. Some have filed papers in the courts to stop it. And, in some places where it has been built, it already needs repair to the holes which have been made near its bottom.

"No, Señor Perez, we do not worry about the fence, and you need not worry about your daughter. Go home to your wife and wait for Juanita to call tomorrow morning."

Hernando nodded and climbed into his Volkswagen.

After Hernando Perez drove away, El Hombre stepped into

the bus and counted his passengers.

"Good," he said. "We are all here. Let's go."

El Hombre moved to the driver's seat, started the bus, and drove twenty miles north on a dirt road. Before he reached the tiny border town of Sasabe, he turned left and followed a thin track into the Baboquivari Mountains. He slowed the bus to a crawl as it wound through the rough country.

The track, barely wide enough for the bus between some rocks, came to an end between low rounded boulders at a ten-foot wide arroyo which ran north and south.

El Hombre turned off his lights and engine, got to his feet, faced his passengers, and raised his left arm with his forefinger aimed to the north. "What you see in the distance there is the United States of America.

"We will sit here a few minutes while our eyes adjust to the darkness. Then we will walk a mile up the arroyo until we come to a cave in the rocks to the west of us. The temperature in the cave is sixty-five degrees. If you think you will need a jacket or sweater, you must remove it from your suitcase now and carry it. We won't stop to open suitcases later.

"La Migra has unmanned drone planes carrying cameras and helicopters which they fly along the border at irregular times. While I have been promised they will not fly in this area tonight, both the planes and helicopters carry infrared cameras which allow them to spot warm bodies in the dark. The less time we are in the open arroyo, the better.

"Though it should not happen, if we see or hear such plane or helicopter coming, I may order you to return to the bus as fast as you can run. Or, if the bus is too far, I will order you to hide in the rocks and bushes along the arroyo. If I order you to hide, hold your suitcase over your head and body so the flying machine will not detect your heat.

"We will not talk while we walk in the arroyo or in the cave. Instead, we must all listen for La Migra's flying machines. If you hear one, call out to me.

"Now, you must listen to my next words very carefully. I will say them only one time."

El Hombre let his eyes wander around the bus until he felt all his passengers watched and listened to him. "We have guaranteed you safe passage to Tucson in the state of Arizona. We are providing an expensive service to you, but we can only do this because we are very careful who we take with us. You have been chosen because I believe you will keep our secrets.

"You have provided us with information about your families. If we ever hear that you have told anyone about us, all of your family members, your parents, brothers, sisters, and your children, will suffer. Their suffering will be so great they will not likely survive it.

"You must never tell anyone, ever, of me, of this bus, or of the place where I picked you up. You must never talk of how we traveled on the highway or in the desert, of the other vehicles we used, or anything about any other person you happen to see while on your journey."

In the moonlight reflecting off the light desert into the bus, El Hombre let a threatening glare rest momentarily on the face of each of his passengers.

"I will now describe to you what will happen during the next few hours if you follow, but only if you follow, my instructions.

"First, in a moment I will call your first name and give you a card with a number on it. This number is very important to the success of our trip. Do not ask me to change your number and do not change with anybody else. If you do that, you will not be dropped off in the correct place when we reach Tucson.

"Second, I will also give every third person a small flashlight. No one will shine a light inside the bus or outside in the open desert. Do not use the flashlight until we are inside the cave, and I tell you it is safe for you to do so. If I see a light before we reach the cave, the person shining it will not take another step toward the United States.

"Third, when I tell you to leave the bus, do so in the order of the number on your card. Number One will go first, Number Two will go second, and so on. You must stay in this order as I lead you north.

"When we turn out of the arroyo, the path will climb into the mountains. Do not turn on any lights, but watch the shoes of the person in front of you. There are loose pebbles in some places, and you must be careful where you place your feet.

"The cave stinks of bat guano in a few places, but all the bats have left for the night. Do not worry about the bats.

"We will walk in the cave thirty minutes until we come to a tunnel. This tunnel is actually a round pipe six feet in diameter so you can walk upright unless you are taller than that.

"We will walk in the tunnel a short distance then I will direct you, in the proper number order, to climb a ladder into another vehicle. This vehicle is a flatbed trailer upon which we have carefully stacked hay. Inside you will find a small red light and coolers filled with bottled water and snacks.

"If you think you will get thirsty during the next hour or so while we are walking, take a bottle of water from the box next to my feet and show it to me as you get off the bus. Drink what you want, but keep the empty bottle with you until you reach the ladder. You will give it back to me at that time. Do not throw the bottle down in the desert or in the cave or you will not be permitted to climb into the trailer.

"One last reminder. It's this cave and the tunnel we have built which get you into the United States unseen. Do not ever tell anyone about them. Not if you want your relatives here in Mexico to remain alive and in good health.

"Stay in line while in the cave and the tunnel with Number One at the head of the line. When you climb from the tunnel into the trailer, find a place to sit on a hay bale.

"Once you are inside and seated, the man with card Number One will collect the flashlights and place them in the box next to the coolers and close the padlock on the box. You will not need to use the flashlights again after you are in the trailer. The red light will be enough until you leave the trailer and it will keep your eyes adjusted to the darkness of Tucson.

"Also, once you are inside and seated, the driver will close the door from the outside. He will open it at the first stop then leave it open. Do not get too close to the door after he leaves it open. If the trailer were to hit a bump and you fell out, you would likely be killed when the rear wheels ran over you. In any event, the driver will not stop for you.

"The trailer has a large canvas cover on the top. We have found that La Migra does not stop and search such trailers because they do not know that people are riding in the center of the trailer.

"If you take a bottle of water or a snack from one of the coolers, place the empty bottle and the trash back in the cooler. Do not let it blow out the door. If a Border Patrol or police vehicle happened to be following the trailer when a bottle or piece of trash fell out the bottom, he would stop the truck and trailer and take all of you to jail.

"The ride to Tucson takes about two and a half hours. The first hour and fifteen minutes will be over unpaved desert roads. Do not move around in the trailer while it is moving.

"I will now explain how we unload the trailer. We use this procedure because it works. We cannot let you all out in the same place and have you walking around carrying a suitcase.

"You must leave the trailer in the order of the number on the card. The man with card number thirty-four will be the last person in the tunnel, the last person to enter the trailer, and he will also be the last to leave the trailer at the final stop.

"When I talked with you privately to arrange your crossing, you may have given me a telephone number of a person in the United States to call with your drop off location. If you did, your relative or friend will be called shortly after you are all on the trailer. Your friend or relative is already in Tucson and will have an hour to reach your drop point.

"The driver will be watching for La Migra, and he controls the red light in the trailer. When it is time to leave the trailer, he will stop the truck and flash the red light off once for each person he wants to leave.

"For example, if the driver wants three people to climb down out of the trailer at the first stop, the light will go off three times with about two seconds between each flash. Our guarantee for your safety requires you to obey the light and leaving the trailer at the proper place and at intervals.

"If anyone leaves the trailer before his or her turn, the driver will shoot that person then drive the trailer into the desert where all of you will be ordered out and left to fend for yourselves.

"So watch the red light. If it goes off three times at the first stop, the people with cards numbered one, two, and three may drop with their suitcases to the ground under the trailer and walk away. Your waiting friends or relatives will be close enough to see you. Do not shout or call to your waiting friends or relatives. Just walk slowly and quietly to them and continue moving away from the trailer.

"The rest of you must stay seated until the red light goes out again. At that time, but not a second before, the person with the next card number may leave the trailer. Then, again, the rest of you must wait until the red light goes out again.

"The driver usually leaves three or four people at each stop, but sometimes it is only one. So it will take several stops and an hour or so to unload all of you.

"Do not get impatient and leave the trailer before it is your turn just because you think you are safely in the United States. The truck driver has a gun and instructions to shoot anyone leaving the trailer out of turn. Even if you managed to get away, your family in Mexico will pay your price.

"If you follow my instructions, you will be with your friends or relatives before the sun rises.

"When I talked with each of you privately, I told you to pack your cell phone in your suitcase. While riding in the trailer you may want to open your suitcase and use your cell phone. Do not do it. La Migra has expensive equipment which allows them to listen to cell phone conversations. They are smart. If you call the person you believe is waiting for you, La Migra will also be waiting for you.

"Also, you must be silent when the trailer is stopped or when the door is open. La Migra has powerful listening devices which can hear people talking inside metal trailers. Your voices in the hay trailer are much easier for them to hear.

"One last thing," said El Hombre. "We have been helping people like you enter the United States for several years. If you follow the instructions I have given you, you will soon be living and working in the richest country in the world. You will be amazed at how much freedom you have and how much wealth there is.

"But do not forget you are in the country illegally and are subject to prosecution and deportation. If you commit a crime, you will serve a time in jail or prison and then be deported. If you ever have contact with the authorities, be polite. Do not run, and do not fight. And, most important, do not tell them about me or this bus or our cave or the hay trailer. Tell them you walked across the desert onto the Indian Reservation near San Miguel.

"If you are caught by the United States authorities, and you have not committed a crime, and you do not run or fight, it is likely you will simply be deported. While it is disruptive, it is merely a matter of finding me again. Three people on this bus have taken this journey with me before today. They followed my instructions and reached Tucson safely. They each enjoyed quite a long time in the United States, but, for whatever reason, they got caught. Because they had committed no crimes, they did not go to jail. They were simply deported back to Mexico, and now they are returning to the United States.

"I advise you to keep quiet, work hard, and not attract attention while in the United States. People who attract attention do not remain."

El Hombre turned and hefted a medium-sized backpack off the floor near his seat and placed it on the driver's seat. He opened it and removed a clipboard and a rubber-banded stack of three by five cards. "Okay. Let's get these cards passed out. I will call your first name and give you a card. You stay in your seat, and I will come to you."

He turned on a light attached to the top of the clipboard by a thin, flexible arm and read the first name. "Ramón." He looked up, and, when he saw a hand, stepped to a young man and gave him card number one.

*　　*　　*

Juanita Perez felt no fear, but, rather, took comfort in El Hombre's words. Though he was Norte Americano, he spoke fluent Spanish, he knew his job, and his confidence in their success calmed her. She did not look forward to the cave, but she realized they could not be seen while under the ground.

Juanita soon heard her name and received card number five from El Hombre. She did not receive a flashlight, but El Hombre had given one to the young man ahead of her. She kept an eye on him while they waited to leave the bus.

Rubio had written to her with instructions to wear sturdy shoes for the desert hike, but Juanita believed her brother had to walk many miles through the rough country to get to Arizona. She wore her best pair of athletic shoes and hoped she did not get them too dirty.

Juanita hefted her suitcase and got in line behind Number Four as they left the bus. She stayed close to him as El Hombre, wearing his backpack and a miner's hard hat with a lamp, led his thirty-four customers into the narrow arroyo. Soon all Juanita could see were dark, steep walls on both sides and the narrow band of lighter sandy soil at her feet.

After a while the man in front of Juanita stopped, and she almost bumped into him. She followed him along a barely visible trail which left the arroyo and climbed into the rocks. Soon they ducked into the near darkness of the cave entrance, walked a few minutes, and stopped.

A light came on ahead of her, and Juanita could see that it was the light on El Hombre's hard hat. She heard him tell Number One he could turn on his light. Soon other lights came on, and the line started moving again. She looked down and saw that Number Four lighted his steps.

Someone had worked on the path through the narrow, rocky cave, and the illegal immigrants no trouble walking. After fifteen minutes or so they crossed a wide white line painted across the path and on the rocks beside it. The letters "USA" had been painted on a rock on the north side of the line.

After another few minutes El Hombre turned and spoke loud enough for most of his customers to hear, "We're nearing the tunnel. We will go slower here."

Then the line slowed as they veered to the right and entered a smoothly rounded section of concrete pipe.

"Get ready to stop," said El Hombre after they had walked three minutes.

The line slowed then stopped. Juanita could see a round glow at the top of the tunnel ahead of them. She watched the light on El Hombre's helmet dance around the tunnel as he lifted a ladder and pushed it through a hole above him.

Then El Hombre doused his lamp, turned to those in the tunnel, and said, "People near the front of the line turn off your flashlights and leave them off."

The glow above El Hombre's head dispelled the fear Juanita knew she would feel in total darkness.

"Give me your suitcase," said El Hombre to Number One.

Juanita could see El Hombre lift the suitcase over his head then a pair of hands pulled it from the tunnel.

"Go up the ladder and into the trailer," said El Hombre.

Number One did as ordered. He could not see the face of the man who held his suitcase, but, as he looked around at the hay bales inside the trailer, the man between the tunnel and the trailer called, "Take your suitcase." Number One pulled his case into the trailer, set it near a hay bale, then turned to help his pregnant young wife up the ladder.

The rest of the loading, the drive into Tucson, and the unloading went as described by El Hombre.

After two men lowered Juanita from the trailer, she turned, caught her suitcase, then ducked and stepped away from the opening into a truck stop parking area.

"Is that you, Juanita?" called Rubio in English.

"Sí," she said.

"Over here," he called from her left in Spanish, "and you need to start saying 'yes' instead of 'sí.' This is America, and you must learn to speak American."

Juanita smiled and raised herself erect between a pair of trailers then hurried to her brother and hugged him.

Rubio took her suitcase in one hand and her hand in the other and said, "Let's get out of here!" He pulled her toward his car.

*　　*　　*

After the hay truck and trailer combination left the loading area, El Hombre climbed from the hole and dropped the ladder into it. He looked around the hundred-foot circle he and his brothers had graded in a narrow box canyon at the very southern tip of their ranch. Two miles west of him the huge Tohono O'odham Indian Reservation offered illegal immigrants many easier places to enter the United States. The rough country on their finger of land in the Baboquivari

Mountains between the reservation and the Buenos Aires National Wildlife Refuge which made the eastern boundary of their ranch deterred trespassing.

El Hombre found a rounded boulder at the edge of the circle, sat, and lit a cigarette.

Ten minutes later the headlights on a gleaming mystic green Hummer H1 Alpha, one of the last of the public versions of the military vehicle manufactured, appeared in a notch the Tuckers had graded at the lowest place at the north end of the canyon. The vehicle stopped.

El Hombre got to his feet, faced in the direction of the Hummer, and switched on his head lamp.

The Hummer responded by switching on four bright off-road driving lights and advancing toward El Hombre. As it neared him it made a half circle and stopped. The driver doused his lights and engine and climbed from the off-road machine.

"El Hombre!" he said with a smile.

"El Jefe!"

"How did it go, brother?"

"No problems, Max," said Emiliano as he handed his backpack and notebook to his brother. "There are twenty-two phone numbers in there you need to call. I arranged them in the drop off order for you."

"Thanks, Emiliano. I bought two new prepaid cell phones. I will make the calls as soon as I'm within range of a cell."

"Our clients' money, my notebook with the phone numbers you need to call, and six kilos of cocaine are in the pack."

"Good. Shall we fix the cover?"

The two brothers squatted by the heavy manhole cover, muscled it into place over the opening, then stood and kicked sand over it. When he could no longer see it, Emiliano rolled a nearby rock atop it and kicked more sand around the rock until it appeared to be a natural part of the desert.

"How many on this trip?"

"Thirty-four. I added a latecomer this morning. Our reputation is spreading. The teenage girl's father said their priest recommended us."

"We have a first class product and an impeccable safety record," said Max. "How many coyotes can brag they've never had a client who had to run from or got arrested by La Migra?"

"None I know of, but I've been thinking about something."

"What's that?"

"We really don't need to be taking these risks anymore, Max. I've got more money stashed than I'll ever need, and I think Lenny's had enough of the Border Patrol's political bullshit. We've never talked about quitting, but I'm thinking we should while we're ahead."

"With Lenny telling us when it's clear to roll, the risks are minimal," said Max. "And think of the quality service we provide to the illegals. We'll increase our fees after the fence is built through here."

"If it ever is."

"Oh, I think it will be. So does Lenny. I also think he enjoys the power he has," said Max.

"He's old enough to retire," said Emiliano.

"He may be that, but are you ready to fork a horse again and try to make a go of a ranch full of scrawny cattle?"

Emiliano smiled and shook his head. "No. One reason I got into this business is to avoid riding horses in the hot desert. The less time I spend sitting a saddle, the better I like it."

"Right, brother. Hummers and A T Vs are the way to go."

"You and your fancy cars."

"That's why you've got more money than I do," said Max. "You don't buy expensive toys like I do."

"Okay, Max," said Emiliano. "I may bring up the topic with Lenny, though. He hasn't been buying expensive toys, either. He may decide he's got enough stashed."

"We can always talk about it, brother." Max looked up at the star filled night sky. "Well, I'd better get on the road and make those calls. I hope to be in Las Vegas in time for a late lunch. You want to come along? I plan to take the Aston Martin, and you can start making the calls when we reach cell range outside of Tucson."

"No, thanks. I'd just as soon those Las Vegas guys not know who I am or what I look like. I'll go stash the bus and meet you at the ranch in a few days."

"I'll be back at the ranch with your share Monday afternoon," said Max. "Give my best to Tina."

"I will. Thanks."

"See you soon, brother."

"Monday or Tuesday."

"Adios." Max tossed the backpack onto the front passenger seat of the Hummer, climbed behind the wheel, started the diesel, engaged the Allison transmission, and headed north.

Emiliano turned and started along a climbing trail lighted by his helmet lamp. His 'desert tour' school bus sat about four miles away as the vultures flew, but he had no need to use the tunnel and cave when crossing the border into Mexico. The trail climbed easily from the tunnel exit in the box canyon and dropped into the arroyo on the far side of a low saddle, and nobody cared about southbound hikers.

SEVEN

I reached Boise about four o'clock, Mountain Time, Tuesday afternoon, and telephoned Steven Reynolds at his clinic. He repeated his invitation to park my trailer near his cabin, and I accepted it with the advice I could find it again.

Reynolds said he would pick up a bucket of chicken after work and meet me at the cabin at around six thirty.

When Reynolds arrived he found Penny and me sitting next to my trailer. My dog stretched in the grass while I sat in my camp chair reading Nelson DeMille's latest novel. The one with the *deus ex machina* ending I saw coming about half way through the story.

Reynolds got out of a four or five-year-old Ford Explorer, called, "Hey! Mister Ballantine. Good to see you. I'll be right there." over the roof, unlocked his garage door, raised it by hand, and parked the Explorer inside.

He walked toward me through the still open garage door and extended his hand. "Thanks for coming, Mister Ballantine. I really appreciate it."

I got to my feet and stuck my left forefinger in the book. Penny got to her feet beside me. "You're welcome. Can we go by 'Dan' and 'Steven'?" I asked as I shook his hand.

"We can, and it's 'Steve.' And thanks." He looked at Penny. "And who's this?"

"This is Penny," I said. "Give him five, Penny."

Penny raised her right paw.

Reynolds shook the paw. "Hello, Penny. Have you taken time to sniff around?"

"She's smart, Steve," I said, "but I haven't trained her to speak American yet. And, yes, we hiked a loop around the cabin. The squirrels are on high alert, and the birds either screamed at us or left the area."

"Good," he said. "Keep them on their toes."

"I didn't see any black boxes on the trees as I drove in."

"I dismantled my warning system," said Reynolds. "I didn't need it anymore after my arrest." He looked at my truck and trailer and asked, "Are you a full time R Ver?"

"I am. Am I parked okay?"

"You're fine. Sorry I don't have electricity for you to plug into. I run a propane-powered generator that sits out back a few hours each evening. It charges a bank of batteries which keeps the small stuff running during the day."

"No problem," I said. "I've got a propane-powered refrigerator and deep charge batteries, too."

"Won't you come inside? I've got beer and a couple of bottles of less than top drawer booze. The chicken's in the car."

"May Penny join us?" I asked.

"Certainly. I'll go through the garage, grab the chicken, and open the front door."

"Okay," I said as my mild paranoia kicked me in the pants. Maybe he lured me out here to murder me as revenge for finding him and disrupting his well-planned fraud scheme. Out of habit I lowered my right hand to the butt of the titanium Smith & Wesson forty-four special in my right hip pocket.

A few minutes later I relaxed inside the cozy cabin. I had a bottle of Corona in my left hand, and I scratched Penny's neck and ears with my right. Reynolds sat on a worn leather couch across a varnished pine coffee table from me. The chicken warmed in his oven.

Brad Gunn had provided the 'police report' version, but I

try to compare such with a 'horse's mouth' version whenever possible. "Before we get to business," I said, "can you catch me up on what happened to you since I visited you in the jail after your arrest?"

"Sure," said Reynolds. "First, I thought about the advice you had given me and decided it had merit. Second, I wrote the letter you requested to Jack Roeper."

"He got it. Thanks," I said.

"Third, I volunteered to work in the jail dispensary. The physician who runs it, Sam Trenton, appreciated my help. He also has a clinic in Boise where he does a lot of work with the poor and homeless. After he learned he could trust me, I basically took over the jail dispensary which gave him more time in his clinic."

Reynolds then told me what Brad Gunn had told me except he added that the year in the penitentiary at Lompoc, California, was mostly more working in the medical facility and trying not to get fat on the carbohydrate diet they offered. He described Marva suing him and securing a judgment against him for eight hundred thousand dollars plus interest at ten percent per year.

"I don't know how she thinks she'll ever get it. The feds get the first half of my earnings and will continue to do so for several years. After I pay on my student loans and buy a few groceries and gasoline, I don't have much left."

"Did her judgment include alimony?"

"She waived it in exchange for the house and cars. She sold the house and my car and got enough to pay for a gastric bypass." Reynolds shook his head. "I couldn't talk her into any sort of treatment while we were married.

"What may surprise you is that her father calls me once in a while. He's in his seventies and comfortably retired. We always got along well, and I think he found my big scheme amusing. The last time I talked to him he said Marva was down to about two eighty and had found a temp job. He doesn't mind paying for her apartment. He said he'd just as soon give her the money now instead of her getting it after he's gone."

"So what about your lady friend?" I asked. "You found somebody willing to spend time with a really poor doctor?"

"What makes you think I have a lady friend?"

I pointed at the knitted doily under the lamp on the table next to me then the curtains over the windows. "Bachelors don't have doilies under their lamps or clean curtains around their windows, Steve." I smiled. "These things look new."

He smiled. "Cynthia comes out and spends almost every other weekend with me here. She's a nurse at the clinic. Divorced. Her daughter still lives with her, but she works as a waitress while she's a sophomore at Boise State University. Her son lives with his dad in town. He's a high school senior.

"I wouldn't say it's love, but we're good friends and enjoy a relationship that's comfortable for both of us. With the debt load I carry, I wouldn't ask Cindy to marry me anyway." Reynolds looked toward his tiny kitchen. "That chicken should be ready. Why don't we get dinner out of the way before I show you what Linda sent me."

I try to limit myself to one tasty, but bad for me, meal per week, and that dinner filled the bill. Battered, deep fat fried chicken, potato salad, cole slaw, a biscuit with butter, and two beers. After we ate, Reynolds threw away the paper and led me back to his living room where we took the same seats.

"May I show you what I received from Linda?" he asked.

"Before you do," I said, "tell me what you think of her."

"Becoming a convicted criminal helped make me a realist, Dan. When I talked with you in the jail that day, I honestly believed Linda loved me, wanted a life with me, got frightened by something, and was waiting for me with the money I got from selling my son's stocks.

"However, as time passed, and I repeatedly examined the circumstances of our relationship, I reached the conclusion she is a murderer and a con artist who completely duped me."

I said nothing.

"That was a low point," said Reynolds. "I sat in a cell in Lompoc and felt life was a totally fucked up deal. I decided happiness did not exist except as a fantasy for fools.

"I had worked my ass off and took on debt up to my ears to become a physician," he added. "Then my son gets killed, my wife eats herself into a lazy, waddling caricature of a human being, and I finally wake up to the fact I made a bad career choice. On top of that, I made another bad woman choice and stupidly lowered myself to a level where I became a thief and a cheat, and I mutilated a corpse and intentionally crashed an airplane I really enjoyed."

I started to comment that prison is a time for self-examination for most inmates, but I didn't.

Reynolds lifted his beer bottle to his mouth and enjoyed a swallow. Then he looked at me and said, "But I've swung the pendulum back, Dan. Sam Trenton is a happy man. He's a fine doctor. He's not rich, but he has many friends, and he truly helps people. Including me.

"Not only did he help me with my legal problems, he helped me learn to like medicine again.

"Many of the people Sam and I see in his clinic either can't pay for medical treatment or can afford the bare minimum. We bill people, but Sam has never turned anyone over to a collection service. Medicare reimbursements make our nut, and whatever else we collect goes to maintain the facility, buy new equipment, or is distributed as an occasional bonus to the staff.

"My Explorer was donated by a fellow whose wife we couldn't save. I had no car when I got out of Lompoc. Sam sent me air fare and met me at the airport with the Explorer because he knew I would need a vehicle to get to and from the clinic.

"So I've mellowed, and I've stopped kicking myself. But I have not changed my opinion of Linda Coleman. I believe she is evil, Dan. A murderer and a thief. I was unable to revive Bill Roeper, and I now believe my efforts were futile because Linda injected him with a fatal amount of morphine."

I nodded my agreement.

"And if she killed Bill Roeper, she probably murdered her first husband like you suggested when we talked in the jail.

"So I misread her, Dan. From two I've spent the most time with, it appears I am a pretty piss poor chooser of women. Cindy is, hopefully, the exception that makes the rule."

I nodded. "Will you show me what Linda sent you?"

Reynolds reached to the floor, lifted a black, three-ring binder, and handed it across the low table to me. A thin stack of one hundred dollar bills was clipped to the outside.

"That's the balance of your fee, Dan."

I pulled his cash loosed and held it toward him. "You can have this back, Steve. It didn't cost me two thousand dollars to come here. I gave you that figure to see how serious you were."

"Thanks Dan. I had to borrow it from Cynthia which bothered me more than you can know.

"And I'm serious, Dan. There's a chance my son's stock money is still available. If it is and you could help me get it back, I could pay off the I R S and Marva and get some new equipment for the clinic."

I opened the three-ring binder and found several plastic pages holding narrow sheets of embossed paper containing writing in blue ball-point pen.

I looked up at Reynolds and asked. "Why did she write to you on toilet paper?"

EIGHT

Linda/Lori found a small table from which she could see the Fountains of Bellagio. She ordered a margarita and received it a minute before the six o'clock show commenced. She recognized Luck Be A Lady from Guys & Dolls.

The water danced and gyrated and held her entire attention for over five minutes. She wondered how many sprayers there were and how they could shoot the water so high.

As the fountains became still, and she lifted her glass to her mouth, a man holding a glass of amber liquid in one hand stepped to her table.

"I am Max Tucker," he said. "May I join you?"

Linda/Lori hesitated. She had not given any thought to the idea a man might hit on her. Well, at least not until she reached San Felipe.

She quickly assessed what she saw. A darkly handsome man. Forty or a year or two younger. No wedding ring. Rolex watch in either stainless or platinum, but not tacky gold. Tailored slacks and sport coat. No tie. Several dark chest hairs visible at the V of his open shirt. Nice, even white teeth. No facial hair, earrings, or tattoos.

Linda/Lori decided to take a chance. "You may." She placed her drink on the table and extended her right hand. "I am Lori Portman."

Max shook her hand firmly, placed his drink on the opposite side of the small table from hers, took a chair from a nearby table, placed it a hundred and eighty degrees from hers, and sat. "What did you think of the show?"

"Fascinating. Amazing. And I'm one of those people who wonders how things work," she said with a smile. "How many nozzles are there? How do they shoot the water so high?"

"I believe the gift shop has a D V D one may purchase which answers those questions," said Max.

"I'll have to look for that."

"Have you ever seen them at night?" asked Max.

"Not yet, but I intend to."

"There's a show every fifteen minutes between eight and midnight. I often sit in my room and watch until I fall asleep."

"You come here often, then?" asked Lori.

Max nodded. "My business brings me to Las Vegas several times a year. If we're having a good year, I treat myself to the Bellagio. So far the I R S has not objected to my deductions."

"If I may ask, what sort of business?"

"My brothers and I inherited the family cattle ranch in southern Arizona. I come up here to sell cattle mostly. Sometimes I make a deal to buy a new breeding bull."

"Do your brothers come with you?"

"Oh, no. I guess you could say I'm the cattleman in the family. My older brother, Leonardo, is a Deputy Chief with the Border Patrol. My younger brother, Emiliano, helps with the ranch and lives in what we used to call the guest house, but he likes Mexico and spends a lot of time there."

"The time you spend outdoors has given you a great tan."

"My coloring comes from the fact I'm one-quarter Yaqui Indian. My grandfather, the patriarch who bought the ranch and built our herd, married a fiery full-blooded Yaqui."

"Did he steal her from Mexico?"

Max smiled and shook his head. "No. She was born in the Pascua Pueblo which is in the northwestern corner of Tucson. The Yaquis lived throughout what we now call the Sonoran

Desert. A fierce and hearty people, they were never conquered militarily by the Spanish, and they defeated several successive conquistadores in battle."

"That's fascinating," said Lori sincerely. "Didn't the Spanish try to convert all the Indians to Catholicism?"

"They sent the Jesuits. The Yaquis worked with them, but they never took to their religion. The Spaniards finally ordered all the Jesuits out of Sonora and planned to send in the Franciscans. But the Yaquis weren't happy with that decision and rebelled to the point the new priests never arrived.

"My grandmother was a Methodist."

Lori smiled.

"My father was already born when our government gave the Yaquis two hundred acres near Tucson in nineteen sixty-four. They formally recognized the Pascua Yaqui Tribe in nineteen seventy-eight."

"When did they build their casino?" asked Lori.

"You're way ahead of me," said Max with a smile. "The tribe opened a bingo hall in 1992 which they expanded to include a casino two years later. They call it the Casino Del Sol, the Casino of the Sun. It's just outside Tucson."

"Good for them," said Lori. "I probably shouldn't say it too loud here in Nevada, but I have no problem with Native Americans building casinos on the land we gave them."

"Often that land is out in the boondocks," said Max. "Many tribes can't feasibly build a casino."

"Aren't the tribes with casinos supposed to share their profits with the tribes that don't have a casino?"

"From what I've read, they've become quite capitalistic which I believe is a popular euphemism for stingy."

Max sipped from his drink. "May I refresh your drink?"

Lori looked at her near empty margarita. "You may."

Max caught the eye of the bartender and pointed at their glasses. Then he looked at Lori. "How long are you in town?"

"One more question first," she said with a smile. "One brother is Leonardo, and the other is Emiliano. How did you get to be Max?"

"It's short for Maximilian. Neither of my parents stood up to my grandmother when she insisted on giving us our names."

Lori smiled. "My grandmother was very British and believed children should be neither seen nor heard. I only remember her as someone to fear and avoid."

Their drinks came and, a few moments later, the Fountains of Bellagio commenced a performance of God Bless the USA. Max and Lori and turned to watch the dancing waters.

"I simply have to find that D V D," said Lori when the music and dancing waters ended.

"So, Lori, what brought you to Las Vegas?" asked Max.

"I needed to get my hair done," she said with a smile.

"It looks very nice."

"Thank you, kind sir."

"You don't have a hair dresser at home?"

"Actually, Max, I'm a single lady on vacation. I'm passing through Las Vegas on my way to spend time with a girlfriend who has a time share in San Felipe starting next week."

Lori smiled like she thought a Wealthy Woman of Mystery would smile.

"One can get an excellent margarita in San Felipe," said Max. "Tequila Herradura Reposado is available there. You should ask for it by name."

"I will remember to do that."

"It's early, perhaps, but I have not eaten since early this morning. Will you join me for dinner, Lori?" asked Max.

"Did you hear my stomach growl?"

"I thought I heard the fountains bubbling." He smiled.

"A true gentleman," said Lori. "Do you want to eat here?"

"Are you craving anything special?" asked Max.

Lori thought a moment. "No."

"Well, I get all the beef and Mexican food I can handle on the ranch. When I come to Las Vegas I like to sample other cuisines. Do you like Asian food?"

"I do."

"Then I know just the place."

Max pulled a cell phone from his jacket pocket and looked at Lori. "This doesn't work on my ranch. I have to use a much more expensive satellite phone." He opened the device and touched seven buttons.

"This is Max Tucker calling. Do you have a table for me and a guest this evening?

"Thank you. We'll be there."

Then Max touched a single button. "Valet parking, please.

"This is Max Tucker. Is Byron available?"

Max smiled at Lori. After a half a minute, he said, "Byron, this is Max Tucker. Would you bring my car out, please?

"We'll be there in about twenty minutes.

"Thank you, Byron."

Max closed his phone, looked at Lori, and said, "Byron and I made an agreement a couple of years ago. I promised to deal exclusively with him, and, in return, he promised to park my car in the safest spot in the covered part of the lot."

"I expect you tip him generously, also," said Lori.

"Enough to make sure he keeps his part of the bargain."

Max and Lori finished their drinks then walked to the valet parking area. An attendant noticed Lori with Max and hurried around a low two-seater to the passenger side and opened the door for her. She handed him her Gucci bag and smiled to herself as she eased her butt into the leather bucket then swung her legs inside.

The attendant returned the bag and closed her door then trotted around to the driver's side and closed Max's door.

Max powered down his window and asked, "You'll save my spot, right, Byron?"

"Yes, sir, Mister Tucker," said Byron.

Max passed a fifty-dollar bill to the young man and added, "We'll be back before you go home."

"I'll be here waiting for you, Mister Tucker."

Max nodded then turned to Lori. "I think your bag will fit behind the seat."

"This is very nice, Max," she said as she turned and dropped the sack behind her.

"It's an Aston Martin Vantage Roadster. It's not too hot out, and we're not going far. May I lower the top?"

"You may."

"Your lovely hair will sustain less damage if you keep your window up."

Lori pushed the button to lower her glass. "And not hear the exhaust music? No way!"

Max smiled, engaged the gear box, and accelerated briskly toward Las Vegas Boulevard where busy Saturday evening traffic stopped him.

"Looks like you needn't worry about your hair," said Max. "We're not going anywhere very fast."

"Will you take me for a drive on the freeway after dinner?"

"That's a deal."

The stop and go vehicles forced Max to crawl the expensive sports car to the Asian district where he pulled under the canopy of a popular restaurant. A valet hurried to open Lori's door. As she climbed from the Aston Martin, Max powered up the top and windows.

The valet hurried around to Max who read the young man's name tag as he held out a fifty-dollar bill. "Here's the deal, Lee. Park it in a safe place, keep an eye on it, and I'll match this when we return."

"Yes, sir. No problem, sir."

The maitre d' greeted them inside the darkened restaurant where a blood red carpet complemented private booths swathed in red leather. "Good evening, Mister Tucker. How are you this evening?" He extended his hand and accepted the folded fifty-dollar bill Max held in his palm as they shook briefly.

"Fine, Mister Wu. Just fine. Sorry about the late call."

"No problem, Mister Tucker. Please follow me."

When Max and Lori had their seats, the maitre d' handed them red velvet-covered menus, met Lori's eyes, smiled shallowly, then looked at Max. "We received some very nice sea bass this morning, Mister Tucker. It is wonderful smothered with the chef's sweet chili sauce."

"Thank you, Mister Wu," said Max. "You just made a tough decision for me."

Mister Wu bowed. "Your waiter will be here shortly."

"Thank you," said Max. He turned to Lori. "Do you have a favorite food?"

"The sea bass sounds good, but that chili sauce must not be the kind of chili I usually have."

"It's basically onions, diced tomatoes, and cubed pineapple in a tangy sauce. It's not too sweet, and its bite is mild."

"Well, then," said Lori, "I really like shrimp, but I think I'll have the sea bass."

The pair made small talk over dinner. Lori declined further alcohol and drank sweet, hot tea with the idea she would be careful not to say anything she did not want to say. As the excellent meal wound to a close, she realized how long her day had been and felt a tiredness creeping over her.

"I can probably get us tickets for the Cirque Du Soleil Mystère show at the Treasure Island," said Max.

Lori lifted her tea cup and said, "It has been a very pleasant evening, Max, but I've had a long day. Rather than a show, I think a nightcap while watching another fountain show at the Bellagio would be a nice way to end it."

Max smiled. "We can do that, but I owe you a Vantage ride. How about I have the Bellagio pack us a luncheon basket and some wine, and we'll drive up to the ski resort for a picnic tomorrow. It will be cool up there."

"The ski resort?" asked Lori. "Where is the ski resort?"

"An hour north of town." Max smiled. "Well, a bit less than that in the Vantage."

"I didn't know a ski resort is that close to Las Vegas."

"Most people visit Vegas for the gambling, the entertainment, and the golf, and I doubt many hard core skiers and snowboarders come just for winter sports. But it's there for the locals who have to see snow now and then in the winter."

"I think a picnic is a great idea," said Lori. "What time do you want to leave?"

"I have some business to take care of in the morning," said Max. "How about one o'clock?"

"I'll be ready."

Max called for the check, paid the bill, left a generous tip, kept his promise to Lee the parking valet, and drove them back to the Bellagio. They watched Elton John's <u>Your Song</u> and Alex North's <u>Singin' In the Rain</u> while the waters performed.

"You should come back at Christmas," said Max. "They have a series of performances with holiday music."

"I should," said Lori. When the fountains stopped, she added, "Thank you for a great dinner, Max. I'll meet you here at one o'clock tomorrow."

"May I walk you to your room?"

"No, thank you," said Lori with a smile. "See you tomorrow."

Lori left Max sitting alone and hoped he would not follow her to the exit and discover she did not have a room in the Bellagio. She got lucky and found a taxi waiting outside.

Lori drove her Toyota to the Bellagio the next morning. She parked in the guest lot and rolled her fat "money" suitcase and one other bag to the desk. When she asked for a room for two nights, the clerk asked for her credit card. She explained was a recent victim of identity theft, and asked if she might leave a cash deposit instead.

The clerk made a photocopy of her "Linda Coleman" driver's license and accepted five thousand dollars in cash.

Lori hurried to her room, dropped her bags, and spent an hour shopping for the proper casual clothes for a picnic, and, additionally, an evening dress with the appropriate accessories.

Max stood and greeted Lori with a smile when she approached him at one o'clock. "I'm happy to see you again," he said sincerely.

The pair spent a happy Sunday afternoon together. Max drove the Aston Martin on the mountain roads skillfully fast and confessed to Lori he had taken the Bondurant High Performance Driving course twice.

They enjoyed a wonderful gourmet picnic packed by the Bellagio staff. As the time neared to return to Las Vegas, Max declared he wanted to spend more time with her, and he asked Lori again if she would attend the Cirque du Soleil performance. This time she agreed, and, after changing clothes, the pair spent the evening together.

As they left the performance, Max took Lori's hand in his, smiled at her, and asked a door man to secure them a taxi. During the short ride to the Bellagio, Max asked, "Have you visited the Skywalk yet?"

Because she recently had seen a television travel program,

Lori said, "A trip to Costa Rica is still on my 'to do' list."

"Costa Rica?" asked Max.

"Are you talking about the suspension walk in the Costa Rican rain forest?"

"No, although that sounds like something I should see some day," said Max. "The Hualapai Tribe has land on the west rim of the Grand Canyon. I guess they decided it's too far out of the way for a casino so they built an open-air glass walkway which juts seventy feet out from the edge. It's supposed to be quite a view of the Grand Canyon.

"I had planned to head home tomorrow, but I did some checking this morning. I hoped you would ride with me in the Vantage to the Skywalk tomorrow, but two things made me change my mind. One, to get there one must drive over Hoover Dam. I understand that, until they finish the bypass bridge, such crossing can be delayed because the Homeland Security people see the dam as a terrorist target."

Max smiled and added, "There's nothing more boring than sitting in an Aston Martin waiting one's turn to cross a dam."

Lori returned his smile.

"The second thing," said Max, "is that the last twenty miles of the road to the Skywalk are not yet paved. I have a Hummer I use for off-road driving around the ranch, and I would rather not take the Vantage off the pavement.

"Would you join me in a helicopter flight over Lake Mead, into the Grand Canyon, then a stop at the Skywalk?"

"I'd love to, but I must be at the Bellagio by four thirty."

"No problem," said Max.

As they entered the Bellagio, Max asked, "May I walk you to your room?"

"You may."

Outside her room door, Lori held her plastic key, turned to Max and said, "I had another wonderful day, Max. Thank you."

"You're welcome, Lori. So did I." He leaned forward and kissed her lips lightly. "Shall I call for you about ten?"

Lori smiled. "I'm looking forward to it."

The next morning their pilot took them over Lake Mead,

the Hoover Dam, an extinct volcano, and miles of rugged desert to the Grand Canyon. There they descended four thousand feet to the Colorado River then climbed and landed near the Skywalk. Lori felt fear when looking down through the glass walkway, but found the outward view wonderful.

At the hotel, Max escorted Lori to her room. "I must return home tomorrow. Will you join me for dinner this evening?"

"I would be happy to, Max."

"Le Cirque here in the hotel has a nice French menu."

"You know what, Max? I'd like a nice little steak."

"I'll make reservations. Seven o'clock too early?"

"I promise to be hungry."

Max kissed Lori on the cheek and said, "See you then."

Joseph Smith smiled when Lori stepped through the front door of A NEW YOU at five o'clock.

"Very good," said Smith. "The best I've seen in quite a while." He opened a folder on his counter, lifted a California driver's license to eye level, and looked from the document to Lori and back several times. "We could not have done better if I had taken your picture. There's just enough difference to make it totally believable."

"Thank you, Mister Smith," said Linda/Lori. She placed a Bellagio envelope on the counter containing the balance of Smith's fee. "May I see for myself?"

After Smith handed her the license, she verified Smith's staff had followed directions regarding her hair. She decided she had almost matched the color.

Smith opened the envelope, counted the money, then pushed the folder to Linda/Lori.

"Thank you very much, Mrs. Portman. It has been a pleasure doing business with you."

"Perhaps we can do more business," said Lori.

"What might that be?" asked Smith.

"I have cash I would like to convert to something more portable."

"What did you have in mind, Mrs. Portman?" asked Smith.

"I was thinking gold coins."

"That's doable."

"I could make the exchange at coin stores," said Lori. "What I need with the gold coins are documents reflecting the dates of purchase."

"Documents are our specialty," said Smith with a smile, "and the nice thing about gold coins is that stores buying them and selling them go out of business all the time. Depending on the dates you wish to appear on the documents, we could show them purchased at a business long since gone. No way the I R S nor anyone else could successfully challenge them."

"Well, you recall I told you I left my husband."

Smith nodded and said, "I remember that."

"Well, for whatever reason, my husband did not trust banks. He had several businesses that generated significant quantities of cash, and something tells me he did not pay taxes on the stash I found before I left him. I think if, instead of cash, I had discovered a collection of gold coins and receipts reflecting their dates of purchase, I could sell them as needed without attracting unwanted attention."

"Most gold dealers demand identification from sellers," said Smith. "I do know some people who purchase gold coins, U S Eagles, Isle Of Man Nobles, Canadian Maple Leafs, and Australian Koalas, without requiring identification, but they do so at a ten percent discount from the market price."

Lori nodded. "I see. Well, let's say, hypothetically, I had three hundred thousand dollars in circulated one hundred dollar bills. How many one-ounce gold coins would you sell me accompanied with documents reflecting multiple purchases over the last ten years up until about two years ago?"

Smith opened a drawer, lifted a small calculator, punched several buttons, looked up and said, "Right this minute half a million dollars would get you seven hundred and sixty-two one-ounce coins. I'm sure you understand the price of gold fluctuates constantly."

Lori looked beyond Smith a moment while she considered her options. The coins would take up less space than the cash, but they would be heavy.

"There are other tools for carrying about such a sum in a small package, Mrs. Portman," said Smith.

"I placed the cash in a safety deposit box, of course, and I will need to retrieve part of it from time to time."

"Diamonds or other precious stones are easy to transport. A stamp or coin collection doesn't take up much space. No one questions deeds of trust. Bearer bonds are available."

"I thought bearer bonds were made illegal."

"In nineteen eight-two in all states except Nevada and Wyoming," said Smith.

"I'm concerned about liquidity, Mister Smith. I would rather not visit my bank every few weeks. I would like to turn whatever asset I purchase into cash with a minimum of questions, identifications, and documents. My father once told me everyone will take gold."

"There have been cases of counterfeit gold coins, but testing devices are available. Most coin stores have them."

"I guess I need to think about it some more," said Lori.

"If there's any way I can help you, Mrs. Portman, give me a call or send me an email." He handed her a business card that read JOSEPH SMITH and contained a telephone number and an email address.

"Thank you, Mister Smith."

Lori left the store with her new documents.

The instant the door closed behind her, Smith opened his phone, touched an instant dial number, and said, "She just left."

"I'm on her," said the voice on the phone.

An hour later Smith's phone rang. He opened it and said, "Where did she go?"

"She drove a four or five-year-old white Corolla with Utah plates to the Bellagio, parked it in the lot, and went inside. I've been watching the car, but she hasn't returned. How long you want me to watch it?"

"Get comfortable. You're on the clock. Call me the instant she returns to the car. If she leaves town, be prepared to follow her to a place where you can stop her and do a thorough search of her and the car. If I don't hear from you, I'll send you some relief before midnight."

"Okay. I'm on it."

NINE

"She claims she's being kept prisoner and can't get any writing paper," said Steven Reynolds.

"Really?" I met my host's eyes.

He nodded. "Read it. It's almost unbelievable. Her pen skipped, and I had trouble with some of the writing. I put it in the folder so I could try to decipher some of the words without damaging the paper."

"You're sure this is Linda's handwriting?" I asked.

"Well, I didn't see her writing very often," said Reynolds, "but the content is convincing."

I began to read, but the writer's faulty ball point pen on fragile toilet paper slowed me. After a few lines, I looked at Steve. "I take it you've studied this enough to figure it out."

"I think so."

"How about you read it to me?"

"Sure."

I handed Steve the folder, lifted my beer, and listened while he read.

"Dear Steven:

"I am in very serious trouble. I fear for my life. I cannot think of any way out, and you are the only person who might help me. If you choose not to, I am doomed.

"I confess I am an evil person, Steven. At first I fell in love with you, but, then, when you did not have the courage to divorce Marva, I thought you were weak. I began to dislike you, and, when you found your son's stocks, I searched for a way to get a piece of the money. I didn't actually expect to get it all. That's just the way things worked out.

"I spotted a Forest Service truck on the road near the cabin when I went for groceries the day before you were arrested. I saw it again when I went out that evening to search for that blue jay's nest. I believed the police had found us and would soon arrest us, so I drugged your drink and left.

"I know you must hate me for not telling you about the truck, for stealing from you, and for refusing to help you after you were arrested. I understand that. If you help me, I ask nothing more than a strict business arrangement.

"I am being held prisoner by a wealthy man named Maximilian Tucker. He and two brothers own a large ranch on the Mexican border southwest of Tucson, Arizona. They raise cattle and hay, but I also believe they are smuggling Mexicans into the United States through their ranch.

"Max's brother, Emiliano Tucker, spends some time on the ranch, but he also goes to Mexico frequently. Another, older brother named Leonardo Tucker has visited the ranch several times. He is a deputy chief for the US Border Patrol in Tucson. I think they are all involved in the smuggling, and I think they are dangerous men.

"I want off the ranch with enough time to get away and hide from Max and his brothers, but I am never left alone. There is no cell phone or internet service here. The brothers use satellite phones, but there must be a code to make them work. I tried to call out on one once, but I could not do so. When Max found out I had tried, he hit me and raped me.

"I cannot leave the ranch without a vehicle. One time I tried to walk off, but it's too far to go in one night. I tried to wait out the heat of day, but Max found me. He took my suitcase containing my water and left me to die. I was in bad shape after I walked back to the ranch house.

"After my escape attempt, Max threatened to kill me and he locks me in my room each night. If Max or Emiliano is not here, Max's foreman, a mean man named 'Gordo' locks me in.

"The absolute worst thing is that Max takes me sexually when the mood strikes him. Almost as bad, when he's been drinking, he beats me for the slightest infraction.

"I have one ally. Isabel Gonsalves does my hair every two weeks in her shop in a small town called Sells. Max usually drives me there, and he sits in the salon and watches me and waits until Isabel is done. When Emiliano takes me, he sits in his truck outside and waits for me.

"One time Isabel saw I had a black eye after Max had punched me. I confessed to her Max beat me, and I had no way out of my situation. Isabel is sympathetic, and she agreed to forward this letter to you. I'm sorry, but the only clean paper I had available is this toilet paper.

"I plan to slip this letter to Isabel the next time Emiliano takes me to Sells. Hopefully that will be soon.

"Isabel has agreed to hold your response, if there is one. I'm not using my real name with the Tuckers. Please address your letter to Lori Portman, in care of Isabel Gonsalves, Isabel's Hair & Nails, 406 Main Street, Sells, Arizona.

"Here's my offer, Steven. Most of your money is safely hidden. If you can get me off this ranch, I will take you to it and give it to you. You also have to promise not to have me arrested, and, after you get your money back, you have to withdraw the criminal complaint you filed against me and have the felony arrest warrant recalled.

"I do not know the exact location of the ranch because Max picks up his mail at a P O box, but I know part of it touches the Mexican border. And there is an Indian Reservation on the western edge.

"Please help me, Steven. Please."

Steven looked up at me. "That's it."

"You believe the letter is legitimate?"

"I do."

"Is there a felony arrest warrant out for her?"

"One of the things I discussed with my attorney before we made the deal with the feds was his suggestion I file a formal complaint with the county sheriff accusing Linda of theft. My attorney said a copy of the F B I report and my court file would go to the district attorney who would most likely file a felony criminal complaint against Linda. He would also probably cause a warrant to issue for her arrest."

"Did you do that?"

"No, Dan, I didn't," said Reynolds. "The money was legitimately mine, well, half of it was Marva's, even though I'd turned my son's stock certificates into cash and hadn't paid the appropriate taxes. But back then I still believed Linda loved me and that she was working on a plan to get me out of jail."

"Did you confess that to your attorney?"

"I did. He laughed at me and told me he had a fool for a client. He also said filing a complaint against Linda might help convince the feds I was victimized by Linda.

"And, with the twenty-twenty vision of hindsight, I now

know he was right. I was a fool. It took several months in prison and several long talks with Sam Trenton to become convinced Linda had played me like she admits to in her letter.

"I'm glad I got her letter. It finally removes all doubt.

"Anyway, after my release from Lompoc I visited my attorney and asked if it was too late to get that arrest warrant. He said the statute of limitations on grand theft is three years. So I took a copy of the F B I report to the Boise County Sheriff and filed a formal complaint. A week or so later the District Attorney called me. He said he would cause an arrest warrant to go into the system, but I shouldn't get my hopes up. Linda's trail was too cold to pursue."

"He was probably right about both of those things," I said, "but the situation has changed. With Linda's toilet paper letter as evidence of her whereabouts, the local sheriff and D A would probably be interested in making the felony bust."

"I considered that, Dan, and I almost took her letter to the D A before I made the effort to find you," said Reynolds. "But the more I thought about it, the more I concluded I would have a better chance of getting my money if I helped her."

Reynolds looked at me, and I decided he sought affirmation of his course of action. "You're probably right. She says the money is 'safely hidden.' If she's being held prisoner on some ranch, I think we should assume the money is some other place. A safe place."

"Where do you think she would hide that much cash?"

"I doubt she invested it or even put it in a safe deposit box because she would have to identify herself. If she believes there is an outstanding arrest warrant, she would not run that risk."

"She had a year and a half to rent a safe deposit box before I got the warrant out," said Reynolds.

"If she didn't do it within the first day or two of leaving here, the fear of that warrant being in the system probably kept her from it," I said. "Her letter mentions seeing a Forest Service truck and fearing immediate arrest. Most criminals, and she knows she's one, would not risk opening an account which most banks require as part of renting a safe deposit box."

"Could she put it in that Swiss bank account you mentioned?"

"She could," I said, "but she would have had the problem of transporting the cash to Europe. Airlines and cruise ships require identification and I understand they X-ray luggage these days.

"Again, I think the risk is too great."

"If she didn't stash it legitimately, how do you think she would hide it? Where would you hide that amount of cash?"

"Oh to have such a problem," I said with a grin.

"Yeah, right." Reynolds met my grin.

"I would probably look into the private storage facilities in a large city. I'm sure there are private vaults available, but even the less sophisticated businesses where people store extra furniture and such offer some security and availability.

"Her use of another name suggests opening an account in that new name. She'd need a valid social security number to go with the name, but those are available for a price."

"She could afford it," said Reynolds.

"That she could."

Reynolds took a swig of beer. "So, Dan, I've thought about it, but I don't know what to do. I have reached one conclusion, though. I don't trust her. Even if, and this is a big if, I could sneak onto that ranch and sneak her away, I doubt she would simply take me to the money and give it to me."

I smiled. "You criminal types don't trust each other, huh?"

Reynolds returned my smile. "Not hardly."

"I don't either. You would need some solid and continuing hold over her to get the money from her. In fact, before I lifted much more than a finger to help her, I would want some token of her good faith."

"Like what?"

"We know she has at least one asset in addition to your money: this cabin. She probably still has the Swiss bank account where she put half a million dollars after the death of her first husband. If she wasn't a prisoner, I would say she should transfer that money to you."

"That would be a nice token," said Reynolds. "With that much money I could pay off the feds and take a bite out of what I owe Marva."

"Would you accept this cabin?"

"I guess I would, but, as far as I'm concerned, I've already got it. I checked the deed, and it's still in Linda's brother's name. Peter Hodges. I pay the taxes on it, and I seriously doubt Linda would ever take any steps to evict me."

"It would still be nice to have clear title."

"It would, but the main reason I wanted to meet with you was to ask you this question: Can you think of a way to rescue Linda that would require her to give me my money back?"

I lifted my bottle of beer, took a drink, then shifted my gaze to the natural rock fireplace. I had nothing against helping Reynolds, and snatching Linda Coleman off an isolated ranch didn't seem all that difficult. My problem is that I didn't trust Linda Coleman, either. I felt she left a lot of important information out of her letter.

"What are you thinking, Dan?"

"I don't have enough information to make an intelligent decision. Finding the ranch and sneaking her away couldn't be all that hard, but I doubt she's telling us the whole story."

"Do you not believe her letter?" asked Reynolds.

"I suppose it's possible she thinks she's a prisoner, Steve," I said, "but her letter points out at least one moment of freedom. Consider this scenario: She's at Isabel's getting her hair done. Emiliano is sitting outside in his truck. What would stop her from having Isabel call the cops to whom she claims she's been kidnapped by the Tuckers?"

"I didn't think of that."

"She could have had Isabel deliver a letter to the cops just about as easily as she got her to mail one to you," I said. "There has to be some reason she doesn't want the cops in on her rescue.

"We don't know if she has discovered there's a felony arrest warrant in the system or if she merely suspects it. Cynic that I am, her letter may be a ruse to find out if you actually made that complaint which resulted in a warrant for her arrest. The sudden appearance of Sheriff's deputies looking for her would be one way she learns she needs to stay out of sight."

"I guess I'd look pretty foolish if I went charging in like some modern Don Quixote to save her, and she was not in any danger," said Reynolds.

"I don't know if Linda's that clever, but if she pulled a stunt like that, how much of your money do you think you would see?"

Reynolds smiled. "The same amount as I have now. Zero."

"We don't know enough, Steve. If she's really a prisoner, seeking your help suggests to me she can't she seek help like a solid citizen in similar circumstances. And, if that's the case, Max Tucker probably knows her limitation.

"She wrote the Tuckers are dangerous men. She may honestly believe her life is at risk. She may not fear a criminal complaint initiated by you, but perhaps she has committed a crime in some other jurisdiction. She can't go to the cops, and, if Max murdered her and buried her in the desert, who would look for her?"

"Nobody."

Reynolds thought a moment. "Can I pay you to investigate her letter, Dan? I'm still on parole. I can't go to Arizona after Linda. Not only that, I not qualified to deal with her allegedly dangerous men."

"On the last case I worked for a fee instead of a percentage of what I saved the insurance company, I got three thousand a week plus expenses," I said. "Can you afford that?"

Reynolds shook his head. "No, Dan. I usually drink Bud in cans which I buy on sale. This Corona is a treat for me."

I finished my beer and placed the empty on the table. I looked at Reynolds and said, "Okay. Here's my offer, Steve. I'll go to Arizona and check out Linda's situation. If it's what she says it is, I will try to rescue Linda and recover your money. If I'm successful, I get half. If it's a hoax, or it can't be done, I'll eat my expenses."

"Half?" asked Steve.

"Half of whatever I recover."

"That could turn out to be a lot of money."

"It could," I said. "I could also leave Arizona with what the little dog left behind. Squat."

"Can I think about all that a while?"

I stood and watched Penny get to her feet. "Sure, Steve. You've got my number. Leave me a message. I won't get it until Saturday. If we have a deal, I'll mail you a contract with a return address. Get your signature notarized, mail the contract back, and I'll head for Arizona.

"And don't forget the alternative of taking Linda's letter to the local sheriff and district attorney. They'll work for you for free. What do you care if Linda gets arrested, prosecuted, and sent to state prison for a couple of years? She stole your money and your freedom."

Reynolds got to his feet and extended his hand. "You're right, Dan. She did."

As we shook, Reynolds added, "And thanks for coming, Dan. Just like the last time we talked, you've given me a lot to think about."

I nodded and stepped to his door. Penny moved with me, but before I turned the knob, I looked back at Reynolds and said, "There's another option, Steve."

"What's that?"

"You did your time for your crime. If you believe the letter, you could do nothing and leave her in the prison she's made for herself."

"I never sat on death row," said Reynolds. "She says her life is in danger."

"She conned you before, Steve, and she may be conning you now."

Reynolds nodded.

"Good night, Steve. I'm glad to see you have a good attitude about life again." I opened the door and stepped through it into the night.

I would have been happy to read for a few minutes and go to bed, but I feared Reynolds would soon knock on my trailer door with some question. So I let Penny sniff and pee a minute then called her to my truck. I drove east on the graveled road to where it ended at the Arrowrock Reservoir.

Comfortable we would not be bothered before sunrise, I parked and let Penny sniff while I lowered my jacks to stabilize my trailer. I looked out over the star lit water and wondered what might sample my bait the next morning.

TEN

In her Bellagio room, Lori thought about having sex with Max. She enjoyed sex, but she never took a man to her bed simply because he wanted to, or she wanted to, or it seemed like a good idea at the time.

As Nurse Linda Coleman, she had relaxed her guard with Doctor Steven Reynolds when she concluded he wanted romance. He seemed safely married, she liked his looks and his personality, and he took her for airplane rides which she enjoyed immensely. He flew to Boise to fish with a pal. During his second trip, the pal agreed to cover for him with Mrs. Reynolds if he wanted to bring a female friend.

The first trip was wonderful. She drove her Jeep to the Lincoln airport where Steven collected her away from curious eyes. They flew over the Sierra Nevada Mountains to Winnemucca where they stopped for fuel and the best piece of French Apple pie she had ever tasted. Rather than stay with Steven's friend, Steven paid cash for a motel in her name, and she enjoyed sleeping in while Steven got up early to fish. They dined alone together, and the sex had been most pleasant.

After Linda told Steven about her deceased brother's cabin in the forest northeast of Boise, they took an occasional weekend trip without telling Steven's pal. They enjoyed each other without worry somebody might see them. Later, when Steven found his son's stock certificates and told Linda he wanted to convert them to cash without telling his wife, she suggested he fake his death and they live in the cabin.

Sex became an easy way to control Steven until Linda became bored with him.

Lori knew Max desired sex with her, but she felt no need to reward him for the money he had spent on her with her body. She had enjoyed being the object of his attention, and she found him attractive, but she didn't feel a spark.

Not tonight, she thought. *I will remain a Wealthy Woman of Mystery and agree to meet him here the next time he comes to town on business. In the meantime I have places to go and money to secure.*

Max and Lori shared a delightful steak dinner that evening. He purchased a bottle, and then a second bottle, of expensive wine, and they shared a Baked Alaska dessert.

As they left the restaurant, Max took Lori's hand and led her to her room. At her door, he asked, "May I come in for a nightcap?"

"Just a nightcap, Max?" Lori asked. "Is that all you want?"

"I want to spend as much time with you as possible, Lori," he said with a small smile. "I told you I must return to the ranch tomorrow."

"And I am on my way to San Felipe," she reminded him.

Lori almost gave in, but she stuck to her plan. "I'm afraid I couldn't resist your charms tonight, Max. I have too much good wine in me."

"Why resist, Lori? Don't you enjoy my company?"

"I do, Max. I really do. But it's simply too soon for me. Perhaps next time."

Max looked into Lori's eyes and thought fast. He wanted her, all of her, but he also wanted more than one night. He had decided he should get to know her better, and, if they got along as well after more time together, perhaps he would consider a long term relationship.

He kissed her cheek and stepped back. "I never know exactly when I'll be here. How shall I get in touch with you?"

Lori suddenly realized a personal weakness: She could not think of everything.

She asked herself, *What would a Wealthy Woman of Mystery do in such circumstance?*

"I don't know my girlfriend's address in San Felipe," she said. "All I have is a cell phone number for her. I would not feel comfortable publishing it."

Max sensed their romantic mood had evaporated. "May I have your cell phone number?"

Lori smiled. "I realize I am probably the only female in the country above age ten who does not possess a cell phone, Max, but I don't like them. I am annoyed by people who walk around polluting the atmosphere with their blather, and I wish it were a federal offense punishable by tongue removal to use one while driving. I do not have a business that requires people call with me, and I refuse to be on an electronic leash."

Max wondered if he received a subtle brush off and tested the possibility with a question, "Could I talk you into visiting me at my ranch when you tire of San Felipe? I have a pool, horses, beautiful sunsets, and a live-in housekeeper and cook. It would be like visiting another resort."

"I do not know you that well, kind sir. I think I would like to see your ranch some day. Perhaps another wonderful weekend in Las Vegas would convince me to do so."

Max pulled a thin leather card carrier from an inside jacket pocket, removed a business card, and offered it to Lori. "If you would call in two weeks or so, I might know when I will be back in town."

Lori took the card. "Thanks, Max," she said. "These last two days have been wonderful. I like you, and I do want to see you again. Please forgive my old-fashioned ways."

Max nodded, took her hand, pulled it toward him, bent, and brushed his lips across the back of her fingers. Then he looked into her eyes and said, "Good night, Lori. I will count the days until we meet again."

"Good night, Max."

Max turned and walked away. He did not look back.

As Lori packed the next morning she decided she had too many clothes. She placed all of her new things, her underwear, and her cosmetics into her rolling bag and her old clothes into the smaller case. She considered leaving the older suitcase in the room with a note to donate the clothing and bag to charity, but she decided such action would be uncommon behavior.

Lori did not want to do any act out of the ordinary.

She wore her Gucci shirt dress, carried her bags to the main desk, checked out, and started for her car. As she stepped into the warmth of ten o'clock in the morning and turned toward the parking lot, Byron approached her.

"Good morning, Miss," he said. "May I retrieve your car?"

She smiled at the eager young man and decided her Wealthy Woman of Mystery disguise might be working. "My car, well, it's not actually my car, is not in your valet lot,

Byron. Thanks anyway."

"If you'll tell me what it is and where it is, I'll be happy to get it for you," said Byron. "Mister Tucker left earlier and made me promise to get your car or your taxi."

"That was thoughtful of him," said Lori. "Well, I'm doing a favor for my niece by driving her car to California for her." She opened her new Coach purse, found the Toyota key, and handed it to Byron. "It's a white Toyota Corolla with Utah plates. I think the letters are W V M, but I don't recall the numbers. I parked it in section C."

Byron took the key. "I'll find it, Miss. If you want to step back inside where it's cooler, feel free. I'll bring your car right about here where you can see it."

"Thank you, Byron."

A dozen minutes later Byron appeared in the Toyota, and Lori took her bags to the rear of the vehicle.

As Byron lifted her cases into the trunk, he asked, "Do you know the man in the red S U V there?" Byron glanced over his right shoulder then looked at her.

Lori followed his eyes to the vehicle then met his eyes. "No," she said. "Why do you ask?"

"He was sitting in his car near where I found yours. I was suspicious so I took the long way here. He followed me."

Lori looked at the SUV again. "I don't know him. It's probably a coincidence he followed you."

"But it could be that he's following you, Miss. Sometimes people who've had good luck get followed by bad people. I could call security, and they could delay him long enough for you to leave the Bellagio."

Lori thought a moment and wondered if she had not said too much to Joseph Smith. She opened her purse, pulled a one hundred-dollar bill from a banded stack Byron could not see, and offered it to him. "That's a good idea, Byron. Would you do that for me, please?"

"No problem." He looked at the bill but did not reach for it. "Mister Tucker took care of me, Miss."

"Max did not contemplate the need for you to search for my niece's car or call security, Byron. Let me thank you."

Byron smiled and took the bill. "You're welcome, Miss. You wait right here with your car a few minutes."

Byron closed the Toyota's trunk and trotted to a kiosk.

Lori watched Byron speak into a telephone, and two minutes later a Bellagio security vehicle stopped in front of the red SUV blocking it from forward movement. Lori waved at Byron, drove to Las Vegas Boulevard and turned toward the airport. She watched her mirrors nervously but did not see any vehicles following her.

As she neared the airport, Lori changed direction and returned to the internet café she had used several days earlier. Inside, Lori bought a sandwich and a diet drink, booted her laptop, and contemplated her situation.

She had planned to drive to Calexico, put the car in storage, walk across the border to Mexico, and find a bus going to San Felipe. There she would stay until boredom or circumstances suggested relocation.

But Joseph Smith knew she had money, and she feared he knew her car. How much better a victim could she be? Lori decided she needed to quit Las Vegas as soon as possible.

She could not fly commercially. An airplane ticket required identification, and Lori had decided to make minimal use of her new documents. The FBI had arrested Steven Reynolds, and she believed they sought her as a person of interest in the insurance fraud case. She dare not use her Linda Coleman identification.

Lori recalled Max had secured their helicopter seats for the Grand Canyon flight without requesting her driver's license. She used her computer to explore private charter flights but soon decided police or FBI agents could too easily place her in both Las Vegas and whichever destination she chose.

Lori learned Amtrak did not service Las Vegas. Yuma, Arizona, had the nearest train station.

Greyhound could transport her north, south, east, and west from its Main Street terminal. A private bus company advertising luxury, nonstop service to Los Angeles and San Diego had coaches leaving McCarran International Airport at three thirty that afternoon.

Lori considered driving the Toyota to the airport and

abandoning it in the parking lot, but she decided against it for
three reasons: One, she felt reluctant to throw away eight
thousand dollars worth of automobile. Two, if the FBI looked
for her, they would eventually find her Jeep in Salt Lake City
which might lead them to find she had purchased the Toyota.
Three, if they discovered her purchase of the Toyota, they
would search for it. If they found it in the airport parking lot,
they would have one more clue about her. If they showed her
picture around town, someone might recognize her.

No, better to hide the car.

With her laptop, Lori found several Las Vegas storage
facilities. She used a public telephone to call one and, upon
learning the cost, advised the clerk she would soon arrive to
rent a garage space.

Lori's Swiss bank had a branch in New York City which
had provided her with a credit card she used two or three times
per year simply to keep it alive. The bank sent no paper
statements; charged amounts were automatically deducted from
her balance. When Lori rented a storage garage using her
'Linda Coleman of Sacramento, California,' driver's license,
she paid with the credit card and authorized an automatic
monthly billing by the storage company. Then she parked the
Toyota inside private space number one hundred eighteen.
There she pulled blue jeans, a blouse, and a pair of athletic
shoes from her 'old clothes' suitcase, and jammed them into
her 'new clothes' case. She left the Toyota unlocked with the
keys in the center console cup holder. She rolled both her
heavy money suitcase and her 'new clothes' suitcase behind
her to the public drive way, and secured the roll down door
with a new, expensive padlock she had purchased in the office.

Four doors from Lori's a teenager closed and locked a door
nearly identical to hers. With her two suitcases rolling behind
her, she approached him and said, "I need a ride to the airport,
and I decided not to bring my cell phone on this trip. Could I
get you to call me a taxi?"

"What does it cost to take a taxi to the airport from here?"

Lori guessed. "About thirty dollars plus tip."

"I could use some gas money," said the lad as he pointed at
his ten-year-old pickup. "I'll take you there right now for

twenty and no tip."

Lori smiled. "You've got a deal."

"Let me help you with your suitcases."

With one stop for gasoline, the young man dropped Lori at the main terminal thirty-five minutes later.

After a quick change of clothes in a ladies room, Lori bought a one-way private coach ticket to San Diego.

The comfortable bus reached San Diego a few minutes after eight o'clock. Lori asked a taxi driver at the terminal to take her to "a Hyatt or a Marriott" and soon found herself pulling her suitcases into the latter.

At one the next afternoon Lori boarded an eastbound Greyhound and reached Calexico a few minutes before four. She reviewed the directions she had printed from her computer in her room, walked across the border into Mexico, found a taxi, and said, "Estacion de autobus de San Felipe, for favor."

The taxi driver took her to the San Felipe bus station on Airport Road.

Bobby, the English-speaking night clerk at the San Felipe Sea Breeze Palms hotel, offered Lori a smile and his acknowledgment they had received her email advising them of her late arrival.

Lori asked what discount she might receive for a two-week stay. The hotel's internet page listed a summer room rate of one hundred and ten dollars per night.

Bobby consulted a chart and quoted her a price of ninety dollars per night if paid in advance.

Lori counted out thirteen hundred dollars and placed them on the counter.

"I will need to make an imprint of your credit card, Mrs. Portman," said Bobby.

"I don't have credit cards, Bobby. I had my purse stolen a few weeks ago, and it will take awhile to get my credit cleared.

"I promise I won't damage anything in my room. I'm willing to leave a cash security deposit if necessary, but if you insist on a card I'll have to find another hotel."

"I can take cash, but the owner insists I get at least a

thousand dollars," said Bobby.

"That's not a problem, Bobby, so long as I get a receipt."

"We're on the same page, Mrs. Portman."

"Please, Bobby. I'm on vacation. Can you call me Lori?"

Bobby smiled. "Lori it is. Let me make you that receipt."

In her room, while Lori unpacked, she considered where to hide the two keys to the padlock protecting the Toyota. Finally she lifted the pad in her right athletic shoe and forced a key under it at the arch. She pushed the second key to the bottom of a face cream jar.

ELEVEN

I fished Arrowrock Reservoir an hour the next morning, but I didn't have any luck. Maybe I needed a boat.

Penny and I drove back to State Route 21, turned north, and headed to Bull Trout Lake. We camped three days and enjoyed feisty trout both bulls and cows. I started my generator long enough midday Thursday to run my computer and prepare a draft contract between me and Steven Reynolds.

The hopeful physician lucky in two ways: One, he had caught me between Ed Logan's gut rumblers, and, two, Linda Coleman stealing his money had aroused a low-level sympathy pang in me when it happened. While searching for Reynolds and Coleman two years earlier, I had concluded he had conceived and planned the income tax evasion scheme which included murdering and decapitating a homeless man. However, when I saw the surprised look on Reynolds' face when the FBI agent appeared from the cabin with his son's empty duffel, I began to question my conclusion. Now, after hearing him read Coleman's written confession, I believed she had more than enough criminal intent to murder and steal.

Part of me hoped her letter accurately described her situation. I don't usually care enough about people to judge them, but I felt Linda Coleman deserved something less than the total happiness she probably thought Steven Reynolds' money would bring her.

I also predicted Reynolds' hope to get part of his money back and learn more about Coleman would combine enough for him to hire me.

With four fat fresh trout in my freezer, Penny and I headed toward Boise after breakfast Saturday morning. I topped my propane and gasoline tanks then parked in a supermarket parking lot and called my dad. He relayed a message from Reynolds: "Send the contract."

I edited and printed the contract I wanted to make with Reynolds. I also prepared a letter to Linda Coleman I wanted him to sign:

"Dear Linda:

"I am sorry to hear you are in trouble. I want to help you, but I have financial limitations. Fifty percent of my small salary working at a medical clinic in Boise is garnished by the government for back taxes, interest, and penalties. Additionally, Marva sued me for conversion of her share of my son's stock money and also for divorce. I owe her $800,000 plus interest at ten percent per year.

Also, I am on parole and cannot leave the Boise area.

"I have contacted and discussed your letter and the circumstances of our relationship with a private investigator. Dan Ballantine is a former police officer and is a licensed attorney in California. I believe Dan can help you, but he suggested I should secure the money you stole from me before he or I take any action.

"Dan will find a way to communicate with you. Please talk with him as you would with me, and he will relay your words.

"Steven."

Instead of searching for a post office and waiting in line to mail the documents, I called Sam Trenton's clinic and asked for Doctor Reynolds. The person who answered the telephone said he was with a patient and asked if he could return my call.

I told her my location and asked for directions to the clinic. I had decided I would not head for Tucson without a signed contract, so I drove to the clinic and waited twenty minutes to meet with Steve. As he led me to a tiny office crowded with file cabinets, I told him I'd been fishing Bull Trout Lake.

"I don't mean to pressure you in any way, Steve," I said after he closed a door behind me, "but the sooner we have an agreement, the sooner I can head for Arizona. If you want to study these documents a couple of days, or consult with your attorney or Sam Trenton, you can mail them to me in care of general delivery to Wells, Nevada. I plan to hit Interstate Eighty there, and I can fish Angel Lake a few days while I wait for your decision. If you don't want my help, I'll head west toward Reno instead of south toward Tucson."

"No, Dan." Steve moved around behind a cluttered desk. "Let me take a few minutes to see what's in here, but I know I want you to do whatever you can to help Linda.

"Please have a seat."

I sat and watched him give the contract and letter a quick read. Then he pulled a pen and started to sign them.

"Hold it a second, Steve," I said. "I don't mean to be a picky lawyer, but we should call someone in to witness both our signatures."

"No problem, Dan." He lifted a phone receiver, pushed a button, and said, "Debbie, would you ask Nurse Scott to come to my office, please. Thank you."

Reynolds put down the phone and said, "Nurse Scott is the Cindy I told you about. We've discussed Linda Coleman's cry for help, and she agrees you should get involved."

Cynthia Scott, in her late thirties or early forties, occupied the distant end of the continuum from Marva Reynolds, Steve's former wife. She stood an inch or two over five feet in pale blue scrubs and could not have weighed more than a hundred pounds. With her light brown hair pulled back from a face that evidenced time spent outdoors, I could see a sense of humor in her flecked green eyes.

After introductions, Reynolds asked her if she would witness our signatures, and she readily agreed.

While we executed the contract, Cindy said, "That woman led Steve down the primrose path, Mister Ballantine. Part of me wishes she could simply rot in whatever private hell she's found herself in, but a bigger part of me would like to see you recover some of the money she stole."

"I agree with you, Miz Scott," I said. "I'll do what I can."

Penny and I headed southeast on Interstate 84, but, since I don't like doing battle with eighteen-wheelers, we turned south forty miles later. State Route 51 took us toward Nevada on lonely two-lane blacktop–my kind of road.

Around three we entered the Duck Valley Indian Reservation which straddles the Idaho-Nevada border like a four hundred and fifty square mile postage stamp. Because it lies too far from a major highway to support a casino, the Shoshones and Paiutes for whom the government established the reservation in 1877 try to make money with big fish.

The reservation contains three lakes. Lake Billy Shaw, Sheep Creek Reservoir, and The Mountain View Reservoir are open from April through October each year. I had read a magazine article which told how the Indians built Lake Billy Shaw in 1998, stocked it with large rainbow trout, and opened it to fishing in 2001. Fishermen could keep one fish between sixteen and nineteen inches per day.

A rainbow trout a foot and a half long will fight to stay in the water, and, when landed and cooked, will feed two adults and three or four children. It would be too much trout for Penny and me, and I did not consider the twenty-five dollar per day permit good value.

So I waved a friendly hand at the greedy Indians as I motored by the fishing shops and drove off the reservation into a four hundred and fifty thousand acre section of the Humboldt-Toiyabe National Forest. Now on Nevada State Route 225, I slowed for tiny, mile high, Mountain City, and, a few miles later left the two-lane for the twenty-two space Wild Horse Crossing campground near the Owyhee River. We were ahead of hunting season, and, for an eight-dollar fee, had the place to ourselves.

Penny and I had a scramble of beaten eggs, diced ham, diced cheddar cheese, and chopped onions for breakfast Sunday morning, then continued south on 225 to Elko. There we jogged northeast on Interstate 80 for twenty miles before turning southeast on Nevada State Route 229. After a fifty mile meander through yet another section of the Humboldt-Toiyabe National Forest, we ran out of 229 at US Highway 93. We turned south and motored through high desert to Ely, Nevada.

At the south end of town I pulled into a fuel station, topped my tank, and cleaned the latest bug collection off my windshield. As I pulled back onto 93, I saw a sign for a bakery-deli and decided a fresh sandwich would do me good. I bought a nine-inch ham and Swiss cheese submarine but decided against eating it in my trailer. I consulted my map, noted a roadside rest about twenty-five miles south, and, when I reached it, let Penny loose to sniff and explore while I ate.

After lunch I drove eighty miles south between the Ely Range on the west and the Wilson Creek Range on the east. We slowed for Pioche and, about ten miles later, Panaca, where we turned east on Nevada State Route 319 and headed for Utah.

I don't often listen to radio when I travel because I can't stand the commercials and drivel between the musical selections. Nor, except in the big cities I try to avoid, can I find a station playing the soft jazz or guitar instrumentals I prefer. So I usually play the dozen or so CDs I have slowly accumulated.

But once in a while, usually in the middle of nowhere, I want to hear what human voice familiar with the area might have to say. My scan picked up a station in St. George, Utah, calling itself The Cowboy.

When and why did radio stations start naming themselves?

I can listen to country while I drive if there's nothing else. I don't mind hearing Toby Keith sing, "You ain't much fun since I quit drinkin'." Or Billy Ray Cyrus warble, "I'm so miserable without you, it's almost like you're here." Or Gene Watson complain, "You're out doing what I'm doing here without."

Jimmy Buffett is not actually country, and I own one of his CDs. Thankfully it does not include him moaning, "My head hurts, my feet stink, and I don't love Jesus."

But I hit the off button when I hear 'Crow' Carroll and Mackinaw sing, "I gave her the ring, and she gave me the finger." Or Don Hicks struggle through "How can I miss you when you won't go away." And Bobby Bare had some hits both amusing and serious, but I don't understand, "Drop kick me, Jesus, through the goal posts of life." What does he mean by "I've got the will, Lord, if you've got the toe."?

I have a map which covers the southwestern states. Boise is not on it, but Mountain Home, Idaho, about thirty-five miles southeast of Boise, is. The light pencil line I drew from Mountain Home to Tucson, Arizona, crossed an obstacle: the Grand Canyon. The shortest distance around it, on the east end, would take me through polygamy country in southwestern Utah and north central Arizona.

That would not be a problem as I have been inoculated against marriage.

Why do most Mormon women stop having children at thirty-five? Because thirty-six is too many.

The Mormon stand-up comedian said, "Take my wives. Please."

Polygamist men believe they can have multiple wives. Can polygamist women have multiple husbands? Can a bisexual polygamist man have multiple wives and multiple husbands? What if one of the husbands is a transsexual?

Polygamy is a felony in Utah. A convicted polygamist goes to prison, and, upon meeting his three hundred pound cellmate, Tyrone "Fancy Pants" Washington, explains he is serving a sentence for having too many wives. And Tyrone says, "Will it mess wit' yo' religion if I makes you one o' my wives?"

Giggles aside, it is not uncommon today for a woman to decide she's a lesbian, divorce her husband, get custody of their children, and take another lesbian into her household as an almost married partner.

Similarly, two homosexual men can raise children together.

So why not multiple marriage partners?

The California Supreme Court declared the state's marriage laws unconstitutional and said the state's domestic partnership law is not an adequate substitute for marriage. Shortly thereafter the voters passed Proposition 8 which says marriage means a man and a woman. Interesting to me as a California attorney, the Attorney General, Jerry Brown, former governor, first came out in support of the voters then filed suit challenging the validity of the proposition. So now the courts get to decide the issue.

Is the day coming when there will be no marriages but only contracts between two or more consenting adults?

My wife dropped, almost literally, my severely autistic infant son in my arms and said she couldn't take it anymore. Then she divorced me for "irreconcilable differences." The baby we made declined to show her any affection, and that was my fault?

Could a contract prohibiting such behavior be binding?

Well, one has to think about something while driving those long, straight sections of two-lane blacktop with the radio off.

I stopped in St. George, Utah, for fuel then pulled the trailer a few miles up Interstate 15 to State Route 9 where I got off and headed east to Hurricane. I turned southeast on State Route 59 into Arizona where it became State Route 389. At Fredonia I took US 89 east through Kaibab, and, about ten miles east of town I turned north on a dirt road along the western edge of the Vermillion Cliffs National Monument. I soon found a safe place to pull off the road for the night.

Pretty country.

Monday morning I stayed on 89 which turned south after it crossed the Colorado River. I drove through the western side of the Navajo Indian Reservation then into the Coconino National Forest to Flagstaff where I topped my fuel tank with regular and my tummy with another fresh deli sandwich.

I probably could have reached Tucson by nightfall had I been willing to travel two interstates, 17 and 10, but I opted for one last chance for fresh fish. A few miles south of Flagstaff I left I-17 on State Route 487 and meandered through the forest down to Clint's Well. I didn't see Clint as I turned south on State Route 87 a few miles to where it joined State Route 260. About thirty miles later 260 headed east, and 87 took me to Jake's Corner. Jake must have been with Clint, so I turned south-southeast on State Route 188 and found a campsite at Theodore Roosevelt Lake.

Penny and I went onto the water in a rented boat and caught several largemouth bass. I released all but a single small one which, back at our camp, I sliced and fried in hot butter. It wasn't bad, but it wasn't trout, and Penny got a larger than usual share.

I stopped on the north side of Tucson Tuesday afternoon as soon as I had good cell phone service. I consulted my RV book and made a reservation for a week at an older park on the west side of town. One rate included electricity, basic cable TV, and WiFi. Most important, the RV facility sat across the street from a large city park where I hoped Penny could run loose.

We checked in, hooked our land lines, and thawed and cooked one of my frozen trout for our dinner. Even formerly frozen, I thought it tasted better than the bass. Penny did not express a preference.

I left Penny in the trailer Wednesday morning with the air conditioner on low. After renting a small sedan in Tucson, I drove southwest on State Route 86 to Sells. My internet encyclopedia had warned me the town, formerly called Indian Oasis but renamed in 1918 to honor an Indian Commissioner named Cato Sells, contained only about three thousand people. The capital of the Tohono O'odham Nation, Sells sits in the southeast corner of the Reservation and twenty-something vulture flying miles from the Mexican border.

I found Isabel Gonsalves' four-chair hair and nail salon on Main Street, entered, and saw three women working on the dark locks of three other women. All six women looked at me as if I had parked my flying saucer on the street outside and crept in on eight legs.

"Good morning, ladies," I said with a smile. "I need to talk to Isabel Gonsalves for about two minutes."

"Good morning, sir," said a dark, middle-aged woman who could not have weighed less than two hundred pounds.

I nodded at her. "I am sorry to interrupt your work, Ms. Gonsalves, but may we speak in private? I promise to be brief."

Isabel stepped to the side of her customer and said, "Excuse me, Mrs. Ramirez. I'll just be a minute."

"Not a problem, Isabel," said Mrs. Ramirez.

Isabel looked at me. "Shall we step outside?"

I nodded and opened the door for her. On the sidewalk I handed her my private investigator card. "I am Dan Ballantine. Doctor Steven Reynolds hired me to help Lori Portman if I can.

May I give you a letter to give to her?"

A cloud came over Isabel's smooth face.

"Is there a problem?" I asked.

"I wish I had not agreed to get involved in Lori's problem, Mister Ballantine."

"Why not?"

"I now fear the Tuckers. When I told my husband about Max beating Lori, he said she should have expected such treatment." Isabel glanced at my card then met my eyes. "My husband's closest friend is an Indian policeman. He said the Indians believe the Tuckers run illegal immigrants and drugs across the border. Dead bodies have been found on the reservation close to the western edge of the Tucker ranch, and they didn't all die from exposure to the desert heat."

"Is that why Lori is afraid to leave without help?"

"I know very little, Mister Ballantine. You look like a capable man, but I warn you to be careful with the Tuckers."

"When will you see Lori again?"

"She comes in every other Friday at eleven o'clock in the morning," said Isabel. "So, day after tomorrow."

"Does Lori visit the toilet when she comes to your shop?"

"Not if Max brings her," said Isabel. "He sits in the shop and watches her the entire time she is here. He makes me nervous, and Lori and I talk very little.

"If Emiliano brings her, she could visit the toilet. Emiliano sits in his truck and listens to music while I do Lori's hair and nails. He only watches the door."

"Can I pay you to give something to Lori?" I asked.

"Money is not necessary, Mister Ballantine," said Isabel. "I only want to help Lori get away from the Tuckers."

I pulled Reynolds' letter and a small walkie-talkie from my left rear pocket. My Smith & Wesson forty-four revolver rested in the right one. "This is a letter from Doctor Reynolds. I will park nearby Friday morning. If Lori wants to talk to me, she can do so with this."

I had printed and taped instructions how to work the walkie-talkie on the back of the unit. Linda, I still thought of her as Linda, only had to turn it on, press the button to talk, and release the button to listen.

"I will give them to her," said Isabel. "Let's hope Emiliano brings her on Friday."

That afternoon I visited the Pima County Assessor's office on North Church Avenue in downtown Tucson. Arizona Revised Statutes 42-13051, if you must know, requires the assessor to maintain an up-to-date ownership list of all privately owned property within the county. I found the legal description for the eighteen square mile Tucker Ranch and learned the brothers inherited the property from their mother who had survived their father. The brothers also held the property as joint tenants with the right of survivorship. That meant they could not split the property, and the last one alive got the whole.

I studied a county map and found the western half of the long, narrow Tucker ranch encroached into the Baboquivari Mountains, but Baboquivari Peak, 7734 feet, sat about three miles west of the ranch within the Tohono O'odham Indian Reservation. The Indian land, the Ironwood Forest National Monument, the Buenos Aires National Wildlife Refuge, the Organ Pipe Cactus National Monument, and part of the Cabeza Prieta National Wildlife Refuge filled the western two-thirds of Pima County. I felt certain the owners of those parcels contributed little tax revenue to the county coffers.

The map provided one other interesting piece of information: State Route 286 ran south from State Route 86, the road I had traveled that morning to Sells, to the Mexican border. Part of 286 separated the Tucker ranch property from the Buenos Aires National Wildlife Refuge. A US Customs Station sat on the Pima County side of the border, but the map's legend painted the road on the Mexican side as unpaved.

If the Tuckers were smuggling illegal immigrants and drugs into the United States, they could leave their ranch almost anywhere along its eastern border and hit pavement aimed at Tucson.

At the RV resort I turned on my computer, got on the internet and searched for the Tucker brothers. Emiliano's name did not appear, but Leonardo's name popped up several times in references to his position as a US Customs and Border

Protection Deputy Chief.

Max's name appeared in a magazine article about ranchers along the Mexican border in three states dealing with illegal immigrants. He had declined to formally join the Arizona Minutemen, a citizens' vigilance organization monitoring immigration, because, in his words, "there are too many armed men with contradictory and sometimes un-American motives patrolling the border."

I did not know what Max meant by his comment, and I had no interest in getting involved in the immigration issue. But if I thought I might sneak onto the Tucker ranch and snatch Linda, I needed to know as much about the Tuckers as I could learn in a short time. The proximity of the Tucker Ranch to the Mexican border provided the possibility for smuggling people into the United States, and common sense told me the men involved in such activity usually armed themselves. They might also employ electronic warning devices on their vehicles and property.

Friday morning I rented another sedan, and Penny and I reached Sells by ten thirty. I parked on a side street such that I had a clear view of the front of Isabel's salon. At six minutes before eleven o'clock, a near new white Dodge Ram four-by-four pickup parked in front of the salon, and a woman fitting Linda Coleman's description left the front passenger seat and entered the business. The male driver remained in the vehicle.

Twenty minutes later my walkie-talkie beeped. "Hello. Is anybody there?"

I thumbed a button and said, "This is Dan Ballantine."

"This is Lori, uh, Linda. I am in the bathroom and only have a minute or two so please listen."

"Who's in the Ram?"

"The what?"

"The big white truck sitting outside the salon. The one you were in a few minutes ago."

"Oh. I didn't know it was a Ram. The man is Emiliano Tucker." Urgency entered her voice. "Please listen, Mister Ballantine. I told Steven, Doctor Reynolds, I think Max and his brothers are smuggling Mexicans onto their ranch where it touches the border. About the only times I am left alone in the house is when they do their smuggling."

"Tell me exactly what they do," I said.

"Every two or three weeks, always on a Tuesday or Wednesday night, Gordo, he's the ranch foreman, hooks a big truck to a trailer load of hay which is kept in the barn and never unloaded. He starts it and leaves the barn heading south from the main ranch valley about ten o'clock at night.

"Max follows the truck in his Hummer.

"An hour or two later the truck and trailer return to the valley, but Gordo drives through without stopping. He brings the truck and trailer back to the barn several hours later. Usually around sunrise.

"Max follows Gordo, but he stops at the house and switches his Hummer for his Aston Martin. Then he leaves the ranch for two or three days. I think he goes to Las Vegas which is where I met him.

"Emiliano has already been out of the house for a week. I think he goes to Mexico where he has a girlfriend or wife, but he always visits the ranch for a day or two after Max returns from Las Vegas."

"How often do they follow this routine?" I asked.

"It varies," said Linda. "The interval between events is more often three weeks, but it's been two several times."

"Who is in the house after Max leaves?"

"I'm left locked in my room whenever Max is gone. On the nights they use the hay truck, I am alone in the house."

"Does Gordo have a wife?"

"Gordo's wife stays in a smaller house about fifty yards away from Max's house. The cook and the housekeeper live in another small house which is a duplex. The three homes form a loose triangle, but Max's house is closest to the barn."

"Did Gordo and Max make a run last Tuesday or Wednesday?"

"No," said Linda. "The last one was two weeks ago."

"So they're due next week then?"

"Yes. If you could watch, and you saw them leave with the hay truck, you would have an hour or so to come and get me from my room. Will you please come and get me?"

"Do you know if Max has installed any electronic devices which would warn him of trespassers?"

"I don't think he has. He has a couple of mean pit bull dogs which are kept in a kennel in the barn during the day but turned loose at night. Before he started locking me in my room, he warned me never to go outside the house at night when the dogs are loose. He said they are trained attack dogs."

"Did you read Steven's letter?"

"Yes. I put it inside a magazine and read it while Isabel trimmed my hair."

"Then you know I need something from you before I will attempt to rescue you."

"I have no way to get anything to you."

"You could recite the number of your Swiss bank account and tell me how to extract the life insurance money you put there after your husband's fatal traffic accident."

"How did you find out about that?" asked Linda.

"Does it matter?"

"No. I guess not, and I've got to stop talking. I'll give Isabel a key. It fits a padlock to garage number one eighteen at Winston's Storage on Jackson Street in Las Vegas. Steve will find half his money in the trunk of a small Toyota. The keys to the Toyota are in a cup holder. Tell him to take the car, too, and sell it if he doesn't want it. The ownership papers are in the dashboard compartment.

"One last thing," said Linda. "Please tell the storage people you have cleaned out my space and ask them to stop the automatic billing.

"I've got to go."

I heard the squawk as she released the button then nothing.

Linda, with shorter, medium blond hair freshly styled, left the salon and climbed into the Ram about twenty minutes later.

I waited another ten minutes then drove my rental to the store, parked, and entered. Inside I approached Isabel and said, "Lori said you would have something for me."

Isabel handed me my walkie-talkie then pulled a key from her pocket and held it out to me. "Please help her, Mister Ballantine. She is very much afraid."

"I will try, Ms. Gonsalves," I said as I took the key. "Thank you for your help."

Back in my rental I tapped the Boise clinic number on my cell phone. Since I had been in a dead zone during most of my drive from Tucson to Sells, I asked the receptionist to have Doctor Reynolds call me in one hour.

My phone beeped a few minutes after I had returned the rental car and climbed into my Tundra. I braked and pulled to a curb parking place as I opened it and said, "Ballantine."

"It's Steve Reynolds, Dan. What's happening?"

"I was a teenager when Geraldo Rivera made a big television deal of opening Al Capone's secret vault. Do you remember it?"

"Yes."

"Well, it's your turn except I don't think you'll want to notify the media. Linda told me an hour ago that half your money is in the trunk of a Toyota she stored in Las Vegas. She said you can have the car, too."

"Really? That's great news, Dan."

"It is if it's true," I said. "Can you catch a plane to Vegas tonight or tomorrow morning?"

"I'll have to charge my ticket on a slim credit card."

"I will drive to Vegas and check for the money by my lonesome if you want me to," I said.

"No. I believe her, Dan, and I want to be there. I think Linda's desperate enough to be truthful. Tomorrow's a day off. I'll get there as soon as I can."

"Well, if we hit pay dirt, you can pay the bill with some to spare. And you might consider saving a few bucks by buying a one way ticket. If there is a car, you could drive it to Boise unless it's too much of a beater to make the trip.

"On the other hand, I've read stories of gamblers selling their cars for bus money home."

"No," said Reynolds. "I would keep it if it's a decent car. I consider my Explorer a loaner from Sam and the clinic.

"Hey! Good work, Dan. Thanks."

I almost said something about not counting one's chickens, but he sounded excited and I didn't want to ruin his mood. "I'll start for Vegas now, but it's almost four hundred miles from here. Call me when you can and let me know what time to pick you up at McCarran."

"Will do, Dan."

Penny and I stopped by my trailer for a few things then headed north. Steve called me back as we neared Tempe. He gave me his flight number and arrival time the next morning.

I reached Bullhead City about eight o'clock and decided to call it a day. I much prefer small towns to big cities. After a quick meal in a chain restaurant, I found a motel with an end room available and no objection to Penny.

We left at dawn and grabbed a cup of coffee and a poppy seed scone before we left town. Who had the bright idea to call the cup 'venti' instead of 'large'? I assume the same guy decided to call the medium cup 'grande' when everyone in the western half of the country has heard a smattering of Spanish and knows 'grande,' as in Rio Grande, means 'large.'

This is America. We speak English. Well, sort of. Okay, I know 'venti' is Italian for twenty, and the cups hold twenty ounces. I still think it's dumb. They should called it 'viente' which is Spanish for twenty and fits much better with grande.

I collected Steve Reynolds and his carry-on bag outside a McCarran International Airport terminal and drove us to the storage business. I parked my truck outside garage number one hundred eighteen, and, using Linda's key, easily opened the heavy duty padlock.

Reynolds rolled the heavy door up out of the way, and we both smiled at the dusty white Toyota behind it. He found the keys in the cup holder, opened the trunk, and we both saw two suitcases. He pointed at a dark blue case whose canvas surface appeared somewhat concave.

I watched another large smile fill Reynolds' face as he unzipped the case and exposed many stacks of banded one hundred dollar bills.

"Damn, Dan, but that's a pretty sight."

"It is, Steve. It is. I wonder what's in the other case."

Reynolds opened it and found women's clothing. "These are Linda's, things" he said as he rummaged through it. "She wore these clothes at the cabin."

"She probably went shopping and bought new stuff."

Steve nodded. "I'll bet some of the women who visit the clinic would love to have this stuff." He looked back at the banded bills. "Let's see how much money she left here."

"Let's," I said.

Reynolds counted the stacks as he removed them and placed them on the clothes case.

I watched and kept a silent count.

When he finished, he looked at me. "I can hardly believe it, but there's seven hundred and fifty thousand dollars here."

"Linda told me we would find half your money."

"Well, she stole over one point six million, but this is close to half. It sure takes some pressure off me financially."

"I'm happy for you, Steve. You can put your half back in the suitcase, and I'll find something in my truck for my half."

His smile faded, but he started counting again.

When I shop for groceries, and I am asked if I prefer paper or plastic, I respond by opening one of several canvas bags I take into the store with me. I took a couple to the Toyota's trunk and watched while Steven counted out three hundred and seventy-five thousand dollars and dropped my share into a pair of my sacks.

As he handed them to me, I said, "I have a severely autistic son in a residential school in Reno, Steve. His care is expensive and will be for the rest of his life. I won't be pissing this away at a crap table."

"I didn't know that, Dan. How severe is his autism?"

"I've never heard him laugh or cry other than in his earliest few months. He's never called me 'Dad.' He has slowly acquired a vocabulary of about twenty words, but he still eats with his fingers and drinks from a Tommy Tippy cup.

"His mother abandoned him with me because she could not accept not being loved by the child she bore."

"I'm sorry, Dan. That's got to be tough."

"Yeah. Like the bumper sticker reads: 'Life's a bitch, and then you die.'"

"Let's see if we can get this Toyota running."

It didn't start. We rolled it from the storage space and noticed the right front tire was nearly flat.

I pulled my safety kit from under my passenger seat. While I plugged the tiny air compressor into a power outlet in my Tundra's dash and started air flowing into the low tire, Reynolds found the ownership papers Linda had described.

"She bought this from a private party in Salt Lake City the same day I got arrested," he said as he stepped to the right side of the Toyota.

"She had a Jeep when she lived and worked in Sacramento," I said. "Did she take it to the cabin?"

"Yeah. I had promised to buy her a white B M W convertible but we hadn't done it yet when the F B I knocked on my door."

"She probably felt she needed to get out of her Jeep before the cops started looking for it," I said. "And she couldn't buy a car off a commercial lot without identifying herself and creating a paper trail."

"You really think she just walked away from her Jeep?"

"That's what I would have done. It's not like she would ever have any money problems."

"No," said Steve. "She had more than she'd ever need. I'm sort of surprised this Toyota isn't a white B M W, though."

"If she thought the law looked for her, she had to buy a plain car from a private party. Maybe, once she got here in Las Vegas and felt safer, she took the time to shop for a B M W."

"Her letter said she couldn't leave the ranch without a vehicle," said Steve. "That implies she doesn't have one there. I wonder why she didn't drive this one down there."

I glanced down at the slowing filling tire then asked, "May I look at those documents?"

Reynolds handed them to me.

"It appears the seller wrote a mileage number on here," I said. "I'd better watch this tire. Can you check the mileage on the odometer?"

Reynolds stepped around the Toyota, turned the key, and called, "The battery must be dead. I'm not getting anything."

"If you'll watch this tire, I'll hook up my jumper cables."

Other than a collection of blue gunk on a battery terminal, I found the engine compartment relatively clean. The yellow sparkplug wires looked like recent replacements, and the dipstick evidenced a crankcase full of clean oil. I started the engine then hopped out and disconnected my jumper cables.

The car settled to an even idle so I stowed my cables. Back in the driver's seat, I compared the odometer number on the dash with the one on the paper I held. I did the math as I left the car and walked around to the right side.

I handed Reynolds the papers. "I don't think Linda drove around much after she got here. Nor do I have no idea why she left this car because it appears to be in pretty good shape. With a new battery and a little more air in the rest of the tires, I think you could drive it to Boise without worry."

"I may as well do that," said Reynolds. "I'll offer it to Sam Trenton and see if he'll let me keep the Explorer."

"Well, based on the car's condition, including the fact the registration sticker on the Utah plate is nearly two years out of date, it appears Linda decided to use it to get here from Salt Lake City then turn it into a private safe deposit box."

Steve looked at the dirty car. "Her letter said most of my money is safely hidden. I wonder where the rest is stashed."

"Good question," I said, "and I think that tire is full enough to get you to a gas station." I disconnected my hose and replaced the valve stem cap.

As I coiled my hose I said, "Linda asked me to visit the office and tell somebody to stop charging her for this space. How about you close the hood and follow me to the office, then I suggest I follow you to one of those large tire stores. If you buy a new battery, they'll be happy to air all the tires including the spare. I didn't check the gas gauge, but you should top the tank with fresh fuel before you leave town."

Reynolds nodded and stepped to the front of the Toyota.

I closed the storage door, removed the padlock, stuck the key in it, and handed it to him. "I don't have any use for this, and you might. It looks like a good one."

"Thanks."

Reynolds followed me to the office then led Penny and me to a nationwide brand tire store.

Penny and I sat in my Tundra with the engine idling and the air conditioner running for about two minutes before Reynolds came out of the store and walked to my door. I powered down the window.

"They've got a battery and said they can get to it in about twenty minutes," said Reynolds.

"Okay, then. You're set," I said.

Reynolds extended his hand, and we shook. "Thanks, Dan. Even if you don't recover any more of my money, I'm grateful for what you have found. I can get the feds off my back and send some to Marva."

"Don't feel bad about stashing some rainy day money, Steve. Marva should be satisfied to start receiving payments which you can make after the feds lift their wage attachment."

"Good idea. No use sending her a lump sum and have her ask where I got it." Steve smiled. "Not that I would answer."

I nodded and smiled my own self.

"One last thing, Dan," said Reynolds. He glanced at his Toyota then met my eyes. "I'm not feeling all that comfortable carrying so much cash. What do you think about me putting it in a bank here in Vegas?"

"That's what I intend to do. There's a Bank of the West a few blocks up the street. I noticed it while we drove here from the storage facility. I'll have to fill out a federal form, but I plan to deposit mine as soon as I leave here."

"Do you mind if I go with you and deposit that cash? I don't really care where I park it for now."

"Not at all."

"I'll go tell the clerk to start on the Toyota when they can and be right back."

Reynolds rode with Penny and me to the bank, and we surprised a local vice president with more cash than he had seen outside his own vault in a long while.

As we left the bank and drove to the tire store, I said, "Well, Steve, we are now committed to getting Linda off that ranch. She said she's left alone one night every two or three weeks while she thinks Max smuggles a trailer load of illegal Mexican immigrants onto his land. Maybe I can simply drive to her front door some night and give her a ride to safety."

"I hope it's that easy, Dan. Can I call you now and then and find out how it's going?"

"I turn my phone on Saturday mornings, but give me a

couple of weeks before you call. I've got some more homework to do.

"While I'm thinking, I need three things from you."

"What's that?"

"First, now that you can afford it, have your attorney prepare a quitclaim deed which transfers Linda's interest in Peter Hodges' cabin, including all furniture and furnishings, to you and me as joint tenants with the right of survivorship.

"Second, have the attorney prepare a declaration for Linda to sign explaining that she was Peter Hodges' sole heir when he was killed and that she simply, through her own neglect, never made the effort to transfer the cabin property from his estate to her after his death.

"If we can secure Linda's notarized signature on a quitclaim deed and that declaration, it will be easier for your attorney to probate Hodges' estate and get a new deed prepared with our names on it.

"Third, I need a certified copy of Linda's arrest warrant.

"I know attorneys like to work at their own pace, but I need to have those documents in hand when I meet Linda face to face which may be in two or three weeks. I'm working on a way to rescue her and convince her to sign those documents before I let her go her merry way."

We reached the tire store. Before he opened his door, Reynolds asked, "How will you do that, Dan? What's to keep her from walking away once you get her off that ranch?"

I grinned. "Wit and charm?"

Reynolds smiled and shook his head, *No.*

"Okay," I said. "She might be the one woman in Tucson I can't sweep off her feet. Perhaps driving her to a police station then showing her a copy of the arrest warrant will secure her cooperation."

"It's good to have a Plan B," said Reynolds. "I can afford to pay my attorney for speed. Where should I have him send the documents?"

I wrote my address at the Tucson RV resort on a card.

"I'll call my attorney Monday, Dan."

"Good. One warning. I doubt you'll see many cops between here and Boise, but I suggest you avoid attracting their attention if you do. The Toyota's plate isn't current, and the story you would tell if detained would take time to verify."

"I'll be careful. Thanks again, Dan. Even if we never see another penny of my son's stock money, you've lifted a huge weight off me. I feel like I can get on with my life again. I'm content working with Sam Trenton at the clinic, and I have no plans to leave. I paid for most of my sins with a year and a half in jail, and now I know I can eventually pay Marva's judgment and get out of debt."

"Debt free is best," I said.

Reynolds extended his hand across my cab, and we shook.

TWELVE

After three days of lying on the beach, reading paperback suspense thrillers, drinking Tequila Herradura Reposado margaritas, and eating rice and beans with her tacos and enchiladas, Lori Portman asked Bobby for directions to the closest gym. She walked there, bought a two-week membership, and commenced a workout program which included a stationary bicycle and light dumbbells.

The resort received daily copies of the San Diego Union-Tribune and the Yuma Daily Sun. Lori got into the habit of reading parts of both newspapers including the private classified advertisements for BMW automobiles. She had lusted for a white BMW convertible for many years and would have purchased one while working at the Medical Center in Sacramento except her salary did not warrant such extravagance.

The first Saturday in Baja California, Lori saw a private party advertisement in the Union-Tribune for an eight-year-old BMW 328i. The ad declared the convertible had less than forty thousand well-cared for miles. She tore the ad from the paper and saved it.

Lori spent considerable time worrying about and wondering what to do with the cash she carried. Other than her early morning visits to the gym, she did not stray far from her room, and the fat suitcase containing the cash, locked and under her bed, did not stray from her mind.

Bancomer had a branch in San Felipe, but Lori felt wary of putting her cash into a Mexican bank.

Lori called Max from a pay phone during her second Monday evening in Mexico.

"Max Tucker."

"This is Lori Portman calling. Hello, Max."

"Lori! Lori!" said Max. "I'm so happy to hear your voice. How are you?"

"I'm fine, Max. Enjoying San Felipe and the Herradura margaritas. How are you?"

"I am better now that you have called. I will be in Las Vegas later this week. Will you meet me there?"

"I can do that, Max, and I look forward to it."

"Great! I'll reserve you a room near mine at the Bellagio."

"That's not necessary, Max. I can pay for my own room."

"No, no. I insist. When will you arrive?"

"Is Friday afternoon okay?"

"I will be there. Please let me know when you arrive. May I get seats for Bette Midler Friday evening?"

"That sounds like fun."

"Good," said Max. "I can hardly wait."

"See you Friday, Max," said Lori. "Good-bye."

"Good-bye, Lori."

Lori then called the BMW's owner. When she learned the car had not yet sold, she introduced herself as Linda Coleman of Sacramento and declared she searched the west coast for the best possible BMW 328i convertible. The ensuing discussion of the vehicle's condition and previous maintenance convinced her she may have found it. She told the seller she would soon be in San Diego for a seminar and asked if he could bring the car to the Marriott the following Thursday morning.

Lori then called the Marriott and reserved a room for Wednesday and Thursday nights.

Following a ten minute drive, the retired gentleman turned the convertible into the Marriott's parking lot and declared he wanted nineteen thousand five hundred dollars for it.

Before he found a place to park, Lori pointed out that the Kelley Blue Book value of the vehicle, even in excellent condition, was only sixteen thousand seven hundred dollars.

The seller reminded her she had reviewed all the service records which not only included all recommended maintenance by a BMW dealer, but an annual detailing of the car which included an exterior polish. Additionally, the annual registration had been paid only six weeks earlier. He parked the convertible in an uncovered corner of the Marriott parking lot.

"I never park under trees," said the seller as he turned the key to stop the engine. He looked at Lori. "Trees drip, and they have birds that also, uh, drip."

"It's a beautiful car," said Lori. She opened the passenger and slid off the cream-colored leather.

"Did I tell you I have the car detailed every spring," asked the seller. "They polish the entire car with the finest paste wax, I won't let them use liquid wax on my cars, and they treat the leather. See how soft and clean it is?"

Lori looked across the open car at the seller still sitting behind the wheel. "You mentioned the detailing, and I agree the car appears to be in excellent condition. But I remind you it is not a new car, and you are selling it, as they say in the business, 'as is and without warranty.' If I bought it and the transmission fell out tomorrow I would have no recourse against you.

"Accordingly, the highest I am willing to pay for it is high book, sixteen seven. Cash."

"You have cash?"

"Yes. I have been looking for such a car for a long time. I have also read articles of forged cashiers' checks, so I visited my bank's local branch this morning, withdrew a stack of one hundred dollar bills, and put them in the Marriott's safe."

The seller looked through the windshield at the multi-story building a moment. Then he looked up at Lori and said, "I suppose I could take eighteen thousand."

Lori extended her hand, "Well, thank you for meeting me here and showing me the car. It really is beautiful."

The seller looked at her hand then eyes. "Seventeen five."

"Say 'yes' to seventeen even, and I'll go get the money."

The seller frowned. He had advertised the car several weeks and was tired of showing it to prospective buyers. "Okay, Miss Coleman. Go get your cash. I'll wait here."

When Lori returned, the seller, still sitting behind the steering wheel, had the Certificate of Ownership in hand. He placed it on the center of the wheel and said, "I must complete part of this document and mail it to the D M V to release my interest in the car. May I have your address, please?"

Lori opened her purse and handed the man her Coleman driver's license. She watched while he copied her name and Sacramento address onto the form. When he finished, she handed him a stack of bills.

The seller counted the money, dropped it between his legs, wrote the BMW's odometer number on the front of the ownership document, then signed and dated it. He removed the buyer's section, handed it to Lori, and asked, "Is it okay if I drive home before I give you the car?"

Lori smiled, stepped around the car, and opened the driver's door. "No way! Not only is it *my* new car, you're not covered by my insurance. I will take you there."

The older man smiled. "I understand, Miss Coleman." He climbed from behind the wheel, and, as he stepped around the BMW, said, "I'm sure you will enjoy the car. My wife did, but now she wants a Chrysler 300 with the big hemi engine. She closes her ears when I tell her how foolish she is and suggest she buy a Mercedes Benz instead."

After dropping the seller at his La Jolla home, Lori stopped at a shopping mall and purchased a medium-sized suitcase. At the Marriott, she moved seven hundred and fifty thousand dollars from her fat "money" suitcase into the new case. When she reached Las Vegas the next afternoon, she visited the storage facility where she had left the Toyota and placed the new case in the trunk. Then she went to the office, told the clerk she would be out of town several months, and verified the credit card billing arrangement remained acceptable.

Before she drove to the Bellagio, Lori found a car wash business, put her top up, and paid for a professional hand wash of her "new" BMW. At the hotel she stopped at the valet parking kiosk and asked for Byron. He arrived a few minutes later, stepped to the kiosk, then hurried to her.

"Good afternoon, Miss," said Byron with a smile. "You must have delivered the Toyota."

"I did." Lori returned his smile. "And I returned in my personal bimmer which you must treat just as well as you treat Mister Tucker's Aston Martin. I am sure I love my car as much as he does his."

"I'm sure you do. It's a beautiful car. I will park it near Mister Tucker's British beast.

"Are your suitcases in the trunk?"

"They are," said Lori. "Let me pull the release."

Byron waived for a bellhop then lifted Lori's cases from the car. "I'll see that these follow you to the desk."

"Thank you, Byron." Lori handed him a folded fifty-dollar bill which discreetly disappeared. "Will you please power up the convertible top when you park the car?"

"I will, and thank you," said Byron. "Be sure to ask for me when you want your bimmer."

"I will," said Lori.

She felt relief when a bellhop pushing a cart appeared for her suitcases. With some reluctance but with the belief a Wealthy Woman of Mystery would do so, she turned her back on the bellhop and her suitcases and walked toward the Bellagio entrance.

Max treated Lori to another romantic and expensive weekend. Sunday evening she invited him to her bed.

Over a room service breakfast Monday morning, Max said, "I want you to visit me at my ranch, Lori. It's wonderful this time of year. It's still warm out, but the searing heat is gone. How soon can you come?"

"I promised my sister in Salt Lake City a brief visit," said Lori. "Is a week too soon?"

Max smiled. "I will count each hour as it passes."

Later that morning, after waving Max off in his Aston Martin, Lori decided to spend another four days at the Bellagio. She shopped, swam, took classes in how to play craps and 21, and decided she would never be a gambler.

Friday morning Lori drove to Tucson and took a room at the University Park Marriott. In keeping with her Wealthy Woman of Mystery persona, she had declined to mention her BMW to Max. She realized some small chance existed that Byron might mention her car in Max's presence, but he had not. Now, in Tucson, she decided flying, rather than driving, to visit Max met with her WWM image.

Saturday morning Lori looked in a phone book and found a storage facility for the car. She stopped at a hardware store and purchased an expensive padlock, drove to the storage lot, and arranged for automatic credit card billing using her 'Linda Coleman' identification and Swiss bank card. As she lifted her suitcases from the trunk, she decided to leave her 'money' case with the car. After moving forty thousand dollars to one of her 'clothes' cases, she dropped the keys into a cup holder, closed the car, closed the garage door, placed her new padlock on it, towed her suitcases to the office, and called a taxi.

Lori took the taxi to the Tucson International Airport and, inside the terminal, studied the arrivals from Salt Lake City. Then she found a pay phone, called Max, gave him the flight number, and told him she would arrive at the airport in about three hours. When her happy host promised to be waiting for her, she found the most expensive eatery in the terminal and enjoyed a leisurely breakfast.

Two and a half hours later, after she verified 'her' flight had landed and passengers were offloading, Lori called Max again. She told him she was on the ground early, and, after taking a few moments to freshen her makeup, she would collect her suitcases and wait for him near the terminal entrance.

While she waited, Lori took off her left shoe and hid a padlock key in it such that she could feel a key under each foot with each step. The second key joined its slightly different sibling in the cold cream jar.

*   *   *

Following his second weekend with Lori Portman, Max Tucker drove his Aston Martin south from Las Vegas with notions of love clouding his mind. The beautiful woman had charmed him by listening to him, complimenting him, and making him feel like a more complete man. In bed she had come alive in his hands and under his body. He looked forward to her visit to his ranch and he hoped to show her such a wonderful time she would want to extend her stay indefinitely.

As the miles rolled under his wheels, Max realized how little he knew of Lori. Other than the unnamed sister in Salt Lake City, she had declined to mention any family. She once described doing volunteer work in a hospital, but she did not name the facility or the city.

When he reached Tucson, Max stopped at an internet café, bought a coffee, opened his laptop, and entered the name Lori Portman and the state, California, in a search engine. He found a hundred and thirty thousand pages, but none of the first five actually presented Lori Portman as two consecutive words. When he re-entered the name alone within quotation marks, the search engine offered only five pages.

Max's facial muscles stiffened as he read of a missing and presumed drowned Long Beach, California, real estate agent named Lorraine Portman.

In a newspaper article published two days after the first describing the capsized sail boat, Michael Portman, Lori's husband, reported to the Long Beach police their home had been burglarized. He complained a safe containing important family documents and a large amount of cash and jewelry had been stolen.

Max found no other California Lori Portmans, and he wondered if his Lori Portman had found an interesting way to leave her husband.

Max telephoned his brother Leonardo at his Tucson office.

"Everything go okay over the weekend?" asked Leonardo.

"Fine, Lenny," said Max. "Stop by the ranch sometime soon, and I'll give you the details."

"I'll do that."

"I need a favor, Lenny," said Max.

"What's that?"

"I've met a woman. I've invited her to visit me here at the ranch, and I want you to run a check on her."

"Is this the woman you met the last time you traveled?"

"Yes. Her name is Lori, I think it's short for Lorraine, Portman. I'd put her age at about thirty-five. She's about five foot eight and around a hundred and twenty pounds. She says she's from California, but she wouldn't say anything about her family, education, or employment other than some volunteer hospital work and a sister in Salt Lake. She's sophisticated, wears very nice clothes, and seems well-read."

"I'll bet she smells good in bed, too, right, Max?"

"She does, Lenny, she does," said Max with a chuckle. "She also accepted my invitation to visit the ranch but won't be here until next weekend."

"I'll run her through our computers tomorrow during the noon hour and let you know what I find."

"Good. Emiliano promised to be here Wednesday, so I'm planning to barbecue steaks that evening. Why don't you and Donna join us?"

"For some damn reason Donna has decided she wants to finish her degree," said Leonardo. "She's got a class on Wednesday evenings."

"Come by yourself," said Max. "It'll just be us guys eating hot meat and drinking cold tequila. Like the old days."

Leonardo chortled. "Right. Okay. I'll get a sitter for Leo and be there about six."

"Bring whatever you find on Lori, will you?"

"Will do. See you then."

Wednesday evening the brothers, Leonardo, Emiliano, and Maximilian occupied comfortable chairs on the Tucker Ranch patio deck and watched the sun's last rays die on Baboquivari Peak five miles northwest of them. After a hearty meal of mixed green salads, pinto beans, and barbecued New York strip steaks, the brothers sipped from icy glasses of expensive tequila. They chatted easily about ranch business, Donna's return to the University of Arizona to complete a useless degree in English Literature, how much money they were making running illegals and drugs, and the construction of the border fence across the bottom of their land.

"Did you get any hits on Lori?" Max asked Leonardo.

"I printed you a list of six Lorraine Portmans with various middle names and initials who have been convicted of various felonies and serious misdemeanors in California. There were more, but I limited the list to white thirty- to forty-year-olds who are out of custody."

"Thanks, Lenny," said Max. "I'll take a look at it."

"You think your Lori has a record?" asked Emiliano.

"No, I don't," said Max. "It's just that I've spent five days with her, and I know very little about her. She'll be here this weekend. You can check her out."

"No can do. I'm meeting with my Hermosillo connection Friday night," said Emiliano, "and I promised Tina I'd be home Saturday."

"Speaking of connections, Vegas says they can handle as much coke as we can deliver, and they want more," said Max.

"I have to assume they expect the same quality," said Emiliano. "If they want shit, I can get a lot of shit."

"No," said Max. "Stick to the good stuff. They test every load I take them. They don't want anything less than ninety percent."

"So they can control the cut themselves," said Leonardo.

"Of course." Max looked at his older brother and nodded. "It's just that we've become such a reliable supplier of quality stuff, they want as much as we can bring them."

"We're doing that already," said Emiliano.

"I told them that," said Max.

"You be careful up there," said Emiliano. "Those guys play hardball." He sipped tequila.

"I've been thinking about that," said Leonardo. "My law enforcement work leads me to the conclusion that personal contacts with drug dealers have a tendency to end poorly in the long run. I think we should hire a mule to carry our stuff to Las Vegas. Let somebody else take the risk."

"And add the risk the mule will dilute our product?" said Emiliano.

"I agree with Emiliano," said Max. "There is some risk with me driving to Las Vegas, but I'm careful. And while I don't trust our buyers, I'm safe so long as I bring quality goods. They don't want to mess with the golden goose."

The next day Max reviewed the Portman list provided by Leonardo. He doubted his Lori appeared among the list of convicted criminals, but the two Long Beach newspaper articles bothered him. After rereading and pondering them, he picked up his phone and eventually reached the office of Michael Portman, Attorney at Law, and, after a brief chat with a receptionist, the lawyer himself.

"I don't recognize your name, Mister Tucker," said Portman, "and my receptionist tells me you have an unusual telephone number."

"It's a satellite phone, Mister Portman," said Max, "and we have never met."

"What can I do for you, Mister Tucker?"

"I want to hire you for one hour," said Max.

"What do you want me to do for one hour?"

"Stand in the Petrossian Bar just off the main entrance to the Bellagio in Las Vegas and be prepared to meet a woman who will fascinate you."

"What?"

"From seven o'clock to eight o'clock, P M, on a Saturday, I don't know which Saturday yet, but it will be within the next month, I want you to stand at the Petrossian Bar in the Bellagio and have a drink or two. There is a woman I may want to introduce you to, but that's all. Just meet her. It'll take no more than a few minutes."

"What's the purpose of this meeting?"

"It means nothing to you, and it may not even happen."

"Your request is unusual," said Portman.

"But an easy one to satisfy," said Max.

"How much notice can give me regarding which Saturday I would have to travel to Las Vegas?"

"At least two days and probably three," said Max.

"As you probably know, Mister Tucker, attorneys charge for their travel time, too."

"I assumed I would pay your reasonable expenses associated with my request," said Max.

"Well," said Portman, "to cover round trip air fare, an overnight in Las Vegas, meals, and my time, I must charge you fifteen hundred dollars in advance."

He flies first class, thought Max. "I will place my check in the mail today, Mister Portman, and telephone your office as soon as I know which Saturday evening I need your services."

"When I receive your check, Mister Tucker, I will prepare a bill which reflects my understanding of the legal service I am to perform, mark it paid, and send it to you."

"Thank you, sir. How will I recognize you in the bar?"

"I will wear an orange tie," said Portman.

Max chuckled. "That will do it. See you in a few weeks."

"I look forward to it, Mister Tucker."

Sure you do, thought Max. An expense paid weekend in Las Vegas. Who wouldn't?

THIRTEEN

With almost half Steven Reynolds' money safely in the bank, I considered how I might rescue Linda Coleman from her "prison." Now that I knew her on sight, I could simply appear at her next hair appointment with a copy of her arrest warrant, and, if necessary, with pistol in hand, "arrest" her as a private bounty hunter, and take her away.

But that risked a confrontation with Max or Emiliano, and, if the local police got involved, I might have to give Linda to them. That would probably kill my chances of recovering more money and getting the cabin deed signed. And, not that I cared all that much, her arrest and prosecution would violate Reynolds' unwritten contract with her to cancel the outstanding criminal charges.

I had not bothered telling Reynolds the Boise County District Attorney did not actually have to dismiss the charges and recall the arrest warrant merely because Reynolds asked him to. The facts Reynolds had recovered his money and would declare a refusal to testify might not be enough. The District Attorney might tell Reynolds the "People of the State of Idaho" were also victims when crimes were committed, and he wanted to get her off the streets a while. He could subpoena Reynolds as a hostile witness, and a judge might order him to testify truthfully upon penalty of contempt of court.

I doubted Reynolds would refuse to testify against the woman who stole one point six million dollars from him.

So an open confrontation on the streets of Sells, Arizona, got put on a back burner as a plan of last resort. In the alternative, I decided to see how much of Linda's "I'm left alone in the house every second or third Tuesday or Wednesday night" I could believe.

With my search engine on the World Wide Web I found satellite photographs of the Arizona border. I soon found the Tucker ranch buildings, and I printed an enlargement of them. I moved my cursor to the section of the ranch which bordered Mexico and studied rugged hills, tight, narrow valleys, box canyons, and the occasional sandy arroyo. I did not find any noticeable trails leading across the international border.

A light round spot near the Arizona-Mexico border caught my eyes. From the satellite point of view it appeared to be a giant's yo yo and string lying on the desert floor. The yo yo rested half a mile or so north of the border and the wavy string stretched northward away from it. I moved in for a closer, grainier look and decided the Tuckers, or one of the previous land owners, had used an earth moving machine to cut a thin road to a small, closed canyon. Then the grader made a flat turn around area at the southernmost wall.

In another part of the country, say western Utah, one might assume a miner had found some colorful mineral ore, or his Geiger counter went crazy, in the area. A road and turning area got graded, a camp established, and some time got spent exploring the area.

But such a circle so close to the Mexican border suggested other activities.

I studied the rough desert immediately south of the circle, but I could see no well-worn trail. Nor did I see any trails on the Mexican side of the border.

So maybe the circle held cattle during round up time.

After I made a note of the GPS number for the circle, I

moved east until I came to State Route 286. I estimated a dozen or more miles of rough country separated the paved road from the circle, and I wondered how much of it could be covered on a dirt bike.

Tuesday morning I found a sporting goods store in Tucson which had a good supply of topographical maps. I told the clerk I wanted to hike the Buenos Aires National Wildlife Refuge, and he pulled a drawer holding the United States Geological Survey Sasabe Quad map. A quick look told me it also covered enough of the Tucker land to serve my purpose, and I bought it and the map adjoining it to the north. After listening to a sales pitch about the latest in handheld GPS devices, I decided to upgrade.

A camera store made my last stop. I had searched the Tucson yellow pages for the largest dealer in town. I had both digital and film cameras, and I needed advice on night photography.

I learned that fast film is not necessary and not always best for night shots. If one is using a tripod, one can lengthen the exposure time and use slower film. But I expected some of my shots might include faces, and I didn't want blurred images.

The Tucson expert told me black and white slide film would give me the best results if I chose not to use my digital camera. When I described my Minolta and my available lenses, he assured me my best photos would be had with the two hundred millimeter lens and a tripod.

Back in the RV resort I lowered the rear wall of my trailer and rolled my Honda XR650L into the warm, late morning sun. I hooked my trickle charger to the battery then prepared for a desert ride. My flat tire repair kit and a heavy-duty wire cutter went into a sturdy carry bag attached to the Honda's tail rack. Then I added my Minolta, four bottles of water, and several snack bars. I rolled my new GPS device into a light jacket and place it into a small backpack.

Penny and I took an afternoon nap, went for a long walk in the park, then I grilled several brats for our dinner. At six o'clock I told Penny to stay in the trailer, pulled on my backpack, helmet, and light gloves, and left Tucson on State Route 86. At State Route 286 I turned south and rolled along the pavement until I could see the Customs Station on the Mexican border.

I stopped, U-turned, and headed back north in third gear while I searched for a route west into the desert. A mile and a half north of the border I saw a faint track leading toward a notch between the hills.

I parked off the pavement, left my Honda idling, made sure I could see no vehicles approaching from either direction, and used my cutter to sever five strands of barbed wire. I curled back the ends of each cut wire then moved my bike through the opening and parked it twenty feet west of the pavement.

With thick rubber bands I rebuilt the fence and hoped people driving by would not notice my handiwork.

After I passed through the notch in the closest hills, I stopped and pulled my USGS map. My track appeared to lead to a spring in the Baboquivari Mountains. Back on the pegs I rode carefully for several crooked miles until I reached a working windmill which pumped a steady trickle of water into a tank. The overflow made a muddy spot with cracked, dried edges and hoof-shaped holes where cattle had crossed it earlier. Dried cow pies marred the desert around the tank, and, in the near distance, I saw half a dozen head of lazy cattle. A few watched me, and the rest nibbled on who knows what.

I pulled my topo map again and studied it a few minutes. After taking a GPS reading, I decided I had strayed north of my target, the man-made circle, which I had hand drawn on my map based on the GPS number I took off my computer.

With the new GPS machine I did not need to ride in a straight line which the mountains did not permit anyway. I took the route of least resistance as I traveled in the general direction of my target. The shadows filled my canyon when I spotted an arroyo leading westerly into the hills. I turned the Honda into it and struggled to stay at its edge and avoid loose sand which might grab a tire. The lowering sun forced me to tilt my head down to keep it from shining directly into my eyes. After I passed between a pair of hills, I found myself in a second narrow canyon which appeared to run north and south. I turned south and, a short time later, found another gap where I could angle westerly.

I zigged and zagged for nearly an hour until I found myself in a box canyon with a wall I did not dare try to climb on a motorcycle.

The shadows made riding the Honda tricky. I shut it off and used my GPS to check my position. I decided I was two miles east of my target. I moved my camera, two water bottles, some snacks, and my jacket to my backpack, and, with GPS in hand, I started climbing in the direction of the fading light.

One sunset, one water bottle, one peanut butter/chocolate chip snack bar, and a strenuous up and down hike later I topped a ridge, stopped, and looked down on a flat, man-made hundred-foot circle in a narrow, closed canyon below me. I sat on a rock on the starlit hill and treated myself to a snack bar.

Two and a half hours later, about the time I decided I must be twenty-four hours or seven or eight days early, I saw a dancing light in the distant sky to my right. Ten minutes later a large truck pulling a trailer loaded with hay pulled through the narrow notch at the north end of the canyon and drove slowly to the circle.

I dropped off my rock, crawled around behind it, pulled my camera and my handkerchief, rested both on the rock, and began to take photos.

The truck made a tight three hundred and sixty degree turn in the circle and stopped heading north. The driver left the diesel idling and, carrying a broom and a lighted, battery-powered camping lantern, walked to the southern edge of the cleared area. There he kicked a basketball-sized rock to one side, set the lantern in the dirt, and began to sweep where the cobble had rested. Soon he uncovered a dark circle about a yard in diameter.

I decided the dark circle was a manhole cover.

The politically correct term is 'maintenance hole cover.'

At some point in my childhood I must have experienced a particularly chatty period. Though I am certain my patient mother hung on my every word, one day my father warned me that a person only had so many words he could use in his life. When he used up his allotted supply, he would die.

Because I was a first born child and wanted to please my father, I chose my words more carefully in his presence.

It is possible Dad's warning applies to syllables, too, so, with insincere apologies to the ladies, I shall use the old term.

The driver set the lantern on the manhole cover, returned to his cab, and stowed his broom.

Is that you, Gordo? I asked myself as I took photos of him.

The driver slowly backed the trailer over the lantern, stopped, got out of the cab, walked back to the lantern, and checked the position of the trailer over it. A small move later he had the trailer where he wanted it. He switched off the big diesel, and silence returned to the box canyon.

Back at the trailer, the driver dropped underneath near the lantern and set a four-foot long bar onto the desert sand.

Through my long lens I had enough light to watch the driver release a latch and ease a hinged three-foot square of steel down perpendicular to the desert floor. Then he moved the lantern off the manhole cover and used the pry bar to muscle the lid off the hole. He left the lantern to illuminate the area, got to his feet, stood beside the trailer.

I saw a lighter flare as the man lit a cigarette, and I silently thanked him for the lighted photo I got of his face.

While the driver smoked, I ducked behind my rock, opened a bottle of water, took a drink, and watched for the next act.

Twelve minutes and a second cigarette lighting later a soft sound caused the driver to stub his butt against the trailer, place it in a shirt pocket, then drop and move under the trailer next to the open hole. He helped position a ladder which emerged from the hole into the opening in the bottom of the trailer.

The lantern provided enough light for me to see and photograph people climbing the ladder into the trailer. Between people the truck driver helped move suitcases and bundles up from the hole and through the opening.

I counted thirty-three people moved from the hole into the trailer before the driver closed the door, pulled his lantern from under the trailer, and shut it off as he walked to the truck cab. I heard the engine start, and the truck and trailer moved north out of the box canyon.

While I wondered if the driver forgot to cover the hole, I noticed movement near it, and a man emerged. He dropped to his knees next to the hole, eased the ladder back into it, then moved to the canyon wall and leaned against a boulder.

Ten minutes later I again saw dancing lights in the sky to the north. Shortly another vehicle, smaller than the truck, appeared in the notch entrance to the box canyon and stopped. Suddenly four bright lights came on the front of the vehicle in addition to the headlights and lit a huge pie-shaped section of the canyon floor.

I could then see the climbing man wore a white helmet. He moved away from the rock, got to his feet, faced the distant vehicle, and switched on a light on the front of his helmet.

The waiting vehicle responded by accelerating toward Helmet Man.

I snapped several photos of Helmet Man in the bright lights of the vehicle approaching him.

When his car passed Helmet Man, the driver made a tight U-turn--I could now identify his vehicle as a Hummer H1--and stopped with his lights shining on the hole in the desert floor.

I took photos of the dark-colored Hummer, and I wondered if the license plate numbers would be readable.

The driver turned off his off-road lights but left his parking lights on and a diesel engine running as he climbed from the Hummer. The two men shook hands, and Helmet Man gave Hummer Driver his backpack.

Is that you, Max Tucker? I asked myself silently as I took several photos of the pair standing in the orange light at the front of the Hummer.

The driver stepped to the side of the Hummer and dropped the pack on his seat. He returned to the hole, and the two men dropped to their knees and wrestled the cover in place. Then they stood and kicked dirt on it until it matched the desert floor.

Helmet Man rolled a rock onto the now invisible cover.

They men stood next to the Hummer, and, I assume, discussed the shortcomings of the now gone W administration a few minutes. Then they shook hands again, and both men moved out of the light.

The driver climbed into his Hummer, switched on his head and off-road lights, and sped away toward the northern notch.

Helmet Man turned south, walked to the edge of the flat area, looked up at the steep, rocky hill in front of him, and commenced climbing.

I waited ten minutes after he cleared the crest before I got to my feet, turned on my GPS device, and commenced retracing my steps. Though I had to be careful climbing and descending in the dark, I found my Honda without difficulty.

I silently thanked the U S military machine responsible for establishing the satellite and GPS system and allowing lowly civilians access to such a useful tool.

No, I did not.

I found the return ride to the pavement more difficult and time consuming than I expected because I needed both hands and both eyes to crawl the Honda through the rough and untracked, except by me, country. Frequent stops to check my position with my GPS slowed me, too, but I reached the pavement without accident.

My Honda, with me and my gear aboard, rolled into a quiet RV park as the approaching sun lightened the eastern sky.

Okay. The sun did not 'approach.' It only looked that way because the earth rotated. I know that.

I got a pot of coffee cooking and took a happy Penny for a long walk in the park while it brewed.

One test of true love is to put your dog in the trunk of one car and your significant other in the trunk of another. Come back in twelve hours, open the trunks, and your true love will be the one who is happiest to see you.

Back in the trailer I fed Penny, filled a large mug with steaming coffee, turned on my desktop, then connected my camera to it.

I sipped coffee while I waited several minutes for the photos to copy themselves from the Minolta to the computer's hard drive. Then I called them up one at a time and made a note of the number and content of each photo while I reviewed them on the seventeen-inch monitor. Though they were in black and white, I was surprised and pleased with the quality. The three men's faces appeared sharp and clear and I predicted they could be easily identified by people who knew them.

At six thirty I telephoned Brad Gunn at home. I could have called his office number and left a cryptic message on the recording machine, but I predicted he would return my call when I was an hour into what I hoped would be a long nap.

"This is the Traveling Dick calling, Brad. Sorry to interrupt your morning routine, but I've stumbled onto something I think you will find interesting. May I send you a collection of digital photos I took during the night?"

"Photos of what, Dan?"

"A smuggling operation on the Mexican border. And don't mention what you see to anybody in the D E A or the Border Patrol until you talk to me. I've been told one of the smugglers may be a high level fed."

"It sounds like you've been having fun, Dan. Are the photos related to the Doctor Reynolds case?"

"Yes, but peripherally."

"I may have to share what you send with Marty in Boise."

"That's not a problem, Brad."

"Good. Send the photos attached to an email to my office address." He recited the address, and I wrote it down.

"It may take a while. There are about sixty photos."

"Well, I won't reach the office until seven thirty or so. I'll look at your email as soon as I arrive. Can I call you back later this morning?"

"The closer to noon the better," I said. "I've been up all night, and I plan to take a nap while it's still relatively cool."

FOURTEEN

Lori, standing just inside the air-conditioned terminal, watched as a green Hummer pulled to the loading zone and stopped. She smiled as Max stepped from the vehicle and looked around for her.

With the handle of a towed suitcase in each hand, Lori stepped into the afternoon warmth. "Hello, Max. I expected the Aston Martin."

Max hurried around the Hummer and kissed Lori lightly on the cheek. He took her bags, opened the rear passenger door, and placed them on the rear seat. As he led Lori to the front passenger door, Max smiled and said, "You know the Vantage has just enough room in its boot for a tooth brush and a bottle of tequila. I assumed you would have at least three suitcases and a trunk."

"These should get me through the weekend," said Lori.

"I'm hoping I can convince you to stay longer than that. Whatever else will I do with all the champagne and caviar?"

Lori laughed. "I'm looking forward to Tucker hand-fed beef and beans and rice and tequila, Max. You promised."

The drive to the ranch gate took most of an hour. Max left Tucson westbound on State Route 86. At a junction called Three Points, he turned south on State Route 286. Twenty miles later he turned onto a graveled road which led to a gate under a steel overhead sign which read TUCKER RANCH.

Max left the Hummer idling while he got out and opened the gate. After he pulled through it, he stopped, got out and closed the gate. Back behind the wheel he looked across the engine compartment at Lori and said, "The most important rule on a ranch is: always close the gate.

"My grandfather got most of the ranch in one piece and pretty cheap," said Max as he maintained a relatively sedate speed on the unpaved road. "As you can see, it's not flat, but it contains many small box canyons where we have placed water tanks for the cattle. I have one man whose main job is to drive a water truck to each tank every day during the summer and keep it at least half full.

"It's every other day in the spring and fall when the cattle don't need so much water. Twice a week in winter."

"Where do you get the water?" asked Lori.

Max glanced at her and smiled. "Ah, water is the key. When he first explored the ranch before he bought it, my grandfather came across a spot in the largest valley that was always muddy. It was a natural seep which he encircled with adobe after he completed the purchase. When he put some money together, he drilled at the spot and hit a thirty-gallon per minute well. So that's where he built his house and barn.

"My father expanded and modernized all the plumbing and installed underground holding tanks. He also bought a tank truck and started hauling water to the cattle.

"And that's one reason you won't see many cattle in the main valley. My mother did not like the nasty parts of the cattle business: the constant smell of manure, the flies, or the dust. Over the years my father moved most of the cattle out of the main valley, paved the valley road, and got the cowboys off horses and into pickup trucks and A T Vs.

"We keep our pleasure riding horses and the cattle we are hand raising for our own freezers in the valley."

That afternoon, after Lori had changed into casual clothes and enjoyed a soup, salad, and sandwich lunch prepared by Max's cook, the rancher took her for a riding tour of the main valley in the air-conditioned Hummer.

The main house had been constructed by Max's father in the shape of a large, squared C. The top arm looked north across the valley and contained the master bedroom, the ranch office, and a small room where guests could change into swim suits. Where the top and western arms met, a great room held a spacious and comfortable den and, nearer the kitchen, the main dining room.

At the southwest junction a huge kitchen included a small nook where Max took most of his meals.

In the southern arm two guest bedrooms straddled a hall which led to a six-car garage in which Max kept his Aston Martin, his Hummer H1, his personal Ford F250 pickup truck, his personal Can-Am Renegade 4x4 all terrain vehicle, and two motorcycles: one off-road Yamaha and a Harley-Davidson Road King Classic.

Max explained the two easternmost spaces belonged to his brothers who had remote openers so they could park their vehicles out of the hot sun when they visited.

An open patio and a covered swimming pool, protected from the occasional west wind and kept warm during winter months, filled the central part of the C.

A fifteen-foot wide hardwood deck with built in benches on the outside of the western and southern arms of the house offered panoramic views of western sunsets over the Baboquivari Mountains. A brick barbecue had been constructed against the outside of the kitchen wall.

The huge Tucker barn, sitting a hundred yards south of the

main house, contained stalls for animals and ten ATVs, a
workshop, and the wellhead. Gasoline and water storage tanks
had been buried beneath the barn, and, in a second story, a
mess hall and apartments had been constructed for a second
cook and the cowboys who worked the ranch.

Max pointed to a neat two-bedroom home east of the barn
occupied by his foreman, Gordo, and Gordo's wife, Dorotea.
His cook, Manuel, and his house keeper, Maria, shared a
duplex a few yards north of the foreman's residence.

Outside the barn Max pointed to a pair of cows and
explained his mother enjoyed a glass of fresh milk every day
and liked to make her own butter. So the ranch always had a
couple of milk cows on hand, and whichever cowboy had
annoyed Gordo the most got stuck milking them twice a day.

Lori's weekend stretched into a week and then a second
weekend. She and Max visited the Old Tucson Studios west of
the city, raced the Aston Martin to Tombstone and back in one
afternoon, enjoyed excellent meals prepared by Manuel, and
shared Max's bed every night. Max took Lori on horseback
trail rides and taught her how to control an all-terrain vehicle.

Emiliano arrived at the ranch Tuesday afternoon. While
Max and Lori went for an ATV Wednesday morning, Emiliano
searched Lori's luggage. That he found both of her suitcases
locked surprised him until he picked the locks and found four
stacks of banded one hundred dollar bills. He also wondered
why his brother's guest possessed several bottles of morphine
and two large hypodermic syringes.

Emiliano reported his discoveries to Maximilian who asked
his younger brother to stay on the ranch through dinner the
following Friday evening. Though he needed to return to
Mexico to supervise another smuggling run, Emiliano agreed.

After several margaritas, an excellent steak fajitas dinner,
and a delicious sexual encounter Wednesday night, Max
complained to Lori that he knew so little about her.

In a moment of weakness, Lori said, "I refuse to go into
any detail, Max, darling, but I left a bad marriage a few months
ago. I've spent time with sister and my best girl friend trying to
sort out my life."

"I hope I'm your friend, too," said Max.

Lori rolled toward Max and rested her head and right breast on his chest and hard abdomen. She lightly touched his flaccid penis and said, "Oh, yes, Max. You've become a friend, too."

"Did you have any children?" he asked.

"I said 'no details,' but no. No children."

"What does your husband do?"

"Last answer, darling. He's an asshole California attorney." She paused and added, "I'm sorry. That's redundant."

Lori felt Max's member stiffening and added, "Not getting enough of this is one reason I left."

"All aboard," said Max.

Leonardo Tucker, his wife, Donna, and their eight-year-old son, Leo, visited the ranch Friday evening for the barbecue.

Lori had found Emiliano quiet to the point of being unfriendly, but she enjoyed Lenny and Donna.

Emiliano left the ranch that evening two hours before his older brother and his family.

The next afternoon, Lori's second Sunday on the ranch, she told Max she had enjoyed her visit immensely and hated for it to end, but she needed to return to California. She asked if he would drive her to the airport Monday morning.

Max responded by advising her he planned to drive the Aston Martin to Las Vegas Thursday morning. He suggested she join him for another weekend at the Bellagio then fly to California from Las Vegas.

Lori smiled and agreed on condition Max take her into town to have her hair done before they left.

Max consulted his housekeeper, Maria. She suggested Isabel's salon in Sells and made an appointment for Lori for Wednesday morning at eleven o'clock.

The sight of the small salon in the Indian town disappointed Lori, but she enjoyed Isabel and decided she had received a styling equal to or better than what she received at the Bellagio.

While Lori had her hair done, Max called Michael Portman's office and left the message to confirm their meeting at the Bellagio for Saturday evening.

That afternoon Max told Lori he had a meeting that evening with a group of ranchers in Tucson to discuss the upcoming cattle sale in Las Vegas. He told her not to wait up for him and asked her to be ready to travel after her breakfast the next morning.

Lori and Max took pleasure in another two days in Las Vegas except for two hours Thursday evening when Max left Lori alone in their room.

After an early casual dinner at the Café Bellagio Saturday evening, Max looked at his watch and said they had time for a drink before their comedy magic show. He steered her into the Petrossian Bar, and they both spotted a man wearing a garish orange standing alone near the waitress station.

Max directed Lori to a nearby table and gave their orders for Herradura margaritas to a waitress. After the young woman stepped toward the bar, Max spoke softly to Lori. "Did you see the guy in the orange tie?"

"Some men will do anything to attract attention."

"I can't stand it," said Max. "I'll be right back."

Max stepped to the man and, with his back to Lori, said, "I'm Max Tucker. I assume you are Michael Portman, and I just said something so nasty about your tie you will not extend your hand to me."

Portman nodded, looked down, and fingered his tie. "I understand," he said. He raised his head and looked at Max. "Don't you like it?"

"It served its purpose," said Max. "Now look over my shoulder, study but do not smile at the lady who came in with me, and tell me if you recognize her."

Portman did as requested then met Max's eyes and said, "I did a double-take when the two you walked in because, at first glance, your lady looks like my deceased wife with a longer hair style. But she's not Lori. Your lady is taller and thinner, a couple of years older, and, most important, she doesn't show Lori's personality.

"My wife would have seen my tie and said something to me about it herself. That's the kind of person she was."

The attorney looked back at Lori and added, "I'm certain

I've never seen her before today, Mister Tucker."

"Thank you, Mister Portman. I no longer require your services. You may leave or stay as you wish."

"That was easy," Portman smiled. "Thank you for your business, Mister Tucker. Call again anytime."

"You're welcome. Enjoy your weekend."

Max returned Lori and took a seat. "He said he lost a bet."

"It must have been important because that is one ugly tie."

Michael Portman drained his glass and left the bar.

Late Sunday morning Lori dropped her suitcases behind the Aston Martin's seats and eased into the passenger side as Max tipped Byron.

"Do you mind if I top the gas tank before I take you to the airport?" he asked as they got underway.

"Not at all," said Lori.

Max stopped for fuel, and, as he left the station, he entered a freeway onramp.

"This isn't the way to the airport, Max," said Lori as the powerful machine accelerated to cruising speed.

"We're going back to the ranch, my love," said Max. "I want to know who you really are."

"What? You know who I am. What's going on, Max?"

"The man in the orange tie at the bar last night was Long Beach attorney Michael Portman. He lost his wife in a sailing accident last year. He said you looked a little like his Lori, but he was certain he'd never seen you before in his life."

FIFTEEN

"So, Dan," said Brad Gunn, "tell me how the photos you sent tie into the Doctor Steven Reynolds case."

"What I tell you has to be off the record, Brad."

"Why?"

"Because I may have located where Linda Coleman is hiding. I also know the Boise County, Idaho, District Attorney, at Doctor Reynolds' request after he got out of prison, filed a complaint against her for grand theft and issued an arrest warrant. The contract I made with Reynolds calls for me to find Coleman, recover as much of his stolen money as I can from her, and, depending on how cooperative she is and how much I recover, Reynolds may try to get the charges against her dropped and the warrant recalled.

"I can't give you information which might cause her arrest for fear Reynolds will never see any of his money."

"Is that why there were some photos missing, Dan?"

"That's correct, Brad. I did not send any photos which contained clear faces of the men near the Hummer or the Hummer's license plates, and I have not yet told you where I was when I took the photos."

"Without the missing photos, the ones I have are pretty much useless, Dan," said Gunn. "I'll admit they are interesting and show a sophisticated level of what I assume is the smuggling of illegal immigrants into the United States, but those floodgates have been open a long time.

"What did you expect would happen when you sent me those photos? The F B I lets other agencies do smugglers."

"I'm working on a plan which calls for me to take certain action at a certain time and place, Brad," I said. "A small diversion such as a team of F B I agents arresting that smuggling crew the next time they load illegals onto their trailer would increase my chance for success."

"A small, taxpayer-paid diversion," said Brad.

"Right," I said. "I pay taxes, too, Brad."

"Sure you do, Dan. But this diversion arrest team cannot include either D E A, C B P, or I C E agents, right?"

"Right. I have evidence there's direct communication with the bad guys from one of those agencies."

"Which agency?"

"Nice try, Brad. I want to be a good citizen, but I do have a contract to fulfill, too. I would have much greater confidence in my plan if we limited law enforcement to your people."

My friend chuckled. "Okay, Dan. I will pass the photos and what you've told me to an assistant F B I director I trust. I'll get back to you."

"One other thing, Brad. There's a clock ticking. As they

say in the lawyer business, time is of the essence."

"How much time do I have?"

"The photos may answer that question, Brad. Suppose you'd dug a tunnel under the border, had advance notice of an absence of Border Patrol activity in the area, and, therefore, could safely smuggle people into the country with impunity. How often would you do it?"

"Probably as often as I could put a paying group together."

"Like every couple of weeks?"

"Thanks, Dan. I'll get back to you."

SIXTEEN

"I don't know why Michael denied knowing me, Max," said Lori, "but I can think of a couple of reasons."

Lori had feigned anger and refused to talk to Max during the long drive back to the ranch. She used the hours to consider her circumstances and formulate both a story for Max Tucker and a plan to get away from him.

"Like what?" asked Max. He sat in a comfortable leather chair in the master bedroom holding a cold bottle of beer.

Lori sat on the bed. "Well, a life insurance policy for one. When Michael has me declared dead, he gets a check for two million dollars."

"Yeah, right," said Max with disbelief in his voice.

"Our marriage had soured, Max. We put up a front for the sake of our respective businesses, but Michael had told me he would prepare the divorce papers as soon as he could borrow the money to buy out my share of our house. He'd already had one talk with his father who wanted us to get counseling before he gave Michael any money.

"My real estate business tanked with the subprime mortgage loan fiasco. I hadn't sold a house in months when we went on that sail boat trip to Catalina. When the weather turned nasty, I put on a sweater, a small fanny pack holding my wallet, and an inflatable life jacket. When the boat started taking on water and the bilge pump quit, I knew we were going down.

When I got a glimpse of the Long Beach shore in the distance, I saw a way out.

"I was a swimmer in high school and college. When nobody was watching, I let myself slip over the side and swam until I was tired. Then I inflated my life jacket and swam until I was a hundred yards offshore before I took it off. It was raining hard and the wind was blowing. Nobody was on the beach when I walked across it to the highway.

"I caught a bus which dropped me a couple of blocks from our house. I took a shower and changed clothes. Then I put my passport, birth certificate, all the cash I could find, a few clothes and toiletries in a small backpack and left.

"Michael later reported we had been burglarized.

"I took a bus to San Diego then Calexico. I walked across the border and took another bus to San Felipe. I lived quietly there six months until I decided I needed a change of scenery. I took buses to Las Vegas on the weekend I met you, Max.

"I'll admit I was shocked to see Michael standing at the bar in the Bellagio, but when he ignored me I decided he was doing so on purpose. It didn't take me but half a minute to figure out why. He's probably got a girl friend, and he'd rather have my life insurance money than me."

"You think he's that greedy?"

"I know he is, Max. He's a lawyer, remember?"

"So I could screw him up by calling the Tucson paper and telling them I'd found you?"

"You'd be screwing me up, too, Max. I'd rather be with you than Michael. If you tell the newspaper where I am, I'll have to answer some uncomfortable questions, and I'd have to go back to California and divorce Michael.

"The best thing we could do is wait until he goes to court to have me declared legally dead then we confront him and demand half the insurance money."

Max took a swig of beer, looked at Lori, and smiled. "While that idea appeals to me because I generally don't like lawyers, and I really don't like lawyers that try to scam the system, hearing you say it makes me wonder about you."

"Wonder about me how?" asked Lori.

"Well, what if you're a good liar?" asked Max. "What if

you really aren't Michael Portman's wife? What if the real Lori Portman drowned in a boating accident and you somehow assumed her identity?"

"That's silly, Max. Why would I do that?"

"Because you're really somebody else and, for some important reason, you don't want your true identity revealed."

"Well, I suppose that's possible," said Lori, "but that's not the case. What I told you is true."

"Okay," said Max. "Tell me something I can verify."

"Like what?"

"When we were in Las Vegas, and I invited you here, you said you were going to Salt Lake City to visit your sister. Give me her name, address, and phone number."

"I don't want you bothering her simply because you don't believe me, Max," said Lori. "It was bad enough I worried every minute afraid she might somehow slip, and Michael would find out I was alive. The next time I talk with her, I'll have to tell her he doesn't give a damn."

While Max took another drink from his beer bottle, Lori said, "You know, Max, I'm not in the mood for the third degree. I'm going to bed." She left her chair, stepped into their bathroom, and closed the door.

Max undressed and waited for Lori in their bed.

When Lori left the bathroom she wore pajamas buttoned all the way to her throat, and, after she entered the bed, she turned her back to him.

Max touched Lori's shoulder, and she jerked it from under his hand. "I'm angry with you, Max. Please leave me alone."

Lori lay awake until Max had been sleeping half an hour. Then she eased herself from the bed, took Max's phone from its charger, and pulled a suitcase from under the bed. In the kitchen she verified she had the bag containing her money then she dressed in jeans, a long-sleeved cotton blouse, and her athletic shoes. She placed several water bottles and Max's telephone in the suitcase and quietly left the main ranch house.

Lori feared one of the cowboys residing above the barn might see her. She hiked northwesterly across the pastures until she reached the north-south paved drive which permitted a faster pace. Her watch read twelve fifty when she came to the tubular steel gate at the valley's north end. She set her suitcase on the road, opened it and removed Max's phone. She tapped the number she had memorized for a Tucson taxi into the phone. She had never before used Max's satellite telephone, and she frowned at it when her tapping got her nothing.

Lori struggled to recall what Max had done when he used the phone. She had seen him lift the phone, punch buttons, then start a conversation. The more she thought about it, she decided he may have punched more than seven buttons. She finally concluded Max must have used a code number before he entered the number he wanted to call.

Lori returned the phone to her suitcase, pulled a bottle of water, uncapped it, and enjoyed a swallow. She leaned against the gate, looked up at the stars, and considered her choices.

I could go back, she thought. *Max is still asleep and won't know I tried to leave. I could plan better, learn how to use his phone, and maybe find a way to get a key to one of his vehicles.*

The moon and starlight shined on the power poles crossing the valley, and Lori's eyes followed the lines to a steep hill on the east side.

I could follow those wires to a highway, thought Lori, but I would have to climb that hill, and I have no idea how far I would have to walk or how many more hills I would have to climb before I reached it.

Lori stashed her water bottle and hefted her suitcase. She turned to the gate, lifted the lever, opened it, stepped through, then closed it behind her. As she resumed walking on the unpaved section of the ranch road, she noticed it narrowed and climbed as it entered rugged hills.

The state highway lay several miles north and east of her, and Lori tried to calculate the distance based on her memories of the three times she had traveled it. Max had driven his Aston Martin slowly on the unpaved road so as not to throw rocks against the sides of the expensive car. When he brought her from the airport in the Hummer, he drove much faster.

The times spent in the Aston Martin weighed heavier in Lori's mind. She estimated forty minutes elapsed between the stop at the main ranch gate and the stop at the valley entrance gate. If Max drove twenty-five to thirty miles per hour, Lori concluded the state highway lay at least fifteen and maybe as many as twenty miles away. If she walked the road at four miles per hour she would not reach the highway before sunrise.

Lori cursed her lack of foresight for not learning how to use Max's satellite phone.

When Max awakened and found her gone, Lori knew he would be angry and he would search for her. When he did not find her in the house, he would expand his search to the area around the house and the barn. She concluded Max would discover she had taken his phone and one of her suitcases.

One good thing, Lori thought, *is that Max will be too proud to ask Gordo or the cowboys to search for her. He could not stand the loss of face at losing control over 'his woman."*

I can use that, she thought. *If I can elude Max until I'm off the ranch, he will tell the others he took me to the airport.*

As she walked Lori shifted her suitcase to her left hand and wished she had paid more attention to the road the few times she had traveled it. She recalled it twisted through hills almost to the paved highway which led north toward Tucson. She had seen a few thin tracks leading away from the road, but she doubted they led off the ranch. The hills on either side of the road offered no shelter beyond the occasional Joshua Tree.

Half an hour after she saw light in the sky on her right, Lori reached a track leading into the low hills. She stopped and stared at a pair of parallel ruts marked onto the desert by truck tires and dried cow pies.

Lori turned onto the track and walked between the ruts. She could see a sliver of sun as she entered a small box canyon which contained several head of long-horned cattle and, near its center, a galvanized metal container the size of a large bathtub. The tire tracks she walked between circled the tub but went no further. She recalled Max had told her a ranch worker trucked water to the cattle almost every day.

Lori wondered how loyal such an employee might be. A hundred dollars might buy her a ride to the highway.

The tub contained a foot of dark water. Lori frowned, looked up toward the climbing sun, and wondered how far she might be from the highway. A hike across the desert might be shorter than taking the ranch road to the pavement, and she would not have to worry about Max finding her.

The small canyon had no obvious openings other than the way she entered. What if she slipped, fell, and twisted her ankle? Did she have enough water? What about rattlesnakes?

After taking a long drink from a bottle of water, Lori decided she needed a break. She sat and leaned against the shady side of the tub.

*   *   *

Max slept until the rising sun lightened his bedroom. He saw Lori's empty side of the bed and concluded she had awakened before he did. Not until after he had showered, shaved, and dressed did he notice the empty phone charger.

Nobody used the satellite phone except Max and, occasionally when he needed to call his family in Mexico, Gordo. And Gordo always secured permission to use the phone before he touched it.

Max immediately searched the house for Lori. When he did not find her, he considered she might be out on the patio, but rather than go outside, he looked for her suitcases.

Max hurried to the kitchen where his cook offered him a cup of coffee. He waved it away, stepped to a nook, and lifted a walkie-talkie to his face. "Gordo."

"Yes, boss," said the foreman from his own kitchen.

"Have you seen Lori this morning?"

"No, boss."

"You didn't borrow my satellite phone, did you?"

"No, boss."

"Okay. I can't remember where I left it. Thanks, Gordo."

Max looked at Manuel and said, "Put my coffee in a travel mug. I'll be right back."

While the cook poured coffee, Max hurried to his bedroom for his Hummer keys, his sunglasses, and his straw Stetson.

Twenty minutes later Max braked his Hummer to a stop at the gate marking the main ranch entrance. He sat a hundred yards off State Route 286 about eight miles north of the Buenos

Aires National Wildlife Refuge. He had not seen Lori near the barn nor on the dirt road. He did not see her in the distance, and he doubted she could have walked all the way to the main gate while he slept. Nor could she have used his satellite phone without knowing the access code.

She had better find a place to get out of the sun, he thought as he Y-turned the Hummer. *It's gonna be a hot one today.*

It may be time to put a lock on the main gate, too, Max said to himself. *She might try to steal a vehicle the next time.*

SEVENTEEN

Brad Gunn called me again that evening while I sat outside grilling hamburger patties for Penny's and my dinner.

"You good guys can be a pain in the ass, Dan," he said.

"How's that?"

"My assistant director colleague, Dave Westlake is his name, looked at your photos and told me he was torn between applauding you for being a concerned citizen and arresting you for impeding a criminal investigation."

"Which criminal investigation is that, Brad?"

"Take your pick, Dan. Based on our recent conversation, I have to conclude Doctor Reynolds got some word from Linda Coleman. That Idaho arrest warrant infers an open criminal investigation into her whereabouts.

"Or how about the smuggling operation you photographed? I'm certain a chat with C B P people would reveal some criminal investigation related to such a successful operation.

"Finally, if the smugglers are so successful with people, wouldn't they also bring in other contraband? Drugs, for instance? Should I check with the D E A to see if they have an ongoing investigation in the area?"

"Maybe all of the above, Brad, but I hope you told Assistant Director Westlake that arresting me on such a flimsy suspicion would one, kill my help with that particular smuggling operation, two, kill any future assistance I might offer the F B of I, and, three, really piss me off."

"Number three brought him around, Dan," said Gunn with a chuckle. "I also reminded Dave of your assistance in bringing down Viktor Vladimirov and Uri Breschev both of whom presently reside on San Quentin's death row."

I interrupted. "And probably will another ten years."

"Probably," said Gunn. "I told him about your help with Doctor Reynolds, and I believe I convinced him you would continue to work with me as a reliable confidential informant.

"The result is that Dave is withholding his applause and giving me a little rope."

"Thanks, Brad. Maybe I was too quick to send you those photos. I might work my rescue plan without the help I hope you will offer after you've seen the rest of the pictures and heard the rest of the story."

"Well, we can't unring that bell, Dan," said Gunn. "I'm calling you from home, and my curiosity level is high. Would you email me the rest of your photos to my home address?"

"You'll soon have them, Brad. After you've looked them over, call me again and I'll tell you about them."

Brad did not call back until nearly eleven. "Okay, Dan. Tell me a tale, and I'll tell you a tale."

I described the cry for help Linda Coleman had sent Reynolds and how my contact with her had resulted in recovery of almost half the money she stole from Steven Reynolds. I mentioned what I had learned of the Tucker family, described my Honda and hiking trip to the turn around spot, and gave him a GPS number for my position when I took the smugglers' photos.

"Your photos opened a can of worms, Dan," said Gunn. "Two cans, actually."

"How's that?" I asked.

"Well, since you told me we could not contact anybody at D E A or C B P, Dave Westlake had our people examine the photos and compare them with existing F B I files which include courtesy copies of files from other federal, state, city, and international police agencies.

"When Dave called me back, he said our people confirmed the identity of the two men in your photos. The man who drove

the Hummer and accepted the backpack is Maximilian Tucker.
The man who climbed from the tunnel is his brother, Emiliano
Tucker, who may also be known as El Hombre."

"The Man?"

"Right," said Gunn, "and that nickname is part of the
problem. Mexican drug cops and our D E A have been looking
for somebody who assembles large packages of cocaine,
among other drugs, in a Mexican town called Altar. Evidently
the Mexicans occasionally bust a low-level mule who only
knows he's supposed to deliver his load to El Hombre in Altar.
But that nickname does not help much."

"I guess anybody high enough on any particular chain of
command could be called The Man."

"You've got it, but a lot of people in Altar have pinned that
nickname on Emiliano Tucker," said Gunn. "He has a
girlfriend who may be his wife there with whom he spends a
lot of time. He's set her up in a nice house, and it is believed he
fathered two of her three children. He has a well-established
network of trusted friends and associates who keep him
informed of strangers in town. Particularly strangers who show
some interest in him.

"The owner of Emiliano's favorite saloon in Altar has two
brothers working illegally in California. In exchange for
information about who talks to Emiliano there, the D E A
leaves the U S brothers alone.

"The copy of a D E A file Dave found mentioned the
saloon owner. Dave made a call and got faxed a supplemental
file containing the saloon owner's reports. He says there
always seems to be somebody looking for El Hombre.

"If a particular somebody, including a Mexican or D E A
undercover agent, gets directed to Tucker, he is willing to meet
and talk. He denies he is El Hombre, but he offers to carry
messages to 'the man.' Tucker never says anything about
drugs or immigration. He says El Hombre will want to know
who they are, and he asks them many personal questions about
their families. Tucker then tells them he will pass the
information to El Hombre and get back to them. But he has
never been willing to meet with an agent a second time."

"The agents obviously failed Tucker's or El Hombre's

'check out' test," I said.

"Right. And several of the non-agent customers who have been seen talking with Tucker have later been caught in the U S and deported."

"I'll bet they don't talk about El Hombre when they're caught, either, do they?"

"No a one," said Gunn. "They usually say they walked across the border on the Indian reservation west of the Tucker ranch or somewhere near Douglas. At least two of the deportees returned to Altar where they were again seen talking with Tucker."

"So the Tuckers have a successful illegal immigrant business complete with repeat customers. You can see from the photos how sophisticated the system is. The illegals climbed into the bottom of the trailer from a tunnel that Max and Emiliano later covered and concealed."

"That's what the photos show, Dan, and it appears you have found evidence that the Tuckers are smuggling drugs and illegal immigrants. Dave said you may also have discovered the cocaine connection between Altar and Las Vegas."

"Las Vegas?"

"Dave said a file copied to us by the D E A describes how, about ten months ago, Mexican drug officers arrested a low level mule on his way to Altar with a half kilo of ninety-five percent pure cocaine. The D E A agent on the scene mixed a chemical marker into the cocaine, and the Mexicans cut the mule loose. One street dealer and three different users arrested in Las Vegas less than two months later had the marked cocaine in their possession."

"I don't suppose the F B of I or the D E A has a monetary reward established for helpful citizens such as myself," I said.

"Good citizenship is its own reward, Dan," said Gunn. "And I need to discuss with you the second can of worms."

"What's that?"

"The oldest Tucker brother, Leonardo, is a long time C B P deputy chief. If he's part of the smuggling team, we want to bring him down, too. So Dave needs to know if you suspect the leak is in the C B P but not the D E A."

"Linda Coleman told me she thinks Leonardo tells Max

and Emiliano when they can safely load the trailer."

"Dave checked a C B P personnel flow chart and learned Deputy Chief Leo actually directs some of the enforcement efforts. He moves agents on the ground and supervises unmanned drone surveillance flights along the border."

"So he would know when agents and drones would not be near the area where the Tucker Ranch touches Mexico."

"Right," said Gunn. "That's our conclusion. So, as far as you know, can we work with the D E A?"

"As far as I know."

"Dave is concerned Leonardo might skate if he isn't arrested at the scene with his brothers."

"I assume that wasn't him driving the truck?"

"No. We have not yet identified that man but it is definitely not Leonardo," said Gunn.

"What about the money?" I asked. "If the Tucker brothers have been smuggling drugs and people so long, why don't you sic the I R S on all of them? Max drives an Aston Martin and a big Hummer and takes frequent expensive trips to Las Vegas. Does the Tuckers' cattle business support such vehicles? Maybe Leonardo has some expensive assets he can't justify on his Border Patrol, er, Customs and Border Protection, income."

"Great minds think alike, Dan. I suggested that tactic to Dave. It may happen, too, at some point, but, for the time being, we fear word of such inquiries might get to Leo.

"Dave has suggested a two-pronged plan of attack. One, he will try to find a federal judge who will let us listen to Leonardo Tucker's phone conversations and read his email transmissions. Two, at the same time, he will describe your photos to D E A and see if they or the Mexican drug people have an agent they can put in the next group of illegal immigrants Emiliano Tucker brings across the border."

"Well, Brad," I said, "I don't mean to be the tail wagging the dog, but I made a commitment to get Linda Coleman off that ranch. The best time to do so is when Emil and Max are loading illegals into the trailer. My plan is to figure out a way to watch the Tucker barn, and, the next time that hay trailer leaves, go in after Linda.

"I can't wait for federal agencies to talk to each other or

plant agents or do financial research, either."

"I was afraid you'd say something like that, Dan. When I told Dave, he asked me how you would react to being taken into custody for a few weeks while he works on his plans."

"Really? Is that how our government works these days?"

"You'd be surprised what powers we have since September eleventh, Dan," said Gunn. "All somebody has to do is use the words 'terrorists' or 'national security' and paranoia falls like a wet blanket over everybody involved."

"I'm beginning to regret asking you for that update on Steven Reynolds, Brad."

"Don't worry, Dan. I've got your back. I convinced Dave a drug and illegal immigrant bust on whichever Tucker brothers are near the trailer would most likely ensnare Leonardo, too. If his brothers don't give him up, the follow up investigation, with the I R S taking a hard look at his assets, surely will.

"And, just between you and me, Dan, so what if he skates? I long ago realized I can't catch every criminal no matter how hard I try or how many hours I work. With Max and Emil doing hard time, Leo won't move any more illegals or dope across the Mexican border."

"Not likely," I said.

"Here's Plan B which Dave and I got approved. The F B I is sending a SWAT team to a staging area near Tucson. Beginning next Tuesday evening, three or four men will hike cross country to that GPS number you gave me and wait for the hay trailer. If it appears and starts loading illegals, they will pass the word to team members waiting on the state highway near the main gate to the Tucker Ranch.

"If all goes as planned, the hiking SWAT team members will arrest Emiliano and Max the instant they see the drugs pass from one man to the other. The main gate men will wait for the truck and trailer and stop it where the ranch road hits the state highway. They will verify the presence of illegals then call C B P to take them into custody."

"That works for me, Brad, but those SWAT guys may sit in position several Tuesday and Wednesday nights before they see that trailer."

"They know that," said Gunn.

"If you have the SWAT team leader contact me, I can show him on my map the route I took to the turn around spot. They could save quite a few steps with dirt bikes."

"I'll give him your number and ask him to call Saturday."

"Okay," I said. "And thanks, Brad."

"Thank you, Dan. And good luck with your rescue."

EIGHTEEN

Maximilian Tucker's father once told him only a fool chased horses or women. "They just keep running, son," said the old cattle rancher. "They only come back when they decide you are no longer interested in them or, more likely, you have something they want or need."

After reversing direction at the main gate, Max drove back to the house and asked Manuel to prepare his breakfast while he saddled a horse. He rode the gelding from the barn to the main house, tied him to the rail, then went inside for huevos rancheros, beans, rice, and coffee.

Max put a walkie-talkie and four large bottles of water in his saddle pockets and carried them and a quartered apple to his horse. While the horse munched, Max tied his pockets in place, mounted, and started across the valley.

When he stepped his horse through the gate forty minutes later, Max spotted Lori's shoe prints in the dirt. He let his gelding walk an easy pace along the road as he followed them.

*   *   *

Lori woke with a start, sat up, and brushed dirt off her arm and blouse. She felt the sun on the back of her head, glanced at her watch, and cursed herself for sleeping so long. She found her bottle of water, drank the rest of it, and dropped it next to her. On her feet she studied the hills surrounding her canyon.

When she concluded the water tank made the only decent shade, Lori sat and decided to wait for the ranch worker to bring water for the cattle. She realized Max on an ATV or in his Hummer might already be searching every canyon on the ranch for her, but that would take time.

*   *   *

Max spotted Lori sitting with her legs pulled up to her chest and her arms wrapped around her legs in an attempt to keep them in the meager shade of the water tank. She looked frazzled and apprehensive about the four steers standing twenty feet away from their midday drink. A pair of uncapped and empty water bottles lay beside her.

Though tempted to wait awhile and enjoy Lori's response when the thirsty cattle overcame their fear of her, Max rode to the tank and dismounted. He met her frown with a smile as he let his horse drink.

When the horse lifted his head, Max stepped to Lori's suitcase, hefted it behind his saddle, and tied it securely with latigo strips. Then he mounted, looked down on her, and said, "I'd better find my phone in this case."

"Will you give me ride back to the house?" asked Lori.

"Nope. You came out here on your own. You can get home on your own."

Lori considered telling Max his ranch would never be her home, but she had seen the holstered pistol riding high on his right hip and she decided not to anger him.

"Go ahead and fill your bottles from that tank," said Max. "Having the screaming shits for a week or so might tell you what a fool you are."

He touched two fingers to the wide brim of his hat in a mock salute, reined his horse around, and lightly touched his boot heels to its flanks.

When he reached the main ranch road, Max stopped, pulled his walkie-talkie from a saddle pocket, switched it on, and touched a button.

"This is Max calling Gordo. Can you hear me Gordo?"

A few second later he heard a scratchy reply. "This is Gordo. What can I do for you, boss?"

"I'm near the road to Tank Number Twelve. I want you to tell the water truck driver he may find Lori at the tank. If he does, he is not to give her a ride back to the ranch house or anywhere else. No ride anywhere. Do you understand?"

"Yes, boss. The water truck driver, it's Tom Travis today, is not to give Lori a ride anywhere. Got it."

"Thanks, Gordo. See you later."

"Okay, boss."

Back in the barn Max unsaddled and brushed his horse. He gave the animal a flake of green alfalfa with a can of sweet grain poured on top.

Max carried his saddle pockets and Lori's suitcase to his bedroom. Before he showered, he opened her case, recovered his phone, and found Lori's money, morphine, and hypodermic syringes. As he put her money in his safe, he wondered why she had morphine and what she used it for.

* * *

Five steers standing a hundred feet from the tank caught Lori's eyes when they raised their heads in unison and looked westerly. She had moved away from the water when they moved in for a drink shortly after Max left on his horse, and she knew they no longer feared her.

When she heard the sound of the approaching truck, Lori, thirsty, fatigued, hot, and sunburned, picked up her empty bottles and climbed tiredly to her feet without touching the tank's hot lip where she had already burned her fingers. She pasted a smile on her mouth as the truck appeared.

Lori watched the driver's side of the cab as the truck slowed and parked next to the tub.

Twenty-two-year-old Thomas Travis stepped down from the cab, looked at Lori, touched his right forefinger to the brim of his straw hat, and said, "Afternoon, Ma'am."

"Hi! I'm Lori Portman. I've been visiting Max."

"Afternoon, Miss Portman," said Travis as he turned away from her and pulled a canvas hose from its holder atop a fender. He dropped the open end into the galvanized steel tub then stepped to the back of the truck where the other end of the hose had been attached to a valve. He turned a handle, looked into the tub, and verified water flowed through the hose.

"I went for a walk last night and got lost," said Lori.

Travis, one hand on the valve lever, glanced at her then looked back at the water.

"I went for a walk after I had a fight with Max, and I'm leaving the ranch. Will you give me a ride to the highway?"

"Nope," said Travis without looking up.

"Why not?"

"Not goin' that way."

"I'll give you a hundred dollars," said Lori.

Travis's answer took the form of the top of his gray Stetson hat turning a few degrees in each direction twice.

"Two hundred," said Lori.

The young cowboy looked up at Lori, studied her a moment, then his eyes returned to the rising water. When the tub reached half full of fresh water, Travis turned the valve to stop the flow then lifted the hose from the tub and stowed it.

"What's your name?" asked Lori.

"Tom Travis."

"Tom, I'll give you five hundred dollars cash money for a ride to the main gate."

The cowboy met Lori's eyes. "The boss knows you're here, Ma'am, an' Gordo give me strict orders not to take you nowhere. Sorry."

"A thousand dollars, Tom," said Lori. "Hundred dollar bills. I really need to get off this ranch right now."

Travis turned toward the driver's door, placed a dusty left boot on the step, and reached for the handle.

"Wait!" said Lori. When the young cowboy looked at her, she asked, "How much do you get paid per month, Tom?"

The young man stared at Lori a moment then said, "My business, Ma'am."

"Whatever it is," said Lori, "I'll double it for a ride to Tucson. I've got ten thousand dollars in cash in a storage facility in town. You can have it if you'll take me there."

Travis thought a moment as if considering her offer. "I don't know how to say this no other way, Ma'am, but men who cross Max Tucker got to have a hidin' place a long ways from here. Else they wind up buzzard food over on the reservation."

"I'll buy you a plane ticket to any place you want to go, Tom," said Lori. "You'll be out of the state before he knows you're gone."

Travis shook his head again. "Good afternoon, Ma'am."

"Wait! Did Gordo order you not to give me any water?"

"No, Ma'am."

"Then will you refill my bottles with potable water?"

"Potable?"

"Drinkable water, Tom. I'd rather not dip into that tub."

"Best not, Ma'am," said Travis. "It's got bugs in it."

Lori, tired, dehydrated, sunburned, scratched from climbing through barbed wire fences, and taking baby steps on sore and blistered feet, reached the ranch house an hour before midnight. She hurried to a kitchen faucet, filled a large glass, and quickly drank it. She refilled and drank two additional glasses of water. As she finished the last one, she lowered her head and vomited most of the water into the sink.

From the doorway behind her Max said, "You drank too much too fast. Slow down, and you'll have a better chance of keeping it down."

Lori turned and glared at him.

Max raced across the kitchen and slapped her hard on the side of her face. Then he took her hand and pulled her into the master bedroom. He threw her onto the bed and jerked her shoes from her feet without untying them. Then he unbuckled her belt, unsnapped her jeans, and roughly pulled her clothing off her legs. He dropped his own jeans and underwear to his ankles, spread Lori's legs, climbed onto the bed between them, and raped her.

After he finished Max rolled off the bed and pulled up his boxers and jeans. While he hooked a large silver buckle onto his wide belt he looked down at Lori and said, "The next time you try to leave this house without my consent, I'll kill you. I'll take your naked body out to one of the canyons, and I'll leave you for the vultures. I'll go back in a few days, collect your bones, and bring them back to my dogs.

"Now get the hell off my bed."

NINETEEN

I spent several hours the day following my conversations with Brad Gunn staring at my computer screen. I found satellite photos of the Tucker Ranch and followed the thin road from the turn around circle near the border to the main ranch buildings in the southwest corner of a large, green valley containing pastures with fences and cross-fences north of the buildings. The dots I saw in the pastures were, I assumed, horses and cattle grazing on the watered grass.

With the up arrows I followed the road northerly around hills and through short canyons until it reached a fence containing a gate about a hundred yards south of State Route 286. From the turn around spot on the border to the watered valley and from there to the paved highway, I noticed twenty or so branches off both sides of the unpaved surface. These thin lines led into smaller dead end canyons which contained what appeared to be small water troughs and cattle grazing. Metal cattle guards contained the livestock within these natural holding pens.

The main gate and adjoining fences ran parallel with the state highway. From my visit onto the ranch property on my Honda, I knew the Tuckers had not fenced their entire ranch. When I followed the photographs along the state highway in each direction I noticed each fence eventually reached an impenetrable, to cattle and dirt bikes, anyway, collection of large boulders.

To rescue Linda Coleman I needed to know when the hay truck left the barn and headed to the border turn around spot. The easiest way would be to leave a walkie-talkie with Isabel for Linda to call me when the Tuckers left her alone in the house. But after I checked the distance from the barn to the state highway, I decided no reasonable sized walkie-talkie had the range.

A satellite phone would work, and I wondered if the F B I had one small enough to fit in Linda's purse.

Then I decided the possibility of the Tuckers running a load of immigrants through their ranch before Linda visited

Isabel did not allow for further communication with her via the hair salon. I would have to take the chance I could find her and get out of the valley while Gordo and the Tuckers loaded their customers into the hay trailer.

I needed to be on the ranch in a place where I could see the barn, and I needed a vehicle to take me to the ranch house and, if I found her, Linda and me off the Tucker property. The ranch road leading away from the large valley twisted through hills for many miles before reaching the paved highway. If I could ride my Honda close to that valley and stash it out of sight, I could hike to a vantage point, watch the barn, then ride in from the north and rescue Linda after Gordo and Max left the valley on the west side.

Thursday afternoon I rode my Honda down State Route 286 to the main entrance to the Tucker Ranch and discovered another problem: the Tuckers locked their gate with the strongest padlock I had ever seen. The lock appeared to be a thick rectangular steel box with about an inch wide opening at the top which exposed a half inch thick loop of steel. I found the name AMERICAN LOCK imprinted in the steel box.

When I returned to my trailer later that afternoon I used a search engine on the World Wide Web and found the lock for sale. The manufacturer advertised a case hardened, chrome plated, solid steel body with a hardened boron steel alloy shackle which could not be reached with bolt cutters.

A man with the right equipment, a plasma cutter, might cut through that lock if he had a power source and enough time.

After examining the lock, I U-turned the Honda and rode from the gate back to the paved highway. There I turned south and held sixty miles per hour until I reached the jumble of boulders at the end of the Tuckers' fence. Then I slowed to about forty and searched for openings in the ranch hills west of the pavement which might be large enough for my bike. When I spotted one I stopped, checked my portable GPS, and made note of my position on the highway.

I passed a sign advising me I had entered the Buenos Aires National Wildlife Refuge and newer barbed wire fences appeared on both sides of the highway. I recalled my map

showed a stubby thumb of refuge land at the north end poked
west across the highway into the Tucker Ranch. A few miles
later the posts supporting fence on the right side of the highway
changed from metal to wood, and I assumed I again rode
beside Tucker Ranch property.

At some point my eyes shifting between the highway and
the ranch property noticed a line of power poles just inside the
fence on the east side, the refuge side, of the highway. If I had
not been wearing a helmet or holding my handlebars, I might
have slapped my forehead as the light came on in my brain. I
glanced over my left shoulder to the north and verified power
poles stretched along the fence as far as I could see. They also
stretched south, and I realized the customs building and
perhaps the refuge headquarters needed electricity.

And wouldn't the same lines feed power to the Tucker
Ranch? Had I crossed under them without realizing it?

I quickly decided I wasn't so stupid I would not have
noticed and stopped to examine power lines leading into the
ranch. Power lines have to be inspected and maintained. While
they occasionally reach across impassable pieces of real estate,
the road the inspection workers use is never far away.

I increased my speed and kept my eyes on the power poles.
Four miles later I reached a set of four lines stretching across
the road over my head. I stopped and studied a row of wooden
poles marching single file westward onto the Tucker property.
Though rutted and rarely used, a thin dirt road led from the
pavement through a flimsy wire gate and cut into the sage-
dotted hills at the base of the poles. The road appeared to be
just wide enough for a four-wheel-drive power company
vehicle which made it a near freeway to a dirt bike rider.

A professional dirt bike rider, perhaps, but after getting
through the gate I stood on my pegs and motored along in
second gear just above jogging speed. A crash that bent my
bike or broke my arm, or something more important, could not
happen while I trespassed on Tucker land.

My thought the power lines stretched across the shortest
distance between the highway and the ranch buildings seemed
logical, but the inspection road, while never losing sight of the
wires, twisted through a series of hills and small canyons. I had

zeroed my odometer when I left the pavement, and, when my path commenced a steep climb five point three miles later, I stopped on a flat spot and parked the Honda.

The motorcycle made little noise at crawl speed, but I could not take the chance I might suddenly pop into view of some cowboy working cattle in the main valley containing the ranch buildings.

I walked the inspection road as it wrapped a third of the way around a pointy hill. The rough track and I stopped at a wide place where power company vehicles could reverse direction. The lines above me crested the hill, and, after a few slow steps to the west, my eyes followed them down a thirty percent drop off to the fenced valley about a hundred feet below me. In the distance southwest of my position lay the main ranch house, the barn, and the other residences.

The path below me switched back on itself three times before reaching the valley floor where it crossed a barbed wire fence then ran straight along a cross-fence to a paved ranch road a hundred yards away. I concluded the power company workers inspected the final stretch of wires from the bottom of the hill to the main ranch road on foot. They used gloved hands to get through the fences, too, as there were no gates.

I thought I could negotiate the hill on my Honda so long as the brakes worked, but I would need my dykes to cut those fences. I would also never make it back up carrying a passenger. Linda would have to make the climb in the dark.

I wondered how badly she wanted to be rescued.

On the ride back to the state highway I rounded a small knob and spotted a man standing next to an ATV which he had parked across the inspection road where it crossed a hundred yard wide valley. I studied the wiry man as I slowed my Honda. He had cowboyed up that morning with faded blue jeans, scuffed brown pointy-toed boots, a long-sleeved denim shirt, a sweat-stained rolled-brim Stetson, and a bread plate-sized silver belt buckle.

The hat may have been a Resistol.

I could see no weapon on his person, but a black plastic rifle scabbard was mounted across the back of the vehicle.

I stopped the Honda ten feet back from the ATV, planted both feet on the ground, and flipped up my dark visor with my gloved left hand.

"You're trespassin'," said the cowboy.

"I am?" I asked with surprise in my voice. "Aren't I in the Buenos Aires National Wildlife Refuge?"

"No, you ain't. You've been on the Tucker Ranch ever since you left the pavement."

"Are you sure? I thought this road ran into the wildlife refuge. I didn't see any signs or cross any fences after I came through that gate."

"I'm puttin' you under citizen's arrest."

"Hey! Wait a second! If I left the wildlife refuge, I apologize. Just point me off the ranch. I'll leave and I won't come back."

"You ain't leavin' here 'cept in a Sheriff's truck."

"C'mon, man. I made an honest mistake. You don't need to bring the law into it. I said I'd leave."

"An' I say, 'No, you ain't.'" He stepped to the rifle scabbard, looked down at it, and reached to release a catch.

"Freeze!" I said.

When he looked at me, he saw my black-gloved right hand wrapped around my forty-four caliber Smith & Wesson revolver. The near half-inch hole pointed at his middle.

He froze.

"Step away from the A T V. Put your hands on your hat."

He did, but his eyes challenged me to shoot him.

I turned off the Honda's engine with my left hand, but I left the key in the ignition switch. I stepped to the back of the ATV and released the three clips holding the rifle scabbard closed. Half the scabbard fell ninety degrees into the ATV and exposed a Winchester rifle. With my left hand I pulled the lever action weapon from its case.

"This feels like it's loaded," I said.

"It ain't no damn good empty," said the cowboy.

"I'm sorry you felt like you had to make a criminal case out of me being here," I said, "but I intend to empty this rifle before I leave. You just stand still there a minute."

"You're makin' a big mistake, mister."

"I've made them before," I said. "You've made them, too. Not only should you not have arrested me for a minor infraction where I've done no harm to you or this property, you should never have tried to arrest me without the ability to control me.

"Think about it, Roy. If I wanted to, I could put a bullet in your heart and be in Mexico before anybody found you."

"My name ain't Roy."

"No?" I smiled. "Well there's another mistake I made. A real cowboy named Roy wouldn't be as dumb as you. I'll bet you're not a Gene or a Hoppy or a Lone or a Randolph, either."

I don't know why I provoked him. I suppose I was pissed at having my ride interrupted.

I placed my revolver on the ATV's fender where I could quickly pick it up and use it, then I worked the rifle lever with my right hand. The .30-.30 rounds landed close to each other on the packed dirt road. When two final workings of the lever brought no bullets, I pointed the weapon at the dirt, squeezed the trigger, and felt the hammer fall on an empty chamber.

After I had my pistol in my hand again, I put the rifle back in its case and latched the clips. Then I collected the live rifle rounds and pushed them into my left hip pocket.

I pointed at a walkie-talkie in a sturdy holster fixed to the center of the handlebars. "I assume that lets you talk to ranch headquarters."

"Yeah, and you're gonna have quite a reception party waitin' for you when you get to the pavement. I expect both the Sheriff and Mister Tucker will be there."

"When you think about this later, Doofus, you'll realize you just made your third mistake. What you should have said was, 'That thing never works unless I can see the guy I'm talking to.'

"I wouldn't have believed you," I said, "but you would have felt better about your words."

I unsnapped the strap holding the walkie-talkie in the holster and examined it. While watching the cowboy, I placed my pistol back on the ATV fender, found a dime in my pocket, removed a large screw and a cover, then pulled a nine-volt battery from the back. I stuck the battery in my pocket with the bullets as I picked up my pistol.

"Here's an idea, Doof," I said. "Next time you catch a trespasser, you pretend to be a nice guy. I know it'll be difficult because, down deep, you're really a mean guy. Dumb as a rock, but meaner than a rattlesnake, right?"

He didn't answer.

"Well, if you can fake nice, you give the trespasser a friendly warning and send him on his way.

"Then, as he rides off, you can do one of two things. You can pull your rifle and, being the tough, mean son-of-a-bitch you are, shoot him in the back. Or you can get on your walkie-talkie and alert Mister Tucker and the other cowboys which direction he's going."

He frowned at me.

"Well, it's just an idea you might consider. Being a tough guy hasn't worked out all that well for you, has it?"

The frown on his tanned and weathered face remained, and his lips did not move.

"When you get back to the ranch, you can get a new battery for your walkie-talkie and bullets for your rifle and nobody will know how hard you stepped on your dick out here.

"I promise I won't tell them." Another smile.

"Fuck you!"

"Aw, now, was that really necessary?" I asked. "I offer you a chance to forget and forgive, and you get nasty."

"This ain't over," he said. "I'll see you again somewhere, and we'll finish this."

I stepped to his side of the ATV and said, "Step back a few more paces and keep those hands on your hat."

After he did, I switched my Smith to my left hand and fished for my pocket knife with my right. I carefully opened the blade and pressed the tip against the valve in the stem at the tire closest to my foot.

"Your bad attitude just bought you a walk," I said, "and now the other cowboys will laugh at you because you didn't check your walkie-talkie before you left the ranch headquarters this morning. If you had, you would have discovered the dead battery and replaced it. And if you had done that, you could have called somebody to bring you a spare for this flat you got.

"Now, before you curse me again, hear this threat: if you can't keep a civil tongue, you'll have to explain how you lost your boots and your probably dirty socks because I'll make you give them to me."

He remained silent while air escaped from the ATV tire.

When the tire was fully flat, I closed my knife and put it away. "Okay, tough guy. Be advised I'm taking your threat seriously. And, because I am, if I ever do see you again, I'll have this revolver in my hand so fast all you'll see is a blur. And if I see anything in your hand that even remotely resembles a weapon, well, to paraphrase Steve McQueen talking to Eli Wallach in The Magnificent Seven, 'I deal in lead, friend.'

"Copper jacketed, hollow pointed lead."

Get yourself a Smith & Wesson, and you, too, can quote Steve McQueen.

I back-stepped to my Honda, straddled it, turned the key with my left hand, and pushed the starter button with my left thumb. When the bike settled into an idle, I slid my revolver into the thin holster in my right hip pocket, pulled the clutch lever, toed first gear, and sped around the offending ATV.

I am certain I picked up all the bullets I ejected from that Winchester, but twelve seconds later, about two-tenths of a second before I raced around another hill and out of the cowboy's sight, I heard a shot and saw a spurt of dirt on the ground ahead of me to my left.

My second thought was: If he had spare ammo for his Winchester, did he also have a spare battery for his radio?

I braked the Honda to a stop and shut off the engine. The cowboy sent no more bullets in my direction, but, then, he could no longer see me or my Honda. He probably assumed I was so scared I would just keep going.

And I would have but for one bothersome fact: I couldn't let the back shooter get away with trying to kill me. I had no way of knowing if that cowboy had ever been shot at, but I refused to leave without giving him a taste of being a target.

I've been shot at more than once, and hit, too, although I only suffered one wound if you don't count bruises. That bullet, fired by a Los Angeles gangbanger, took out my hip joint and ended my career as a police officer.

My bullet took out the gangster.

That Tucker Ranch cowboy probably thought he'd put the fear of God in me, and a lot of time would pass before I trespassed on another man's land.

I would have bet he was wrong about the trespassing, and the only fear I had right then was that I might accidentally hit him while I put a measure of fear into him.

I pulled my revolver and climbed the hill above my Honda until I stood a hundred feet higher than the inspection road. Then I eased my way back around the mound until I could see the cowboy standing next to the ATV about a hundred and fifty yards away. He still held the rifle, but the muzzle pointed at the ground on the far side of his body.

With my pistol in a two-handed grip and aimed above the ATV, I took a modified Weaver stance, kept both eyes open, and squeezed off five shots with a one-second interval between each round.

My first bullet struck the inspection road beyond and to the left of the ATV, and I saw the cowboy glance my way then dive for cover on the far side of the ATV. I walked my bullets down with the second raising dirt close to the vehicle and the third, fourth, and fifth rounds striking it.

I stepped down until my head could not be seen by the cowboy, opened my cylinder, and ejected five hot empty cases into my gloved left hand. After I dropped the brass into my pocket, I pulled a speed strip and reloaded. I returned the Smith to my back pocket, straddled my steel steed, and rode as fast as I dared for the pavement.

My telephone rang at eight o'clock the following Saturday morning. I did not recognize the calling number.

"Ballantine," I said.

"Call me 'Duke.' Our Reno acquaintance said we should meet. Are you available this morning?"

"I am."

"Are you willing to come to my location?"

"If it is reasonably close to Tucson, I am."

"It is. Can you come right now?"

"Yes."

"Good. What do you drive?"

"A white Tundra pickup."

"Okay. Drive south from Tucson on I-Nineteen about a dozen miles to Sahuarita. Turn east in town, that'll be a left turn, on Sahuarita Road. In a few miles you'll see a desert camo Humvee with government numbers parked beside the road. That'll be me. Get behind me, and I'll lead you where you need to go."

I felt no such need, but I said, "Okay. See you in about half an hour," I paused briefly then added, "Duke."

"Good," said Duke before he broke the connection.

Duke? Well, his voice had an air or either royalty or FBI, and I've met a couple of fibbies who acted as if everyone near them were mere peasants.

I took a quick peek at my Arizona highway map and noticed a square of land east of Sahuarita marked 'Sahuarita Air Force Range.' My search engine found an article which declared the Army Air Corps from the Davis-Monthan Base first used the twenty-seven thousand acre hunk of desert for bombing runs in April, 1942. They completed a fifty-five hundred-foot runway and a dozen support buildings the following year. The Air Force quit using the facility in 1962 but did not lease the land to the State of Arizona until 1978.

A local rancher had grazing rights, but the Army Corps of Engineers still had people on the site searching for unexploded munitions.

Why not ask the rancher to drive his herd around the site a few times? He might get more hamburger than he needs, but the government would save the cost of paying humans to search for unexploded ordnance.

I spotted Duke's Humvee which carried Army Corps of Engineer numbers and followed it off the main road to one of the smaller buildings on the old Air Force facility. From the outside I could tell our tax dollars had modernized it with air conditioning, a satellite dish, and several lengthy antennas.

I parked next to Duke's vehicle and called Penny to follow

me from my truck.

A fit-looking man a few years older and a few inches shorter than me in military-style sunglasses, blue jeans, baseball cap, hiking boots, and a tee shirt with a photo of Yosemite's El Capitan above the words "Go climb a rock," approached me around the back of the Humvee. He extended a hand and said, "Special Agent Richard Duchovney, F B I. Call me Duke."

I shook and said, "Dan Ballantine. I don't need to seem picky, Duke, but I would like to see your identification."

"Not a problem," said Duke as he pulled a badge wallet from a back pocket and held it open for me to examine.

I read the identification document next to the badge and said, "Thanks."

Duke said, "Come on in and meet the rest of the team," as he stowed his wallet.

"May Penny come, too?"

"Sure. It's too hot to leave her outside in the truck."

Inside the air-conditioned building Duke led me to a ready room. Five casually dressed, but athletic looking young men in their late twenties to mid-thirties with military-style haircuts, that is, white sidewalls, sat around a large government issue table with coffee cups in front of them. Multiple enlarged copies of my photographs were spread on the table. Duke introduced them as Bob, Rod, Doug, Jeff, and Les, and he told them I was Dan.

"Have a seat, Dan," said Duke. "You want coffee?"

"Sure, but I can get it myself."

"No problem," said Duke as he stepped to the end of the room where a table held a large coffee pot and a microwave. "The guys and I came in singly or in pairs over the last couple of days. We've been told to stay out of sight because our intel says an old time, high level C B P honcho is in on the smuggling. The powers that be are afraid he might have tentacles in the Tucson community who would report an F B I SWAT team if they spotted one."

"I'm sorry my hearsay is keeping you guys out of the Hilton," I said with a small smile.

"Black okay?" asked Duke.

"Fine."

"Well," said Duke as he placed a mug of coffee in front of me, "Agent in Charge Gunn vouched for you and said you'd tell us why we're here."

"You want the long or short version?"

"We're sort of bored," said Duke.

I looked around the table. "Well, stop me if I prattle.

"It all started a couple of years before Desert Storm. A young U S Army tank lieutenant named Steven Reynolds, Junior, bought penny stocks. He bought Cisco Systems for less than twenty cents a share. He bought Microsoft for less than two dollars a share. And a bunch of others that, in hindsight, made him look like an investment genius.

"Then he got killed in action while commanding a tank unit somewhere in the Arabian Desert."

I told how the young officer's father found the stock certificates a decade later and schemed with Lori Portman to turn the stocks into cash, keep the loot hidden from the fat wife he hated, fake his death by crashing his plane in the desert, and live happily ever after in an Idaho mountain cabin. I described why I brought Brad Gunn into the case and how both Portman and the money turned up missing when the FBI arrested Reynolds for tax evasion. I concluded the story with the toilet paper letter Portman sent Reynolds and my walkie-talkie chat with her.

I did not tell them about recovering half the money and splitting it with Steve Reynolds, nor did I tell them Lori Portman was an alias for Linda Coleman. FBI guys have a tendency to check out the names they hear, and my contract with Steven Reynolds required I at least attempt to avoid Linda's arrest.

I concluded my tale with, "I have to confess I have an ulterior motive for reporting the Tuckers' smuggling activities to my friend Brad Gunn."

"What's that?" asked Duke.

"I want to use you guys as my personal police force. While you trek across the burning sands and arrest the Tuckers with a truck load of illegal immigrants and drugs, I plan to sneak into the ranch house and rescue Lori Portman."

I looked around the table, but none of the SWAT team members appeared to have a problem with that. I decided they were all action junkies, and they looked at me as a source of something to do.

"You gave Gunn a G P S number," said Duke.

"Right," I nodded. "That's where I sat when I took those photos." I pointed at the enlargements.

"How did you find that spot?"

I described my bike ride and hike.

"Shit!" said Bob or Rod. "I hate hiking in desert heat. Iraq or here. It don't matter."

"I did it at night," I said.

"You won't all be making that hike," said Duke. "Two of you lucky devils, you'll draw straws, will wait up the road and arrest the driver of that truck and trailer full of illegals when he unlocks the main gate."

So you've seen that lock, too, I thought.

"And the rest of us will ride out in or on Maximilian Tucker's Hummer," added Duke.

"I'm hearing that!" said one of the men not Bob or Rod.

Duke looked at me. "Dan, could we drive a Humvee to that tank you rode your bike to?"

"No," I said. "There are tight places where a Humvee is way too wide. A Jeep Wrangler-sized four-by-four might make it, but it might lose some paint on some rocks, too."

"How about A T Vs?" asked Bob or Rod.

"They would work," I said. "Can we back up a second?"

"Back up what?" asked Duke.

"I need a key to the lock on the Tuckers' main gate."

TWENTY

A month after Lori tried to walk off the Tuckers' ranch, she knew she had to escape the house which had become her prison.

After he ordered Lori to move her clothes and toiletries out of the master bedroom and bathroom and into the guest bedroom, Max converted it into a prison cell. He had an iron lattice work bolted to the windows near the garage including a small collection of iron leaves over the bathroom window. He installed a deadbolt lock on the door with the keyhole on the inside and the twist knob on the outside. He purchased a two-cubic-foot refrigerator and a small microwave oven and told Lori she should keep some food handy for when he left the ranch overnight.

In the event Lori escaped her room and stole a vehicle, Max put an expensive padlock on the main gate, had extra keys made, and delivered them to his brothers and Gordo. He had a sign made for the gate warning trespassers and asking visitors to call his satellite phone number and request entry. ·

Max no longer took Lori horseback or ATV riding, and he limited her outside activities to maintaining what he called the flower beds which contained mostly cactus.

The often triple digit temperatures kept Lori indoors except in the earliest two hours of daylight. During those minutes she often took a cup of coffee onto the patio outside her room, away from other household members, to watch the sun rise.

Max did not ask Lori to do anything. His housekeeper, Maria, kept the house, including Lori's room, clean and the sheets changed. Manuel prepared meals for Max and Lori, and they often ate together. When Max was absent, Manuel told Lori he did not want her in his kitchen.

Lori learned not to complain about what she did not have, but she discovered that if she asked for something, Max often got it for her. He had a satellite dish installed, paid for many premium channels, and bought a large screen television which he had installed in the main room of the house. Lori learned Max or Emiliano could preempt her television plans simply by holding out an empty hand for the remote control device. They enjoyed television boxing matches which she did not watch with them.

Max usually brought her the books and magazines she requested, and, when she asked him, he subscribed to a movies-by-mail service which she controlled. She told him she used to visit a gym regularly, and he brought her a small treadmill for her room. Max took her to visit Isabel every other week.

When Lori told Max she had used all of her birth control pills, he asked for the empty container. A few days later he brought her a six-month supply.

But Lori had no computer, no internet connection, no telephone, and Max would not let her talk with anyone by mail. Lori noticed the poles and lines bringing electricity to the ranch, and she asked Max why they did not also provide telephone service. Max explained his father paid for the installation of the power lines before telephones were common. When he learned the cost of adding telephone wires to the poles, he decided he could do without one as he had for so many years.

When the Tucker brothers inherited the ranch, they, too, decided the cost of installing a phone line exorbitant, and they rarely used the satellite phone.

Max, Emiliano, Gordo, Manuel, Dorotea, and, when they visited, Leonardo and Donna were civil to Lori, but by no stretch of the definition could she say anybody was friendly. Nor did anyone discuss ranch business in front of her. Lori once heard Emiliano refer to her as "Max's woman" and decided she knew the true meaning of the word chattel.

In addition to reading and watching television, Lori, while not appearing to have any interest, paid close attention to the ranch activities and soon learned those regularly scheduled.

On all but the coldest winter or stormy days, a group of cowboys left the south building at seven each morning except Sundays on ATVs. Occasionally a pair pulled a horse trailer with a ranch pickup truck. These same men trickled back to the ranch late in the afternoon, and Lori learned they ate their dinner promptly at six each evening.

The water truck also left each morning including Sundays during the summer time.

Manuel and the cowboys' cook drove a pickup truck to town each Wednesday after lunch, returned four hours later, and unloaded groceries into their respective kitchen pantries, refrigerators, and freezers.

Max cloistered himself in his office the last two days of each month then handed out pay envelopes on the first day of the next month. By picking up pieces of conversations, Lori learned that most employees received a paycheck reflecting minimum wage. However, a generous cash bonus based on a supplemental hourly rate also found its way into each envelope from which no taxes were withheld and no reports were sent to the Arizona or US governments.

Lori never heard a single grumble from any employee about the level of his or her wages. She also noticed nobody quit during the time she spent on the ranch.

Every two or three weeks Gordo drove a truck pulling a hay trailer through the west gate at ten o'clock in the evening. Max followed him in his Hummer.

The truck returned to the valley through the west gate an hour and a half to two hours later, looped around the buildings, and left through the north gate. Max followed the truck through the west gate, but he drove his Hummer to a garage stall and left a few minutes later in his Aston Martin. He returned in two or three days and, immediately after arriving, spent an hour behind his closed office door.

Within two days of Max's Aston Martin trip, Lori assumed he drove to Las Vegas each time, both Emiliano and Leonardo visited the ranch and Max's office. Lori, standing on the patio outside with her hand on the wall, could feel someone closing the heavy safe door near the conclusion of the office visit.

Max did not lock his office door. After Dorotea and Maria got used to Lori's presence and stopped paying close attention to her, she visited Max's office and studied its contents. An off-white painted safe stood in the office closet. The size of a five cubic foot refrigerator, the door held both a key hole and a keypad but no numbered dial.

A sturdy oak four-drawer filing cabinet filled one corner of Max's office, and a matching desk sat near the center of the room such that light from a window streamed onto it from behind the main chair. Though Max did not lock the room, he did lock his desk and the filing cabinet drawers.

With hopes she might find something she could use to secure her release, Lori got into the habit of checking Max's desk and filing cabinet whenever possible.

By declining Max's gentler sexual overtures, Lori became his sex slave. After he raped her the first time when she was physically debilitated, he came to her room whenever he was in the mood for sex and took it.

Lori knew Max would be back after that first time, and she considered finding something to use as a weapon. But she feared she might not survive Max's strength and his wrath.

Lori learned to keep lubricant on her bedside table for when Max used her for his sexual desires. And, after she realized Max had no intention of releasing her until Michael Portman made a life insurance claim based on his wife's death, she decided to murder Max. She knew her plan for doing so must include a way to steal a vehicle and leave the ranch undiscovered.

TWENTY-ONE

I described to Duke and the SWAT team my motorcycle ride along the power line service road, but I declined to mention my encounter with the cowboy on the way out.

I suggested I could wait atop that knob overlooking the ranch's main valley, advise them when the hay trailer left the barn and headed toward the immigrant collection point, then I would ride my Honda down that steep trail and rescue Linda.

"So you're expecting her to leave the ranch on the back of your Honda?" asked Duke.

"Yes, but after due consideration, I decided not to ask her to climb that hill while I tried to ride up that trail in the dark. That left too great a chance for one of us to fall.

"So, after I made the call that warned you guys the truck and Hummer were headed your way, I planned to put Linda on the Honda and ride to a hiding place near the main gate. Then when Gordo arrived driving the truck pulling the hay wagon and unlocked it, I would race through the gate before he relocked it.

"But, if you guys can get me a key to the lock, I can have Linda off the ranch before Gordo reaches the gate."

"You are still assuming, Dan," said Duke, "that Linda will ride on the back of your bike. What will you do if she takes one look at the Honda and says, 'No way I'm riding on that!'?"

"Well," I said, "she's the one who wrote a letter on toilet paper asking a man she stole one point six million dollars from and who she let spend a year in federal prison to rescue her. I'm assuming she's desperate. As with beggars, rescuees can't be choosers about their choice of escape vehicles."

"What if she wants to bring her clothes or her makeup kit or something she stole from the ranch?" asked Bob or Rod.

I looked at the speaker. "Is it Bob?"

"Yeah."

"Well, Bob, I suppose I could bring an empty backpack, a small one, and give her a few minutes to fill it. But I happen to know she can afford to walk away from her clothes."

"How do you know that?" asked Duke.

"I found a newspaper account of the car crash that killed her first husband. I asked my insurance company contact to look into it, and he told me Linda received a check for half a million dollars in life insurance benefits which she stashed in a Swiss bank. While I don't know the current balance, I suspect there's enough left for a new wardrobe."

Duke nodded. "So you can probably get her off the ranch without a key to that padlock."

"Probably," I said, "but if you guys are planning to arrest Gordo at that gate and call the Border Patrol to collect the illegals, wouldn't it be cleaner if I had Linda off the ranch before that trailer arrived?"

"It would," said Duke. "And we put in a request for a key for ourselves just in case. We'll get you one, too."

"Thanks," I said. "One more thing. I would prefer my name and any report of my personal rescue agenda not appear in the press. I'm hoping to sneak Linda off the ranch and be well away from Tucson before the media gets involved. I don't know if the Tuckers or their employees will mention Linda's presence, but, if they do, I'm hoping neither one of us will be found to answer questions."

"If we do your bidding and arrest the Tuckers and anybody else involved in the smuggling, may we assume you are willing to testify at the criminal hearings that necessarily follow such arrests?" asked Duke.

"Yes," I said. "Of course. On the other hand, Brad Gunn once labeled me an R C I, a reliable confidential informant. I would prefer to maintain that role with an emphasis on the confidential part. In my experience as a California cop and lawyer, such persons are often questioned in the judge's chambers and off the public record." I smiled. "Who can tell when I might have some future usefulness to the F B of I."

Duke returned my smile. "We'll do what we can, Dan. Does your plan allow time for you to lead us to that water tank tonight? We'd like to get the lay of the land."

"Sure, but I saved my last trip in my new GPS machine. I'm no techie, but I'll bet there's a way to download my twists and turns into your equipment."

"There is, and we can do that," said Duke, "but I'll bet the trip would go much faster with you taking the point."

I took Penny back to the RV park, enjoyed an afternoon nap, grilled trout, previously frozen by me, for dinner, then rode my Honda to Duke's Headquarters at nine o'clock. I enjoyed a cup of coffee and a cupcake while Bob downloaded my trip information from my new GPS into several of their similar devices.

The SWAT team had loaded six ATVs into a trailer with Army Corps of Engineer markings. They carried backpacks into the trailer then I led the driver on my Honda to the thin tank road. The trailer's rear door dropped, and the team rode their ATVs onto the shoulder parallel to the pavement. They all wore desert camo clothes, backpacks, and pistol belts with flap holsters containing forty-five caliber semiautomatic pistols.

When they had all the vehicles out of the trailer, the truck driver made a U-turn onto the highway and headed north.

I got off my bike and stepped to the cut fence.

Duke pointed at my rubber bands, looked at me, and asked, "Did you do this?"

"Guilty," I said. "I planned to come back and make a proper repair after I rescued the damsel."

"Those rubber bands won't last a week in this heat," said Duke. He turned to Rod and added, "Make a note to bring some wire the next time we come out here."

"Roger that," said Rod.

Duke looked at me. "We'll take care of the fence. Taxpayers' dollars and all that."

"Okay," I said. "Thanks. I really would have repaired it, though. I know the Code of the West."

"I don't doubt you," said Duke, "but we wouldn't want to slow the Traveling Dick."

I could only smile.

"Can you turn your Honda's headlight off?"

"Not with the engine running. I suppose I could remove the bulb, but it would take me a few minutes."

Duke removed his backpack, opened it, and removed a device that looked like a small pair of binoculars mounted to a head strap. He held them toward me. "These are the latest in night vision goggles. They're built onto our helmets as are mikes and transmitters."

I took the goggles and examined them while Duke continued.

"You probably can't wear them under your motorcycle helmet in which case you'll have to choose between the helmet and the goggles. I suggest you aim your bike up the road after we get through the fence and see how bright your headlight is while wearing the goggles. If you find it's too bright, we've got some tape we can put over all or part of the headlight.

"Whatever you choose to do, you'll be leading the way. Also, even if we tape over most of the light, do not turn back in our direction unless you want to blind all but one of us."

I must have put a questioning look on my face.

"I always ask for one volunteer to 'go blind,' that is, not wear the goggles because it takes about ten minutes for one's eyes to adjust to ambient light should one have to take them off. I want one guy ready for action without that wait."

"Got it," I said.

Duke looked to the line of ATVs and his team members standing beside them. "Bob, you unhook those rubber bands then Traveling Dick will roll his Honda through the opening without starting it."

"Roger, Duke."

"Traveling Dick, as soon as you're through the fence, start

your bike and ride about a hundred feet. Keep your headlight
aimed west, and we'll fall in line behind you. While we're
doing that, you decide about using the light or the goggles.

"Bob will close the fence after we're through, and I will
dismount and walk to your rear tire. Tell me what you've
decided about the headlight, and I'll let you know when we're
all ready to roll. Then you can lead us to that tank. We're not in
a big hurry, but you don't have to watch your speed because of
us. Just remember to keep your headlight aiming west at all
times including when you stop at the tank.

"Okay?"

"Got it," I said.

I rode onto the Tucker Ranch property, stopped, and tried
the goggles. I liked them, but my headlight made the desert too
bright. I knew the road to the tank did not present any
particular dangerous sections so I got off and strapped my
helmet to my rack as the SWAT team lined their ATVs behind
my Honda.

When Duke approached he carried a roll of duct tape and
said, "I was pretty sure you would want to dim that light."

I nodded, took the tape and covered all but a one-inch wide
horizontal stripe of headlight glass. After giving Duke his tape,
I started the Honda and found I still had enough light
amplification with the goggles to feel like I looked at the desert
at high noon.

I looked over my shoulder, got an okay from Duke, and led
the group to the tank without incident. I stopped a minute until
everybody caught up, then, using my GPS when necessary to
remind me where to turn, led the team to the box canyon where
I dismounted and turned off my engine.

Duke and his team parked their vehicles, and Duke and I
removed our goggles. The others did not, and Jeff, the "blind"
volunteer, donned a pair.

"So far so good, Traveling Dick," said Duke. "After
everybody has a drink of water, you can lead us out of here."

I took a drink, checked my GPS, and started climbing.

I like to think I'm in pretty good shape. I'm six four and
weigh about one seventy, and I jog four or five miles most
mornings. I set what I thought was a pretty strong pace, but

those SWAT guys not only kept up with me, I got the feeling they wished I would travel faster.

The men who wore their goggles and helmets could see better than I could. I decided that made climbing and hiking easier for them. I finally asked Duke if he wanted me to use my goggles and pick up the pace, but he said we were doing fine.

At one point we walked in pairs through a valley, and one of the men behind me broke wind loud enough for all to hear.

"Jesus, Jeff!" said Bob. "You just killed a poor dumb coyote that's been stalking us. Poor doggie."

"It's that Afterburner Chili Duke cooked up for dinner last night," said Jeff. "My intestines are still filled with hot molten magma that threatens to erupt at any minute."

"Hey!" said Duke walking beside me. "That was a mild, black bean chili with a hint of pork and almost no spices."

"Hah!" said Les. "After two spoonfuls my nose felt like I'd snorted a two-foot line of Drāno."

Doug nodded his head. "When I finished my bowl, sweat poured off me like rain, my eyes fell out of focus for an hour, and I scraped a brown crust off my tongue."

"That's nothing," said Rod. "I filled my pants with brown lava when I farted this morning, and I feared it would eat through my shorts and my chair. I wish I could wipe my ass with a snow cone right now."

"Not only could I not feel my lips after the first bite," said Bob, "that chili burned a two-inch hole through my stomach. If you hadn't of brought a case of beer to wash it down, Duke, I would have pulled my Colt and put you out of my misery."

My chuckles grew into out loud laughter.

Duke looked at me and, with a serious face, said, "It was a mild chili with a slight habanero tang. I was disappointed in it my own self. I only ate three bowls."

When we reached my GPS point above the manhole cover, I sat on my favorite boulder and watched them climb down to the flat spot and scout the area. They appeared to pick places of concealment on the hill south of the pick up point then Bob and Les, wearing their helmets and goggles, moved the marker rock, moved the manhole cover, hooked a line to the rim of the hole, and lowered themselves out of sight.

The others climbed to my position, and, when they arrived, Duke said, "Okay, Traveling Dick, we can travel back now."

"What about Bob and Les?" I asked. "Didn't I see them drop into the hole?"

"They'll be along soon," said Duke. "The honchos want to know where the Tuckers' tunnel comes out on the Mexican side. We'll take our time getting back to the A T Vs, and they'll probably catch us. They'll be sure to leave the place like we found it, too."

We had been sitting at our vehicles half an hour when Bob and Les returned.

"Their tunnel is a piece of six-foot diameter storm drain conduit which leads to a natural crack in the earth under the mountain," said Bob. "It runs generally south for about a mile and a half, and they've cleared a path in it for their customers. It was nice and cool in there, too. I thought I smelled some bat shit, but I decided Les's deodorant had worn off.

"We made note of the G P S number at the Mexican entrance in case we want to pass the location to our Federale colleagues."

"Did you find any other exits?" asked Duke.

"No," said Bob. "We searched several of the larger offshoot cracks, but we didn't find any rooms nor did we feel any drafts.

"The passage is not a cave in the common meaning of the word. It's an earthquake fault that opened up a gazillion years ago and got covered with rocks and dirt sometime since."

"Interesting," said Duke. "Did you leave a little present for the Tuckers at the Mexican entrance point?"

"We did."

"Okay, then. I'll call for the trailer to meet us at the road. Let's saddle up and ride."

The following Monday I received a thick envelope from Steven Reynolds. It contained the legal documents I had requested and a letter describing how he had paid the IRS all back taxes with penalties and interest. He had offered the

Toyota to Doctor Trenton' clinic and had been permitted to take title to his "loaner" Explorer.

I phoned him during the noon hour, and he took time to chat. Without revealing detail, I told him I thought I might get Linda off the ranch within the next two weeks. He wished me luck at both the rescue and the recovery of more of his money.

TWENTY-TWO

As the December and the winter holidays approached, Lori overheard employee chatter about time off and trips to Mexico. She concluded Gordo and Dorotea visited family and friends south of the border the last two weeks of December and the first week of January each year. Manuel and Maria left three days later than Gordo and his wife, and they, too, traveled to Mexico.

At nine o'clock in the morning the day after Gordo and Dorotea left for Mexico, Lori sat in the den reading a novel. She overheard Max in the kitchen tell Manuel he should ask Lori what she wanted for lunch as he would be driving into Tucson to eat with Leonardo. An hour later Manuel told Lori he would be making tuna sandwiches for lunch.

Max left the house at eleven o'clock. Five minutes later Manuel told Lori she could find her sandwich in the refrigerator, and he and Maria walked to their apartments to pack for their holiday trips.

Alone in the house, Lori hurried to Max's office and discovered his first significant mistake since he had made her his prisoner: he had left his desk drawer unlocked. When she pulled the center drawer out a few inches, she found she could also open the other drawers.

A quick search revealed little more than files pertaining to ranch business. The "little more" was a heavy-duty folder containing nearly two dozen unlabeled keys taped inside it. Many of them had plastic heads stamped with the name of a vehicle manufacturer. Those for the all-terrain vehicles appeared quite similar. Lori also noticed spare keys for the

Aston Martin, the Hummer, Max's pickup truck, and several for the padlock on the entrance gate.

Lori stepped to the filing cabinet, noted a small brass marker with the maker's name, and returned to the open key folder where she found a brass key marked with the same name. A smile came over her face. She hurried to her bathroom and returned with a nail file which she used to carefully lift the tape off the key.

Max's filing cabinet contained more files including income tax returns, both state and federal, going back many years. Lori also found several photo albums and a surprisingly large collection of commercial DVDs containing hard core woman-on-woman pornography.

A folder marked WARRANTIES caught her eye, and Lori carried it to the desk. She opened the folder and found warranty and operational documents for everything from the kitchen appliances to the well pump. When she found the one for the safe in Max's office closet, Lori pulled it and began to read.

On page twelve the brochure contained instructions to change the factory keypad setting, blank boxes in which to write the new number, and bold print instructions to secure the booklet in a memorable and risk-free place other than the safe.

With the brochure in hand, Lori stepped to the safe, punched 89523 on the keypad, heard a click, and turned the handle. She pulled the door open, and her eyes widened at the many stacks of banded bills. Suddenly nervous and fearful of being caught by Manuel or Maria, Lori dropped the brochure and verified each stack consisted entirely of one hundred dollar bills. She made a quick count of the stacks and concluded Max had over three hundred thousand dollars in cash.

On a shelf above the cash, next to a black revolver, Lori counted twenty-five plastic tubes each of which contained ten one-ounce Maple Leaf coins.

Lori closed the safe, returned the brochure to its proper place in the warranty folder, put the folder back in the cabinet, slid the key under the tape, replaced the key folder in the desk drawer, and closed the desk.

From the hallway, Lori stood and stared at the desk a full minute. She decided Max would be less suspicious if he found his desk locked. She decided to keep the desk key, but she did not want to leave an open space in the folder.

Lori walked through the house to make sure she remained alone. In her room she pulled from her cold cream jar the mate to the padlock key she had given Isabel to give to Ballantine. It did not match the desk key, but she thought that Max, if he happened to open the key folder, would see an open space and realize he had a problem.

She returned to Max's desk, reopened it, and lifted the key folder. She located the desk drawer key, removed it, inserted her padlock key, replaced the folder, and locked the desk.

Back in her chair with a book in her lap, Lori hit on an idea which would free her from her prison and Max's abuse of her body and mind. She knew it needed more consideration, but she believed she finally had a plan to get away from Max and his ranch. The thought of carrying a suitcase filled with his cash and gold coins and driving his pickup made her smile.

The second Sunday before Christmas, Max told Lori they would have to fend for themselves until the second week in January as Manuel and Maria were taking their annual vacations beginning the next day.

Max had given most of the cowboys two weeks off, too, and he spent his even-numbered days driving the water truck to the various tanks around the ranch, and, on odd numbered days, he hauled hay to the same locations. When he returned to the ranch house each afternoon, he showered, dressed, then made himself a pitcher of strong margaritas.

After several drinks Max often wanted sex. He would find Lori, take her by the hand, lead her to her bed, lower his pants, and insert himself into her. When he finished, he would pull up his underwear and pants, buckle his belt, go to the kitchen, and search for munchies.

The instant Lori undressed and lay on her bed, she would lubricate herself then stoically tolerate the rape.

On Christmas Eve day Lori saw Max mix his pitcher and start drinking. She went to her bathroom, drew a fatal dose of morphine into her largest hypodermic syringe, and placed it under her pillow.

When Max pulled her to her bed an hour or so later, Lori undressed and reached for her lubricant.

"All ready for your Christmas present I see," said Max as he finished removing his jeans and underwear. He grinned at her and climbed onto the bed between her already opened legs.

Max inserted himself into Lori and began to hump.

Lori slid her right hand under her pillow, encircled the syringe, and placed her thumb on the plunger.

As Max reached his climax he turned his face to his right and lowered his head to Lori's left shoulder.

Lori pulled her hand from under the pillow, swung the syringe around until the needle almost touched the outside of Max's left buttock, then jabbed it an inch into the thick muscle and thumbed the plunger.

"What the ... ?" Max raised himself up on his arms, looked over his left shoulder at the syringe, then met Lori's eyes. "Are ... you ... trying ... to ... kill ... me?" he asked as he lowered himself onto her.

Max's left cheek touched Lori's left cheek then his face dropped heavily to the pillow next to her head.

Lori jerked the empty syringe from Max's buttock and tried to roll him off her. When she found his weight heavier than she expected, she dropped the syringe to the floor, got her right hand under Max's left shoulder and pushed.

Lori felt Max's weight shift against her then his body shuddered. It took her a moment to realize he was laughing.

Max became still, raised his head, looked at Lori, and said, "You stupid bitch! I found your needles and morphine the day you thought you could run away from me. I replaced your drugs with water just in case you tried something like this."

He pushed himself off her and pulled up his underwear and jeans. Instead of buckling his belt, Max jerked it from the loops and said, "Now you're gonna get a whipping like my ol' daddy used to give me and my brothers when we fucked up big time."

Max laid the thick leather across Lori's naked body with all his energy. When she tried to roll away from him, he stepped around the end of the bed and struck her again and again.

Lori leaped from the bed and ran toward her bathroom, but Max caught her left forearm with his left hand. The pair danced a tight circle with Max lashing Lori's legs, buttocks, abdomen, and breasts. Finally she collapsed to the carpet, curled in a fetal position, covered her face with her free arm, and shouted and cried as Max continued to hold her left arm and beat her.

Max finally tired and stopped. He dropped her arm, threaded his belt, bloody along the edges, through the loops of his jeans, buckled it, and left the room. He returned shortly with a small glass bottle marked with a brand of cough syrup. He took the syringe from the floor, removed the cap from the bottle, and pulled clear liquid through the needle.

Lori watched Max through teary eyes and with a face twisted with pain.

"Here's your morphine," said Max. He knelt on the floor beside Lori, rested the needle against her naked thigh, and asked, "Okay. One last chance. Who are you, really?"

"Do it, you bastard," Lori said softly. "Just do it."

"I want to know who you are before I take your body out for the vultures."

"Fuck you, Max," said Lori. "Not that it matters, but I am Lorraine Portman.

"Now kill me, damn it! Do it!" Lori turned her head and moaned in pain. "I can't stand to live like this any longer."

"Okay," said Max. He pushed the needle into Lori's thigh, took the syringe in his left hand, and used his right palm to slowly push the plunger to the bottom.

Max pulled the needle from Lori's muscle, got to his feet, and laughed down on her. "I can't let you off that easy, Lori. That was just water. I wanted you to suffer for thinking you could kill me.

"Besides, if you really are Lori Portman, you're worth a million dollars to me. I won't put you out of your misery until your husband has you declared dead and puts in a claim for his life insurance benefits."

Max laughed loudly, left the room, and Lori heard the deadbolt slam home in the door jamb.

Lori lay on the floor and tried to think what she might have to alleviate the great pain she felt from her feet to her face. While working in the emergency room with Doctor Reynolds she had assembled a varied collection of drugs which she stored in the medicine cabinet in the cabin they shared. In her haste to put miles between herself and the drugged physician, she had failed to take the drugs.

I had Vicoden, Percodan, Darvocet, and Hydrocodone, she thought, but now all I have is a small bottle of aspirin. Damn!

Lori heard the deadbolt move, turned her head, and saw Max enter the room. She watched him step to her and place a green can about two inches cubed next to her face.

"We use this on our milk cows," he said with a laugh. "You might try it." He left the room laughing.

Lori read label on the can: "BAG BALM. For chapped teats, superficial scratches, abrasions, windburn, and sunburn. After each milking apply the BAG BALM thoroughly and allow a coating to remain on the surface."

She turned the can and found a list of the ingredients: 8 - hydroxyquinoline sulfate 0.3% in a petrolatum, lanolin base.

You're an idiot, Max, she thought. *This is an antiseptic. Your 'teat' joke will come in handy because my tube of first aid cream is almost empty.*

Though her body felt like one huge painful wound, Lori forced herself to her hands and knees and crawled to her bathroom. There she swallowed four aspirin and bathed the bloody, overlapping welts she could reach with a warm washcloth. When the seeping blood slowed to a minimum, she applied antiseptic to the wounds then, lacking sufficient bandages, wrapped toilet paper around her legs, arms, buttocks, and torso.

Each movement added pain, but she managed to step to her bed, don pajamas, and lay on her back. She positioned herself close enough to the bottom of the bed to rest her feet against the footboard and raise her knees a few inches.

Lori stayed in that position, wide awake, throbbing with pain, until pressure forced her to the toilet. After urinating she stood, looked down, and saw lines of blood where her buttocks had touched the seat. She used toilet paper to wipe the blood then took four more aspirin.

By the time Manuel and Maria returned from their vacations and resumed their usual duties, Lori could move about the house without attracting unwanted attention. She still had scabs from the worst of the overlapping lashes, but the BAG BALM had helped her avoid infections and speeded the healing process. She kept her arms and legs covered and her mouth closed.

The second day after the employees returned, Max called them together in his den. There, with Lori standing next to him, Max admonished Gordo, Dorotea, Manuel, and Maria to never open Lori's locked door in his absence. "There will be absolutely no exceptions to this rule. None! I don't care if she cries out that she's dying and she pours blood under the door to prove it. Her door stays locked! If I come home and find her dead, so be it. Better her than any of you."

Max watched Lori closely and locked her in her room whenever he left the house. He gave her advance notice of his Las Vegas absences, and she put enough hard-boiled eggs, lunch meats, cheeses, and soft drinks in her small refrigerator to last several days.

The cooler winter weather did not last long and, by the spring, Lori had healed except for several faint lines on her skin where deeper welts left fine scars. She resumed her routine except the opportunity to visit Max's office never again presented itself.

Though she had missed two standing appointments during the holidays, Lori resumed her visits to Isabel's salon in Sells. Max accompanied her every time, sat inside the business while the owner cut and styled Lori's hair, then paid for the service.

In midsummer Max had a conflicting appointment, and he asked Emiliano to take Lori to Isabel's. The younger brother knew Max kept Lori on the ranch against her will. He did not know why, but he respected Max's right not to tell him. When he drove Lori to Isabel's, Emiliano circled the business, verified she could not leave through a back door, and assumed he could keep an eye on Lori from the front seat of his truck while parked outside Isabel's door.

Their words had been limited to questions and answers about how Lori wanted her hair cut and styled while Max sat a few feet away. With Emiliano outside in his truck, Lori and

Isabel chatted freely and eased into a friendship.

Several months later Isabel noticed a bruise on Lori's cheek and asked who had hit her.

Lori had looked at Emiliano's head bobbing gently in time to the music he heard and told the stylist Max had punched her after he had been drinking.

Isabel saw and heard of such treatment more than she liked, and she eventually learned Lori was not married to Max but had no way to leave his ranch.

The friendship between the two women grew in spurts as Emiliano occasionally drove Lori for her hair work. In late March after her second Christmas on the Tucker Ranch, Lori told Isabel she had thought of an old friend who might help her if he knew of her situation. She asked the stylist if she would place postage on and mail a letter for her.

Isabel agreed, but the opportunity for Lori to pass a letter written on toilet paper and addressed to Steven Reynolds did not present itself until late the following summer.

TWENTY-THREE

Before I met with Duke and his SWAT team Monday at noon, I found the hot wire to my Honda's headlight and installed a small toggle switch. Over submarine sandwiches from a store in Sahuarita, we reviewed our respective plans another time, and I accepted from Rod a key to the lock on the main Tucker Ranch gate. He assured me he had tested it at two o'clock that morning and found it worked.

Duke loaned me one more toy before I left. "These night vision binoculars have lens doublers which increase the image magnification to six point five times. I think you'll read the license plate on that hay trailer if you want to.

"Just don't forget to give them back."

With my headlight off and my borrowed night vision goggles on, I started my Honda along the power line inspection road at eight thirty the following Tuesday evening. I reached the knob overlooking the main ranch valley at nine fifteen. Starlight painted the pastures and the ranch buildings pale green, but the moon had yet to rise.

I removed my small backpack, stowed the goggles, and removed a case containing the expensive night vision binoculars Duke had loaned me. They magnified ambient star light thirty thousand times and turned night into slightly green-tinted day.

Duke and his team insisted on using the unofficial code name created by Brad Gunn, and, after I settled on my belly with the binoculars aimed at the Tucker barn, I thumbed the button on the high-powered walkie-talkie Duke had loaned me and said, "Traveling Dick is on the knob."

"Roger that," came the surprisingly strong response.

Three hours later I again thumbed the button and said, "Traveling Dick is traveling home."

Again I heard, "Roger that."

Wednesday evening started the same, but at nine fifty I watched a truck and hay trailer combination leave the Tucker barn and drive slowly to the west side of the valley. A Hummer H1 left a garage at the main house and followed it.

"Traveling Dick here. The hay truck and the Hummer are leaving the valley southbound." I recited license plate number on the back of each vehicle.

"Roger that," said Duke with a chuckle.

Through those wonderful binoculars I watched Gordo stop the truck, get out, wave to Max in the Hummer, open the gate, and drive the truck and trailer through it far enough so the Hummer had room to clear the gate and drive around the truck.

While Gordo closed the gate and climbed back into his cab, I thumbed a button and said, "The Hummer is now the lead vehicle. Repeat. The Hummer has pulled ahead of the truck and trailer and is leaving the valley."

"Roger that."

Two minutes later I added, "The truck and trailer are out of the valley. Traveling Dick is leaving the knob."

"Roger that. Good luck, Traveling Dick."

I stowed the binoculars and the walkie-talkie in my backpack, put the night vision goggles back over my eyes, started my Honda, and eased it slowly down the steep trail. At the bottom I stopped, dismounted, pulled my wire cutters, and, with unspoken apologies to Randolph, Roy, Gene, Lone, and Hoppy, removed a six-foot section of barbed wire fence.

Two minutes later I cut another section of fence then accelerated onto the paved road and raced toward the building in the southwest corner of the valley. I slowed to a crawl past the barn and the residences and held my speed down as I neared Max's house.

When I saw the first dog, I hit my brakes, stopped the bike, and got off fast. I kicked down the side stand and pulled a 260-gram can of bear pepper spray from my left hip pocket. Unlike 'people' pepper spray which usually shoots out a stream of liquid, most bear-type sprays eject a fog up to thirty feet. With hair-covered mammals one must get the pepper into the nose, eyes, and, hopefully open, mouth to have effect.

The bigheaded pit bull, running toward me at top speed, remained silent, but his bared teeth and dripping tongue told me he would rather bite off my leg than give it a loving hump. When he hit an imaginary twenty-foot line, I pulled the trigger and held it two full seconds.

The beast hit the noxious fog, skidded to a halt a few feet from my boots, turned ninety degrees to his right, and, while whining, huffing, and shaking his head wildly, increased his running speed.

The second dog ignored the first, but, when he hit my next pepper blast, he exhibited the same reaction and effort to put space between us.

With the can back in my pocket, I remounted and motored to the westernmost garage door. I parked, turned off the Honda's engine, and stepped onto a wide porch. I kept my feet close to the bottom of the building to avoid creaking planks and stepped to the nearest window which, unlike the other windows I could see, had a decorative metal latticework bolted over it.

The darkness coming through the windows gave my goggles no light to magnify. I saw nothing inside the house until I peeked into a kitchen where a hidden bulb over a huge stainless steel stove cast light, bright to my goggled eyes, on counters, appliances, and an island. I stepped by the kitchen door and around a corner to a main door which I found unlocked.

I entered the house, stepped on an oak entryway, and spotted light to my left. With drawn pistol in hand, I stepped into the doorway and saw a shaded lamp on an end table but no people. I hurried through the room and into the north wing of the house. A search of the master bedroom, bathroom, and an office verified Max had left that part of the building. I retraced my steps back to the main entrance and passed through the kitchen into another hall. I found one bedroom door open on my left, and I stopped at a closed door on my right. Unlike the open door, this one had a deadbolt knob on the outside.

Unusual, I thought. Is this the prisoner's 'cell?'

I knocked lightly.

"Who is it?"

"Is that you Linda?"

"You're here! Thank God!" Then, "Yes. Can you take me away from here?"

"Yes. Are you dressed?"

"Yes."

"Good. I will open the door, but make the room dark first and don't turn on a light. I'm wearing night vision goggles, and you'll blind me."

"All the lights are off. Please hurry."

I opened the door, said, "I'm Dan Ballantine. Please follow me." I led her back through the kitchen, out the main door, and onto the porch.

As Linda followed me around the corner she called to my back, "Can't I bring anything with me?"

I reached my Honda, turned to face her, and said, "No. I know you can afford to replace whatever you leave here, and, as you can see, we're traveling light."

I looked her over carefully while I spoke. Though she appeared to be a petite, attractive, middle-thirties housewife dressed in a short-sleeved blouse, blue jeans, and sneakers, I considered her a dangerous, conniving suspect who had probably committed more than one murder. I considered patting her for weapons, but other than a knife taped to a lower calf, her clothing told me she was not carrying.

"I have to ride on the back of that?" she asked.

Duke's accurate guess at her response at the sight of my Honda led me to conclude he was married.

"There's a reason for it that I don't have time to explain," I said, "but, yes, this is our ride."

Linda looked into the dark toward the barn. "We have to be careful out here, Mister Ballantine. Max has a pair of pit bulls. He told me never to go out at night because they have been trained to attack."

"I convinced them we wouldn't taste good," I said.

"How did you do that? I didn't hear any shots."

I pulled my can from my back pocket and showed it to her. "Grizzly bear spray works on dogs if you hit them in the face."

"Good idea," said Linda. "Gun shots would have awakened the cowboys."

"I know these are merely words, Linda, but I've had some training. I have a plan, and if you cooperate with me we should be off the ranch before anybody realizes I've been here."

"Okay, Mister Ballantine, but I know where Max keeps a spare key to his vehicles. We don't have to ride that motorcycle. We can borrow his pickup and leave it at the Border Patrol office in Tucson where his brother works. There are a few things I would really like to take with me."

"I won't leave my bike here because I don't want to have to come back for it. I can't imagine the welcome I would get."

Linda looked at my face. "Can you take those goggle things off a second? It's hard to talk to you."

I removed my goggles.

"We've got time, Mister Ballantine," Linda said. "Max left twenty minutes ago. He's always gone at least an hour and often longer.

"Please come with me a second."

Before I could object, Linda turned and trotted back along the porch toward the main door.

I followed her through the kitchen, past the two bedroom doors, and through a door at the end of the hall into a garage.

"May I turn on a light now?" she asked.

Smart girl, I thought. "Yes."

Linda flipped a switch near the door.

In the huge garage I looked over an empty parking space at an Aston Martin roadster, a late model Ford double-cab pickup truck, and more space.

"Over here," she said.

Linda led me to the far side of the pickup and pointed to an ATV. On the floor next to it lay an aluminum loading ramp.

"Somebody shot at a cowboy last week, and Max used his truck to go get the man and this A T V. He's keeping it in here to show the Sheriff the bullet holes. You could use the ramp to load your motorcycle into the back of Max's truck while I go get the spare key and grab the bag I've kept packed."

I had not mentioned it to Duke and his team, but my plan had one additional potential problem: What would I do if Linda balked at signing the declaration and quitclaim deed for her brother's cabin?

Though I had asked Duke for, and he had provided, a key to the padlock on the main gate, my solution called for me to carry Linda on the Honda to the bottom of the knob. I would ride the Honda to the crest and wait for Linda to climb it. When she reached the top, winded and weak, I would handcuff her to my wrist, present her with the documents I carried in my backpack, and explain what I needed from her. She could sign the documents, she would have to sign them again before a notary later that morning, or I would walk her back down the hill and handcuff her to the gate where Gordo would find her when he left the valley with the hay truck.

I wanted to stick to my plan, so I said, "You may not know it, but there's a very serious padlock on the main gate at the highway. I came onto the ranch on the power line inspection road. We have to leave the same way."

Linda pointed to the north garage wall which held a pegboard and a selection of hand tools. "No, we don't, Mister Ballantine. There's a wire cutter right there. We can cut a hole in the fence near the gate. This truck is four-wheel-drive. We can take it off the road and drive through the hole we made."

"Well, there's one other thing," I said. "I'm not a thief. I'd rather not steal the man's truck."

Linda put her hand on my forearm. "Listen, Mister Ballantine. Max Tucker has kept me prisoner in this house for over twenty months. He raped me at least twice a week during that time. I have scars from where he beat me with his belt.

"I've got no qualms about stealing his damn truck! I'll drive it if you don't want to."

Linda did not add, but I could hear it in her voice, I am *not* riding on your Homda, and I *am* taking some things with me!

Well, I thought, *the best laid plans and all that.*

I looked at her. "If you can open the garage door behind the truck, you can have five minutes while I load my bike."

"Thanks, Mister Ballantine!" Linda offered me a smile. I would have bet Head Emergency Room Nurse Linda Coleman used a similar smile on Doctor Steven Reynolds when he first came to work with her.

I wondered if she had use it while they cut off Bill Roeper's head and stuffed his corpse into the pilot's seat of Reynolds' Piper Cherokee.

*   *   *

Linda ran to her room in a jubilant mood. After her talk with Dan Ballantine while in Isabel's toilet, she had allowed hopes of a rescue to build. Each evening Max left in his Hummer she added her toiletries to a suitcase packed with her favorite expensive clothes and lay on her bed fully dressed.

In her room Linda pulled both her packed suitcase and an empty one from under her bed then ran with them to Max's office. She unlocked his desk, found the key folder, pulled loose the spare key for his pickup truck, and put it in her pocket. She replaced the folder in the file drawer, relocked the main drawer, hurried to the safe in the closet, tapped in the code, and pulled the door open.

"I got you, you bastard," Linda said softly. "Payback can be a bitch!" She dropped to her knees and quickly moved the cash, the tubes of Maple Leaf coins, and the heavy Smith & Wesson Model 327PD into the empty suitcase.

TWENTY-FOUR

Duke led Bob, Les, and Jeff to the water tank and the box canyon on their ATVs. They hiked to the pick up point and found their well-spaced positions behind rocks and bushes as close to the hole as they considered safe.

The SWAT team members remained calm when the truck's lights appeared in the distance. All except Les shifted their views to the right to reduce the increased brightness in their night vision goggles.

Les did not wear goggles because he held a digital video camera to his face and made a record of the truck and hay trailer entering the turn around area. He got a clear picture of Gordo uncovering the hole and opening the bottom trailer door. A few minutes later Les captured thirty-four illegal immigrants climbing from the hole in the desert floor through the hole in the bottom of the trailer.

Gordo closed the trailer door then drove the truck from the turn around area.

The camera recorded Emiliano aka El Hombre climbing from the hole, sitting on a nearby rock, and lighting and smoking a cigarette. When the Hummer appeared, Les's camera captured the smuggler getting to his feet, facing north, and switching on his helmet light.

Les aimed his camera at the Hummer and got ten seconds of the vehicle sitting immobile before everything went white.

Duke, Bob, and Jeff groaned involuntarily as their night vision goggles multiplied the light from four bright off-road driving lamps, flooded their retinas with painful white light, and blinded them.

*   *   *

Maximilian Tucker drove his Hummer around the hay truck and trailer as Gordo got out to close the gate behind them. He drove four miles along the dirt road until it entered a long valley. He slowed and stopped the Hummer then backed it next to a large boulder at the west side of the elongated depression.

Max sat patiently listening to a Johnny Rodriguez CD as Gordo drove the truck by his position, and, fifty minutes later, drove by again headed north.

Max started the Hummer, aimed it south, and hurried to meet his brother. He slowed then stopped as he reached the notch they had graded between a pair of low hills above the tunnel exit point. In the four-inch tall by ten-inch wide display on his windshield, Max clearly saw the white image of his brother projected by the grill-mounted infrared camera of his night vision system. He cursed aloud when he also saw pieces of four other white figures in the near distance behind Emiliano. They were partially hidden by rocks, but he could see dark, gun-shaped objects in three hands. One of them held something in front of his face.

La Migra! thought Max.

After half a second Max changed his mind. He decided La Migra would have detained Gordo and the trailer. He concluded a Mexican gang had been watching Emiliano. They cared nothing about the illegals; they wanted the cocaine.

Max wondered why the gangsters didn't shoot Emiliano and take the drugs.

After a few more seconds Max decided the gang also wanted his Hummer. They had hiked in from Mexico, but they wanted to ride off the ranch.

Max switched on his off-road driving lights and raced forward. He drove clockwise around the hole and skidded to a stop next to his brother.

"THERE ARE ARMED MEN BEHIND US, EMILIANO! THEY WANT TO STEAL OUR DRUGS! GET IN!"

Emiliano looked toward the elevated land to his south and watched four men get to their feet. Three of them stood in place and removed helmets while one held a camera to his face.

"Take the coke and go, Max! They can't catch you! I'm going back to Mexico!"

Emiliano tossed his backpack through the open driver's window onto Max's lap, stepped to the hole, sat with his feet in it, then pushed off and dropped from sight.

As Emiliano disappeared from view, Max floored the Hummer and raced north.

*   *   *

Duke, helmet and goggles in one hand and a forty-five caliber semiautomatic pistol in the other, cursed. "God damn it! I can't see shit! What's happening?"

"Max Tucker is leaving the area in his Hummer," said Les. "Emiliano just dropped back through the hole into the tunnel." The FBI agent lowered his camera and pushed the OFF button.

"Are you guys okay? Bob? Jeff?" asked Duke.

"Blind as a bat," said Bob.

"What he said," said Jeff.

"Can you feel your transmitter, Bob?" asked Duke.

"Yes, sir."

"When you can make out the FIRE button, close Emiliano's back door, will you?" asked Duke.

"Roger that," said Bob. Five seconds later he added, "Fire in the hole."

The four men felt as much as heard the detonation of the explosives they had placed in the cave's Mexico entrance.

"Can you see the hole, Les?" asked Duke.

"Yes, sir."

"Be careful, but get your head down and tell Emiliano he does not want us to have to come in there after him."

"Yes, sir." Les knelt next to the hole, slowly lowered his head inside, and called, "EMILIANO TUCKER THIS IS THE F B I. YOU ARE UNDER ARREST FOR SMUGGLING IMMIGRANTS AND CONTROLLED NARCOTICS. THAT EXPLOSION CLOSED THE MEXICO ENTRANCE TO YOUR CAVE. COME OUT NOW."

The men waited for a response but heard nothing.

Les added, "IF YOU DON'T COME OUT NOW, TUCKER, WE WILL DETONATE THE DEVICE WE LEFT AT THE INTERNATIONAL BORDER LINE PAINTED ON THE FLOOR OF YOUR CAVE."

When they heard no response, Duke said, "Let's give him a minute. He may have been closer to the Mexican opening than we thought. The blast may have stunned him."

"While we wait, I'll tell Rod, Doug, and Traveling Dick

about our new problem."

From the hole a faint voice called, "Okay! I'm coming out. Don't shoot me!"

TWENTY-FIVE

I loaded the Honda into the truck bed, found straps and secured it, folded the ramp, and stowed it in the back of the truck alongside the bike. I lifted Max's wire cutter from his garage wall, stowed it my backpack, then I went looking for Linda. In the main room I spotted her coming my way from Max's part of the house carrying two suitcases.

I held out a hand, accepted a key and one of the suitcases, then turned and led Linda to the truck.

I opened the driver's door as Linda hurried to the far side.

"It's locked," she called after she tried the handle.

I found a button on the door which unlocked the other three doors. I pressed it then opened the second left side door and placed Linda's suitcase on the floor behind the driver's seat.

Linda did the same with her suitcase on the passenger side then climbed into the front passenger bucket and pulled her seatbelt across her chest and clicked it into place.

I looked at the garage and noticed the double doors had chain driven openers. "I don't want to open the garage door with the light on," I said. "I'm going to take a minute to remove the bulb."

"Okay. There's a transmitter which opens that door here in the truck." He aimed a thumb over her shoulder.

"Do the other doors stay down?"

"Yes."

I found a ladder, climbed to the door opener, pulled a white plastic cover off on side, and unscrewed a bulb. After I put the ladder back in its place, I stepped to the switch by the door to the hallway and turned off the main garage lights. Back at the truck, I removed my backpack, climbed behind the wheel, dropped the pack on the wide center console, and fastened my own seatbelt.

"Open the garage door, please."

Linda reached to an overhead console and pushed a button.

In my mirror I watched the door behind the truck lift. I started the truck and backed it from the garage. Then I pushed the button and watched the door close.

As I opened my backpack for my night vision goggles, I heard Duke's walkie-talkie squawk. I pulled the communicator, thumbed a button, and said, "Traveling Dick here."

"We've got a problem," said Duke. "Something spooked Max. He switched on a bunch of off-road driving lights which blinded us. We left our hiding places to arrest him, but he took off in his Hummer. He's headed your way."

I quickly searched my memory and decided I had failed to mention the Hummer's bright off-road lights to the team. While I decided that confession could wait, I said, "Roger that!

"I've had a minor change of plans, too. My client found a spare key to Max's Ford pickup, and I've decided to borrow it for an hour or two. I loaded my bike in the bed, and we just backed from the garage."

Duke's laughter came through the speaker as he pushed his button. "We promise not to arrest you for grand theft auto."

"I won't plead to anything more than joyriding."

"Right, Traveling Dick. I suggest you vacate the premises before the angry owner arrives to disrupt your joy."

"Roger that. Traveling Dick is on the road again."

I set the walkie-talkie in a cup holder at the forward end of the center console, pulled the night vision goggles from my backpack, put them on, then dropped the backpack between Linda's suitcases on the floor behind the console.

"What's going on with arresting Max?" asked Linda.

"I used to be a cop," I said as I accelerated the unlit truck toward the starlit barn. "After you told me your suspicions about the Tuckers, I studied their ranch property on a computer search engine full of satellite photographs. Then one night I hiked to an interesting spot I saw on their ranch close to the Mexican border. I watched and photographed them loading people into the hay trailer and got a shot of Emiliano passing a backpack to Max. I sent the photos to an F B I friend in Reno."

I rounded the barn, turned the truck north and, with

increased confidence in my goggles, upped my speed.

"The F B I talked to the D E A," I added, "but, because you told me about Leonardo, not the Border Patrol. The D E A believes the Tuckers are a major source of cocaine to the Las Vegas area. So the feds sent in a SWAT team to arrest the Tuckers tonight which I thought would give me time to find you and get you off the ranch. The SWAT team leader just told me something went wrong, and Max is headed this way."

"Are you Traveling Dick?" asked Linda.

"They chose that handle, not me." I said. Then I asked, "Have you ever been on the road south from the ranch?"

"No," said Linda. "Why?"

"The SWAT team's plan called for them to let Gordo leave the ranch through that locked gate with the hay trailer before they stopped and arrested him. I assume he left the loading area ahead of Max, and I just wondered if there was room anywhere on the road for Max in his Hummer to pass the hay trailer."

"If Max wants to get around the truck and hay trailer, he will. I've ridden with him in his Hummer. Sometimes he drives it like an oversize A T V.

"In the past he's always stopped at the house after Gordo drives the hay truck through the valley to switch the Hummer for his Aston Martin which he prefers to drive to Las Vegas. If we can get out of the valley before he sees us, we'll get a few extra minutes while he does that."

"Unless he loans this truck out a lot, we only have until he opens a garage door and finds it missing," I said.

"I don't think Max loans anything to anyone," said Linda.

I decided I could spot a loose horse or steer on the road in plenty of time to stop, and I increased my speed to eighty on the straight part of the pavement. "Keep an eye out across the valley and let me know if you see any headlights."

I had just let off the gas to let the truck slow for the gate at the north end of the valley when Linda called, "There he is!"

I glanced over my left shoulder and saw bright moving lights across the valley. I used the parking brake to slow the truck so the red rear lights would not flash. "He can't have seen us. Can you find the switch for the interior lights and turn them off before we open a door?"

She did, and, as I stopped the truck at the gate, Linda released her seat belt and said, "I'll get it."

I drove onto the dirt road on the other side, stopped again with the parking brake, and watched Linda in the rearview mirror. She stood at the gate half a minute staring westerly.

"He's coming this way!" called Linda as she turned and sprinted to the truck. She hopped inside and said, "He didn't stop at the house. Whatever spooked him must have made him decide to drive straight to Las Vegas in the Hummer."

"Can you tell if he's in a big hurry?"

"It doesn't look like he's driving as fast as you did, but I can tell he's moving faster than usual."

TWENTY-SIX

My widower father lives in a two-story house in Davis, California. He subscribes to The Western Channel from his local cable service. When I visit him, he often turns on the large flat-screen television he has hanging on one wall and says something like, "Did you know they're running the Maverick series now?"

Dad thoroughly enjoys the 50s and 60s television westerns such as Gene Barry as Bat Masterson, Chuck Connors as The Rifleman, or Gene Autry as, well, Gene Autry catching bad guys in twenty-two minutes of black and white action per episode. Dad complained he never saw his favorite, Richard Boone as Paladin in Have Gun - Will Travel until he found the first three seasons for sale on DVD at a Borders store.

One trick those heroes of yesteryear often used came to mind as I hustled the Ford along the unfamiliar and twisting dirt road. Like the cowboy who would ride his horse behind a big rock and let the chasing bad guy get ahead of him, I turned right on the first thin road I saw, raced ahead until I believed we could not be seen, and used the parking brake to stop.

"What are you doing?" asked Linda.

"I'm pretty sure Max can travel faster on that road in his Hummer than I can in this truck, and I'd rather have him ahead of us than catching up to us.

"Wait here a minute." I shut the Ford's engine off, removed the key from the ignition switch, hopped from the seat, and sprinted back toward the main road.

Our dust had settled about a minute when I saw the Hummer's bright lights in the sky ahead of me. I could not see the vehicle itself, but those off-road lights threw so much light toward the stars I could easily follow the Hummer's progress.

I returned to the Ford and lifted my walkie-talkie, thumbed the button, and said, "Traveling Dick calling Duke."

"Duke here."

"Traveling Dick left the main valley just as Max entered from the west side. He did not stop at the house to change vehicles. I left the road in a small valley and Max get ahead of me. He should reach the main gate in fifteen minutes or so."

"Here's Plan B, Traveling Dick," said Duke. "Rod and Doug will arrest Max when he leaves his vehicle to unlock the main gate. They will secure him, and Doug will drive Max's Hummer back here to collect the rest of us.

"Rod will arrest Gordo when he stops to unlock the gate.

"Are you carrying?" asked Duke.

"Traveling Dick always carries."

"Good. You can help us by keeping an eye on Max while Rod arrests Gordo. Leave all the illegals in the hay trailer until C B P sends I C E agents to take them into custody."

"Roger that."

"Who are C B P and I C E?" asked Linda after I set the walkie-talkie in the cup holder.

"The former U S Border Patrol is now the Customs and Border Protection division of Homeland Security. Immigration and Customs Enforcement is the police division.

"The F B I kept C B P and I C E out of the Tucker loop because of Leonardo's position."

"Will the F B I arrest Leonardo, too?"

"I can't speak for the F B of I, but I expect they will be searching for evidence of his involvement."

I started the engine and drove a short distance to a place where I could make a Y-turn.

"Why did you turn off the engine and take the key?"

"Steve Reynolds trusted you, Linda, but I don't. This road may lead out of here for all I know, and I would be in a world of hurt if you drove off and left me on foot."

"I wouldn't do that."

"There's something else I need you not to do," I said as I reversed the Ford's direction.

"What's that?"

"Now that my plan to get you off the ranch unseen, and Duke's plan to arrest Max at the loading point have changed, I need you to be invisible. If the feds see you, they will ask for identification and run a check on you. When they find the Idaho arrest warrant, they will take you into custody."

"The only identification I have shows I'm Lori Portman," said Linda. "I bought it in Las Vegas."

"My Reno F B I pal gave Duke and his team the story on Doctor Reynolds so they know your true name. I did ask my pal not tell the locals about your arrest warrant because of the deal you made with Steven. As far as I know, he didn't.

"Duke and his team know I came down here to rescue you, and they know I brought them in and told them about the smuggling to give me time to get you off the ranch. As I told you, my plan called for me to get you to Tucson without anybody seeing us.

"But now I've been roped into playing a role in the arrest of Max and Gordo," I added. "I hope you can understand why you can't let anyone see or hear you."

"I understand, Mister Ballantine," said Linda. "And I will do exactly what you tell me to do. The sooner we get off the ranch and the hell I've been suffering for way too long, the better. I had thought, too, if I ever did get away, I would hire an attorney and sue Max for raping me, beating me, and keeping me prisoner, but I like the idea of him going to prison better."

"I'm curious how that happened in these modern times," I said, "but I don't have time to hear about it now."

"Things aren't so modern on that ranch," said Linda.

Back on the road I raced Max's Ford until I saw raised dust in the distance. I had hoped I could get close to his Hummer before he reached the locked gate just in case he saw the

SWAT guys and decided to tear out a section of his own fence rather than stop at the gate.

I slowed as I entered the open space between the hills and the fence. When I saw the Hummer's brake lights flash, the driver's door open, and a man leave the driver's seat, I fed gas to the Ford. We raced toward the Hummer as Max stepped toward the gate.

My world got too bright for night goggles, and I pulled mine off as Max pulled a key and reached for the padlock.

"Slide down in your seat as far as you can, Linda," I said without looking at her. "We don't want Max to glance this way and see you."

Linda released her seatbelt and lowered herself until she could just see over the top of the dashboard.

A camouflaged man emerged from the desert floor on each side of the Hummer. Each man aimed a handgun at Max.

The rancher surprised me by ignoring the commands he heard from the armed men. Well, I assume they did not order him to turn, run back to the Hummer's open door, jump behind the wheel and close the door.

I turned on the Ford's headlights as I braked to a stop an inch behind the Hummer's rear bumper. I saw the white backup lights come on, and, when Max looked over his shoulder, I hit the high beam switch.

"Stay where you are," I said to Linda.

As the Ford's engine slowed, we could hear Rod calling to Max, "F B I! LET ME SEE YOUR HANDS! F B I! LET ME SEE YOUR HANDS!"

Max seemed to want to think about things a minute.

Rod yelled, "IF I DON'T SEE YOUR HANDS NOW, I WILL ASSUME YOU HAVE A WEAPON, AND I WILL SHOOT YOU!"

Max put both his hands on the top of the steering wheel.

"USE YOUR LEFT HAND TO OPEN THE DOOR."

Within a few seconds Rod and Doug had Max flat on the desert sand next to the road. They handcuffed him and moved him away from the Hummer.

I backed the Ford away from the road a hundred feet into the raw desert and turned off the lights. I looked at Linda. "I want you to get out of the cab, duck down, and walk to the back corner of the trunk."

When I met her at her at the rear bumper, I surprised her by slipping a handcuff around her left wrist and closing it. I pulled her toward the ground and closed the remaining cuff on a ring of steel which was part of the tow hitch.

"What ... ?" she asked as she sat heavily on the sand.

"Be quiet!" I said softly. "I couldn't leave you in the cab because I have not searched your luggage for weapons. So you get to sit out here a few minutes. Stay out of sight and do not talk. Remember what I said about attracting attention.

"I'll get us out of here as soon as I can."

"The handcuffs aren't necessary, Mister Ballantine."

"Remember what I said about trusting you?" I asked.

Linda nodded.

"Nothing has changed."

As I walked to where Rod had Max sitting in the sand, Doug backed the Hummer away from the gate in a ninety-degree turn then accelerated away.

Rod knelt on the sand five feet from Max and opened the backpack he had taken from the Hummer. He lifted a clear plastic-wrapped bundle of white powder so I could see it as I approached.

"Bet you a dollar this is coke," said Rod. "Thanks for the heads up."

"No bet," I said with a smile. "And you're welcome."

Max looked up at me. "Who the fuck are you and what the fuck are you doing with my truck?"

I looked at Rod and asked, "Tell me, Agent, have you advised Mister Tucker of his right to remain silent?"

"I was just about to do that, sir," said Rod. "Would you please be a witness?"

"I'd be happy to," I said.

Rod got to his feet, pulled a card from a back pocket, and read through the Miranda advisement.

Max answered, "Fuck you!" to Rod's questions.

From his pleasant tone of voice and "sir," I assumed Rod recorded our words. I said, "I am willing to testify, Agent, that it is my opinion Mister Tucker was alert, sober, and should reasonably have understood your questions."

"Thank you, sir."

"You're welcome."

"I demand answers to my questions, asshole," said Max.

I decided to have some fun. I looked at Rod and asked, "Are you an asshole, Agent?"

"This gentleman is not the first gentleman who has referred to me by that term, sir, but, to tell the truth, I am not completely sure," said Rod with a large grin.

"Well," I said with open haughtiness, "I do not believe I am one so I shall defer his question to you."

"I'm talking to the taller of you two assholes," said Max.

I looked at Rod and said, "It appears I have a couple of inches on you, Agent. Are you standing in a hole?"

"I believe I am standing in a shallow one," said Rod. "The desert surface is deceptively uneven."

"Then I remain confused," I said.

"Fuck both you assholes," said Max.

Rod and I exchanged smiles.

Gordo arrived forty minutes later. I'm sure he saw the white pickup parked near the road, and he probably saw Rod and me standing next to his boss sitting on the desert floor.

And, of course, he had to have met the southbound Hummer at some place on the ranch road.

"Have you got the suspect, sir?" asked Rod.

"Yes, Agent," I said. I felt confident Max knew the well-done condition of his goose and would cause no trouble.

Gordo left his cab, and Rod arrested him. The foreman did not resist, and he soon sat on the sand ten feet from Max. After Rod read him his rights, Gordo declined to answer questions.

Rod called Duke who said CBP would arrive soon to unload the illegals and take them to Tucson. He gave his ETA.

I checked on Linda twice during the half hour we waited for the federal cops.

Duke and the rest of his team arrived in Max's Hummer a few minutes before the ICE agents. The SWAT guys put Max and Gordo in the Hummer which Duke told Max the FBI was confiscating as an instrument of his crimes. Rod and Doug hauled them from the scene.

When the ICE agents arrived, Duke unlatched the door on the bottom of the trailer, and we all watched as a group of unhappy folks got moved to comfortable federal vans.

I had watched the activity while leaning on the front of Max's truck. After a brief conversation with the ICE man in charge, Duke approached me and said, "May I ask you for one last favor, Traveling Dick?"

"You may."

He winked and said, "The F B I has commandeered this truck to assist in the transportation of persons and equipment. Would you drive it to the federal facility in Tucson for us? If you need to stop for a donut or anything else on the way, I have no objection. So long as you leave the vehicle at the facility in a couple of hours, the F B I will be happy. You may leave any equipment you may have borrowed in the locked vehicle. Just give the key to the receptionist and tell her you are the Traveling Dick."

"Don't you fear she may file a sexual harassment claim?"

"If she does, you may be called upon to testify."

I extended my hand. "Thanks for your help, Duke."

"Same to you, Traveling Dick. You may leave anytime."

"We can go now," I said to Linda as I unlocked her from the back of the Ford. I placed the open cuff around her right wrist and led her to the front passenger seat.

"Good," said Linda, "but I wish you would remove these handcuffs."

"Wait until I tell you about the rest of our deal," I said.

I stepped around the Ford and soon had us rolling toward Tucson on the state highway.

"So what's the rest of our deal?" asked Linda.

"Before I give you your freedom, I need your notarized signatures on a declaration and quitclaim deed which release your interest in your deceased brother's cabin to Steve and me. I will also expect you to give me money from your Swiss account for the balance of any of Steve's money you don't have plus interest at ten percent per year on the whole amount for the time you've had it."

"Ten percent? That's pretty steep."

"That's what fat Marva's judgment against Steve is charging him. All he's asking is that you make him whole."

"Plus the cabin."

"Right. Plus the cabin," I said.

"And then you'll let me go?"

"Yes."

"What if I don't think that's such a good deal?"

"I drive you to the nearest police station and tell them I have arrested you as a private bounty hunter on the Idaho warrant," I said. "I'll show you a certified copy of the arrest warrant when we stop.

"You get extradited to Idaho to face prosecution for stealing Steve's money." I took a chance and added, "Actually, before that happens, the local District Attorney will prosecute you for whatever you stole from the Tucker Ranch."

Linda blinked, thought several moments, then asked, "Do you realize that Steve won't get any more of his money if you turn me in? If I go to jail, I'll never give up another nickel."

"Steve understands that the money we recovered from the Toyota in Las Vegas may be all he ever sees."

"And I wouldn't give him the cabin."

I looked at her and smiled. "Well, he'd probably get to use it another two or three years while you sit in an Idaho prison. You might find an attorney to evict him, but a case like that could drag on a long time. He might even present a quitclaim deed which shows you gave him your interest some time ago."

She gave me a hard look. "You'd forge my signature?"

"Not me, Linda," I said. "Not me."

Linda stared at the highway ahead of us. "I think you and Steve are gambling I don't want to go to prison. For three-quarters of a million dollars, I might."

"Unless you cooperate with me, Linda, your time behind bars has already started," I said firmly. "And you will soon learn that Max Tucker fed you better and had a larger screen television than the Idaho penitentiary. You might also learn that women can get raped by other women in prison.

"It's your call."

Linda said nothing.

After a minute of silence, I said, "You don't have to be happy about all this, Linda, but you were the one who wrote a letter to Steve asking to be rescued. Steve couldn't do it, but I could, and I don't work for free. You still have your Swiss bank account to tide you over a while."

"Have you or Steve calculated the interest?"

"We got two hundred and seventy-two thousand dollars, but I have Steve's authority to review your numbers."

"So he wants half my Swiss money?"

"Steve doesn't know how much Swiss money you have, Linda. He only insists on being made whole."

"Plus the cabin."

"Steve did a year and a half behind bars," I said. "Max Tucker kept you on his ranch long enough for you to know that's worth something."

"What do you get out of all this?"

"Steve and I have a contract, but I can't think of a single reason to share its terms with you."

In Tucson I pulled the truck into the parking lot of a twenty-four-hour coffee shop, found a space, and turned to face Linda. "Well," I said, "It's decision time. You want to cooperate, have some breakfast while we wait for a bank to open, or do I go on to the police station?"

"What if I jumped and ran?"

"A fleeing felon, huh?" I smiled. "I won't shoot you, but I will chase you in the truck while I'm calling the police with your description. The handcuffs will make their job easier."

Linda stared out the windshield.

"Is that what you're thinking?" I asked.

Linda turned her head to look at me and gave me another of her killer smiles. "No, Mister Ballantine. You win. I'll sign your documents and write Steve a check for what I've spent. I'm feeling too good about getting out of one prison, and I don't want to risk being put in another. Life's too short.

"And I want some hash browns," she added. "Max's cook never wanted to take the time and trouble to make hash browns. He always said mashed beans were just as good."

I smiled as I pulled my handcuff key from my pocket. "Put

your hands over here," I said.

Linda frowned as I unlocked the cuff from her right wrist and snapped it around my own.

"I refuse to trust you for a second, Linda, and I don't want the trouble that might come if you jump from the truck and run. We stay hooked together until our business is done."

I drove us to a fast food restaurant that had a drive through lane. Linda got her hash browns, if you can call that flattened, football-shaped mass by that term, a breakfast sandwich, and an orange juice, and I got nothing. Then I drove her to a Bank of the West branch and parked.

Between bites, Linda asked, "Will we just sit here until the bank opens?"

I nodded. "Your signatures have to be notarized."

"The rest of Steven's money is here in Tucson. Why don't we go get it now instead of later?"

"Where is it?"

I drove to a public storage facility and, following her instructions, parked near a garage door.

Linda pulled off her left shoe and handed it to me. "The key to the lock is between the pad and the shoe."

I found the key and gave her back her shoe. While she slipped into it, I said, "We'll get out my door. You'll have to climb over the console."

"This would be a lot easier if you just unhooked me."

"I explained why I won't do that."

We got the garage door open, and I saw a dusty white BMW convertible. "Steve told me he had promised to buy you one of these. I'll have to tell him he kept his promise."

"Does that mean I can keep that part of the money?"

I smiled. "No."

"Did Steven take the Toyota from the Las Vegas garage?"

"Yes. He donated it to the clinic where he works."

"Will you give me credit for the eight thousand dollars I paid for it?"

"No," I said.

With the suitcase full of money on the seat behind me, I

drove us to the bank and parked. Then I called Brad Gunn.

"Have you heard the latest on the Tucker caper?" I asked.

"No."

I brought him up to date.

"Good work, Dan. Other than the bright light glitch, it sounds like all is well."

"I still have one little problem," I said.

"What's that?"

"I'm sitting in a Bank of the West parking lot with Linda Coleman handcuffed to my right wrist. She has cooperated with me to this point, but I trust her not.

"I need a favor from you."

"How can I help you from here, Dan?"

"I want to give you the address of the bank. When it opens at nine o'clock, I want you to call whoever is in charge for me. Tell him I'm a private detective presently assisting the F B of I. I want to make a large deposit, and I have a suspect in custody who wishes to sign a document before a notary.

"I would like somebody from the bank to come and get us and lead us to a private office where we can conduct our business."

"That's easy, Dan," said Brad. "What's the address?"

Five minutes after nine the local president approached my open window and asked, "Mister Ballantine?"

Inside his office the president witnessed Linda's execution of the declaration and the quitclaim deed.

While Linda, still handcuffed to me, listed the amounts she had spent on the cars, clothes, and the San Felipe trip, I gave the president the money case and asked him to divide the contents equally and deposit it into Steven's and my accounts.

The money case also contained a leather portfolio which Linda said contained identification documents and a checkbook. After I reviewed her numbers, we agreed on a figure and she wrote me a check on her Swiss account.

I asked the president to verify the check was good then to split it and deposit it as he had the cash.

With our business done, I unlocked the handcuffs and offered to drive Linda back to her BMW. When we reached her garage space at the storage facility, I left the engine running and asked her to listen while I telephoned Reynolds.

She sat in the Ford's cab while I tapped the clinic's number and asked for Doctor Reynolds.

"Good morning, Dan," he said. "How's it going?"

"It's going good, Steve. I'm in Tucson. I rescued Linda last night, and I have just deposited money into your Bank of the West account. While at the bank, I secured Linda's notarized signature on her declaration and the quitclaim deed and placed them in the mail addressed to you."

"Really! That's great! How is she?"

I looked across the Ford at Linda.

She looked back and shook her head, *No.*

"She was fine, Steve. She was happy to be rescued, and she said to tell you, 'Thanks.'"

"Where is she now?"

"She had another car stashed in a storage facility here in Tucson," I said. "A white B M W convertible."

"No kidding!"

"Really. After we did our business, I left her there."

That was a lie by about two minutes.

"Okay," said Steve.

I think the fool still felt something for the woman who double-crossed him and cost him a year and a half in jail.

"I'll trust you to get the declaration and the deed to your attorney per our contract, and you need to meet with the District Attorney to get those charges against Linda dropped and the warrant recalled."

"I'll call the D A today," said Reynolds. "And thanks, Dan. Thanks for everything."

"You're welcome. I'll call you when I'm up your way."

"Do that," he said. "I know a good fishing hole."

I broke the connection and looked at Linda.

"Can I go now?"

"It may take a few weeks to get that warrant out of the system. I suggest you avoid attracting law enforcement attention for a while. For example, I noticed the registration sticker on your bimmer is out of date. If a traffic officer stopped you and ran a warrants check, he might be forced to take you into custody until the authorities could verify it has been recalled."

"I understand."

"There is one other problem with the felony filed by the Boise County D A. He doesn't have to drop the charges merely because Steve, the victim of the theft, requests it."

"I'll be careful. Anything else?"

"No."

Linda got out, retrieved her suitcases from behind the front seats, and turned to unlock the padlock on her garage door.

I drove Max's big Ford to the federal building and took the key inside. Then I unloaded my Honda and rode to the RV resort.

I had had a long night, but I took Penny for a walk in the park and fed her before I took a nap.

EPILOGUE

Maximilian and Emiliano Tucker hired an expensive Phoenix criminal defense firm to represent them and Gordo. A senior partner arranged for them and Gordo to be released on bond the day after their arrest. The court clerk that accepted the deed to their ranch as security for their future court appearances failed to consider the government might later seek the forfeiture of the property as an instrument of their crimes.

Max's Hummer H1 had been impounded because he used it to commit crimes, but the prosecutor advised him, through his attorney, of the location of his Ford truck. The government never offered an explanation for how his truck happened to be parked in the lot at the federal building.

When Max, Emiliano, and Gordo reached the ranch house, Maria and Dorotea waited for them. The women reported they had not seen Lori in the house or on the ranch for two days.

Max immediately ran to his office and verified his desk remained locked. Then he opened his safe, and his curse, "THAT BITCH!" could be heard by all in the house.

The next time he met with his attorney, Max reported the theft by his house guest, Lori Portman, who had disappeared.

The attorney assigned the matter to an investigator who, after many hours of work which included trips to Long Beach and Sacramento, California, reported the woman who lived in the Tucker Ranch house was not Lori Portman.

The investigator had found and lifted several fingerprints in Max's house which Tucker assured him had been made by his house guest. He traveled to Long Beach, California, and had a lengthy conversation with Michael Portman. He learned about the attorney's trip to Las Vegas at Max Tucker's request, and he secured Michael's signed declaration the woman he saw in the Bellagio bar was not his wife.

The investigator traveled to Sacramento, California, and compared the fingerprints he had from the Tucker house with those provided by Lorraine Portman to the California Department of Real Estate.

The prints did not match.

The attorney advised Max to report the theft to the authorities and offer the fingerprints as evidence. The attorney suggested the police might identify the woman from her prints.

Max Tucker declined to make such report. He confessed to the attorney the money Lori stole came from smuggling drugs and illegal immigrants. If the authorities did find her and the money, which he doubted, the government would confiscate the cash as evidence.

Emiliano Tucker had appeared with Maximilian and Gordo at their joint formal arraignment a week after their arrest, but he declined to make any additional court appearances. When the Attorney General promptly commenced forfeiture proceedings against their ranch, Emiliano decided he had little to lose by relocating south of Arizona. With the huge stash of one hundred dollar bills he had accumulated over the years, he moved with Tina and their children to Brazil where they lived under different identities.

A team of diligent federal investigators worked eight weeks before presenting prosecutors with zero hard evidence of

Leonardo Tucker's involvement in his brothers' criminal activities. The recorded telephone calls and emails they recovered contained no incriminating words. The investigators concluded the brothers used combinations of code words which no jury would ever find conclusive.

No criminal charges were filed against Leonardo, but he received notice he would soon be transferred to an office on the Canadian border in Maine. He not only realized his government career had permanently stalled, he heard his unhappy wife emphatically declare she would not move to Maine with him. He decided to retire.

Leonardo used the federal investigators' accumulated documents and formal conclusion to successfully fight the attempted seizure of the Tucker Ranch. The court ruled his undivided one-third interest sufficient to prevent a public auction of the property. Leonardo sold his house in Tucson, moved onto the ranch property, and reluctantly became a mediocre cattle rancher.

Five months after his arrest the criminal trial of Maximilian Tucker commenced in the U. S. District Court in Tucson, and Max felt the depressing weight of many years in federal prison hanging over him.

Citizen Dan Troop Ballantine appeared in the judge's chambers   and gave sworn testimony as a Reliable Confidential Informant. His words were read to the jury in open court.

FBI Special Agent Richard Duchovney and his SWAT team members appeared, testified, and made a clear and damning case for the federal prosecutor.

Max drove home after each court day wondering if Emiliano had not made the right move.

Late Tuesday afternoon on the fourth trial day, Max drove to the ranch and stopped his pickup outside the locked gate. He left the truck and pulled his key as he stepped to the lock.

On the main highway behind Max a white BMW 328i convertible with the top down turned onto the ranch road and raced toward the gate.

Max opened the padlock then turned and watched the

BMW hurry along the packed dirt and stop behind his truck. A woman with short, dark hair and large sunglasses sat alone behind the wheel. Max assumed she was lost, and he stepped to the left side door. His eyes opened in surprise when he got a closer look at the driver.

"Lori! Or whoever you are. What ... ?"

"I am Linda Coleman, Max. And you should never have raped or beaten me." Linda raised the Magnum revolver she had stolen from Max's safe above the level of the door, pointed it at him, and squeezed the trigger.

A small hole appeared in the center of Max Tucker's shirt, and the bullet's energy pushed him back three quick, short steps. He sat hard on the desert sand, felt a great pain in his chest, and saw blood pumping from his wound.

Max slowly toppled onto his back and looked up at a cloudless blue sky. He heard Linda reverse the BMW's direction of travel, and he died as the car turned onto the pavement and accelerated toward Tucson.

Printed in the United States
141164LV00001BA/39/P